FAKE OUT

FAKE BOYFRIEND BOOK 1

EDEN FINLEY

Fake Out Copyright © 2018 by Eden Finley

Cover Illustration Copyright ©

Kellie Dennis at Book Cover By Design

www.bookcoverbydesign.co.uk

Edited by Deb Nemeth

http://www.deborahnemeth.com/

Copy-edited by Xterraweb Edits

http://editing.xterraweb.com/

All rights reserved.

This book or any portion thereof may not be reproduced or used in any manner whatsoever without the express written permission of the publisher.

For information regarding permission, write to:

Eden Finley - permissions - edenfinley@gmail.com

DISCLAIMER AND TRADEMARKS

Please note that these characters—particularly Maddox—have strong opinions on things. These are their own opinions and not that of the author. Eden thinks veganism is admirable, Canada is gorgeous, and New Jersey ... well, it has a great airport ...

In her defense, Newark Liberty International is the only place she's been in NJ.

She's also an Australian girl, so please excuse her serious lack of knowledge when it comes to American sports. She grew up on soccer, cricket, and rugby. Google and her American beta readers can be blamed for any Australianisms that sneak through.

This is a work of fiction. As such, team names—like the Bulldogs—are completely made up. The views in this book in no way reflect the views and principles of the NFL or any of their real teams.

Names of some colleges have been fabricated so not to misrepresent their policies and values, curriculum, or facilities.

Names, characters, businesses, places, events and incidents are either the products of the author's imagination or used in a fictitious manner. Any resemblance to actual persons, living or dead, or actual events is purely coincidental.

To anyone who has discovered they aren't as straight as they thought they were, and to the people who made them realize it.

CHAPTER ONE

MADDOX

Fuck my life.

Staring at a ghost from my past is a slap in the face from reality.

What are the chances of my one and only ex-girlfriend walking into the very same bar as me? And in *New York*. Chastity-freaking-Wells.

Like any self-respecting twenty-three-year-old guy in this situation would do, I scan the room for an emergency exit.

I need to leave. Right now. I slip off my barstool and throw down cash on the bar, but Chastity and her three friends head straight for me.

Sweat drips down my neck as my gaze darts around the small space in search of an alternative route to freedom. Slasher movie music plays through my head when I realize I'm trapped. Not being melodramatic or anything.

Turning on my heel and walking toward the bathrooms as fast as I can, I get cut off by some drunk guy stumbling into me. He drops his glass and it smashes on the ground, the sound of breaking glass dashing any hope I had of going unnoticed.

When I glance over my shoulder, I lock eyes with the

woman I almost married. Ironically, she's wearing a tiara and veil. Along with a flashing badge and sash that read *Bride to be.*

Her eyes widen as she recognizes her past staring back at her.

I have to go say hi now, but I can't get my feet to move. If I make a run for it, she'll tell her mother, and then I'll never hear the end of it from my Mom. Gotta love the suffocating gossip mill of small towns.

Chastity and New York do not mix. That's what she told me when I said I was going to Olmstead University. Right before she begged me to stay.

Every step I take toward my ex-girlfriend, the more memories flash through my head.

Wear this, Maddy. Don't go out with your friends, Maddy. Go to college in Pennsylvania so we can stay together, Maddy. Everyone expects us to get married when we graduate, Maddy.

Maddy, Maddy, Maddy.

With a deep breath, I plaster on a fake smile as my heart tries to hammer a hole in my chest. "Hey, pretty girl."

Tears well in Chastity's eyes. "Maddy? Oh my God, *Maddy*." Her arms wrap around my neck, and I get a face full of veil.

She still smells like cherry blossom, and something familiar rips through my gut. Affection. Young love. Idiotic behavior on my part.

The truth is, Chastity didn't do anything wrong back then. Granted, she might've turned a deaf ear to my concerns about our future and my attempts to break up with her nicely, but what I did to her when I left for college was unacceptable. I lied to her and ran away, and I've been running ever since.

I didn't have it in me to be the guy she wanted. I was never the settling down type. I'm still not that guy. Probably never will be.

"Has Halloween come early or is a congratulations in order?" I tug on her veil. I'm proud of myself for sounding like a normal human when I'm freaking out on the inside.

She pulls back, but her hands stay on my shoulders. "It should've been us," she whispers.

The tightness in my chest twists. "You know why that wouldn't work."

She wipes her nose with the back of her hand. "I know."

God, I'm still a shithead. And still lying to her after all this time. I should tell her the truth; I owe her that much. I've managed to avoid her every trip home for the last five years, but then I run into her at her bachelorette party?

"We need tequila!" her friend screams.

That's an understatement. I think I need a silo full.

Chastity's face lights up. "Stay and drink with us?"

"Umm ..." No, I should go. Tell her the truth, turn around, and leave.

But she pulls that face—the one I used to give into so well. Her bottom lip droops, and she stares at me with shiny, puppy-dog eyes.

"I can stay for a drink." *One drink*, I tell myself. But I obviously haven't learned from old mistakes and I'm lying again, because twenty minutes and five tequilas later, Chastity falls into my arms and sways to an imaginary beat that doesn't match the house music.

"I miss you, Maddy. Maybe this is, like, a sign. Some higher power. Of all the people to run into—"

The walls start to close in. Suddenly I'm transported back to my eighteen-year-old self, and I need to run away. The pressure to marry the girl in front of me—not only from her but our whole hometown—was, and still is, too much.

More lies fly out of me without thought. "I have a boyfriend."

Chastity's smile is warm. "Figures. I'd love to meet him." She gasps suddenly. "You should come. Bring him to the wedding next week."

Uh ... what?

"I'll text my mom right now."

"No, no. Don't need to do that. We ... umm ..." Of all the times to draw a blank ...

"Done. It's no problem at all. We had two people who RSVP'd yes only to turn around this week and tell us they can no longer make it. You and ..."

She waits for me to tell her my imaginary boyfriend's name, but I remain still with my mouth agape.

"You and your boyfriend can take their places. We'd love to have you. Everyone at home misses you. You never visit anymore."

Yeah, there's a reason for that. "Umm, okay."

Wait, not okay ...

Did I really just agree to go home next week for my ex-girlfriend's wedding? With my *boyfriend*?

I reiterate what I thought the second I laid eyes on Chastity tonight: Fuck my life.

The staccato rhythm pounding in my brain has but one name. Tequila. That cold-hearted bitch.

My head rests on the table in front of me while my usual coffee shop bustles with my worst enemy: people. There are too many people for this time of morning and this type of hangover.

"Shhh," I say into the table. No one listens.

"Wow," Stacy says, startling me, and I lift my head. I didn't hear her come in or sit in front of me, but there she is. With two cups of coffee. I officially love her. "How hungover are you?"

I rub my temples. "On a scale of one to ten? One hundred and twelve."

She laughs, and her green eyes shimmer in amusement.

"Thanks for the sympathy."

"It's self-inflicted. Suck it up."

"Why am I friends with you again?" I'm officially not loving her so much anymore.

"Because I refuse to sleep with you. Had I fallen victim to your charms when we met, you never would've seen me again."

She has a point. I met Stacy at a frat party freshman year, and she shot me down for six months straight before I gave up trying. Probably a good thing she stood her ground. Stacy is the one constant person in my life. We got each other through college, and then we interned together at the same marketing firm where we work now.

"I found myself at a bachelorette party last night," I say.

"If you tell me you slept with the bride, was hired as the stripper, or had a three-way with two of the depressed single girls freaking out over their friend getting married, I'm out of here."

I take a large sip of my scalding hot coffee and swallow hard with a wince. "I have slept with the bride. But not since high school."

"Oooh, shit. Your ex-girlfriend is getting married?"

I tell Stacy the events of last night and how I'm in yet another situation I don't know how to get out of.

"Wait, wait, wait. Back this up. Your whole hometown thinks you're gay? How did that happen?"

"I ... I may've told Chastity I was gay to break up with her ..."

She's trying to hide her smile. I know she is. "I'm so glad I made the effort to come this morning." Her glee is my misery.

"Even your parents? How does that work, and how did I not know about this already?"

"I haven't introduced you to my parents for a reason. And you know me—I never get serious with anyone. I keep telling my parents I'm single and haven't met the right person yet, and I make sure to stay gender neutral in all conversations."

Her smile finally fades. "You've been lying to everyone for five years. I thought you were sad before, but this ... this is—"

"You don't need to say it. I'm a shithead. Tell me something I don't know. But last night, I'm at this bar and in walks my small-town girl in the big city, drunk off her ass. So, I make my way over to her, and she's throwing her arms over me, saying it should've been us. *I have a boyfriend* fell out of my mouth. And then ..." I blow out a loud breath.

"Then what?"

I lower my voice. "I said I'd go to her wedding next weekend. With my boyfriend." My head hits the table again and bangs against it repeatedly. Why the fuck did I agree to that? Not that she gave me much choice. That's exactly how I ended up staying in a relationship with her for three years.

"You what?" Stacy shrieks.

"I was expecting a 'I was so drunk. Maybe you shouldn't come' text this morning. Instead, I'm woken up by a phone call from my *mother*. Chastity had texted her mom, who called mine, and now everything's screwed. Mom's asking why I didn't tell her I was seeing someone and how disappointed she was to find out from the Wellses. She demanded I come home and bring my boyfriend with me to stay the weekend while I attend the wedding."

Stacy sniggers.

"Real helpful, Stace. Have you ever had to endure a guilt trip from a small-town mom? I'm surprised by the time we hung up this morning I hadn't agreed to move home with the boyfriend I don't actually have."

She bites her lip. "What are you going to do?"

"Well, I was kinda hoping ..."

"I'm not dressing up as a dude and pretending to be your boyfriend."

I laugh. "I was actually hoping you could convince your brother to do it." I've never met him, but she does talk about him a lot.

Stacy purses her lips. "Damon's always working or studying. It's pretty sad. I don't know if he'll be able to take the weekend off."

"He's a sports agent, right?"

"Soon-to-be, yeah."

I don't want to play this card, but it's all I've got. "What if I could get him a meeting with a high-profile hockey player in the NHL?"

Stacy's brow furrows. "Who?"

There's a reason I don't tell anyone I'm related to Tommy Novak. I barely know the guy. He's married to my sister, who I've never been close to, and family gatherings are few and far between. It feels wrong asking him for favors, but I'll do it if it means Stacy's brother will help me. "All I can say is he plays for Boston."

"And you're really going to go through with this charade if I get Damon to agree? Why can't you tell the truth? Come out of the closet. But in reverse."

"It'd be a big scandal if the town found out the truth, and that's definitely not what Chastity needs right before her wedding."

"So, you're doing this for her? She's your ex. Why do you care?"

I rub my neck. "She's the only relationship I've ever had. I was a dick for lying to her, and I don't want that to come out during her wedding to some other guy. I figured if I ever found a girl I got serious with—which I've always doubted I'd do anyway—that I'd tell everyone then. I'll tell them eventually, but this weekend is not the time to do it."

"Why don't you just say you can't make it?"

"Do I need to give you the guilt-tripping mom story again? And if I go home and say we broke up, she'll force comfort food into me and make me stay a week to wallow. That's the type of mom she is."

Stacy searches in her bag and pulls out her phone. "I'm on it."

"Really?"

"I'd love to say I'm doing this because I'm your friend, but honestly? The thought of you having to pretend to be gay for forty-eight hours entertains me immensely."

Of course, it does.

CHAPTER TWO

DAMON

"I can't believe I let you talk me into this," I grumble as Stacy and I leave the subway. I tug down my ballcap—a nervous habit I've had since my pitching days. The coach always knew I was struggling on the mound when I fidgeted with my cap. "You're the worst sister ever."

"Hey, it's not like you're not getting anything out of this."

"Yeah, well, this mysterious meeting with an NHL player better come through. How do you even know this Maddox guy is telling the truth about it?"

"He doesn't lie to me."

"That you know of."

My bosses at OnTrack Sports want to promote me from paid-intern-slash-assistant to agent as soon as I finish my law degree, but I need to show them I can bring in my own clients. I'm desperate enough to spend a weekend pretending to be someone's boyfriend to get that chance.

Maybe my family has a right to call me a workaholic.

"I promise it'll happen," my sister says. "Besides, you're going to love Maddox."

"I'm sure I'll love the straight guy who's pretending to be

gay because he's a womanizing asshole with no balls to tell everyone the truth."

She slaps my chest. "See, you already know him."

The closer we get to Maddox's apartment, the more uneasy I become. "Seriously, Stace. I'm starting to wonder if this is worth the possible client."

"Two nights. He gets his ex-girlfriend and mother off his back, you get a new client, and I get hours of entertainment on Monday when Maddox fills me in. It's a win-win-win."

I really need to build my client list. Right now, it's sitting at an unimpressive *zero*.

As soon as we reach the lobby of Maddox's apartment, we're approached by none other than a guy in boy shorts, leather straps crossed over his naked chest and wearing angel wings on his back.

"What the fu—"

"Hey, you must be Richard," my sister says.

The guy tips his head, and cash exchanges hands.

"Stacy, what did you do?" I ask.

"It's all part of my fun."

"Your sister is evil," Richard says.

"Whatever she's paying you, it's not enough."

We follow Stacy into the elevators and head up to the ninth floor.

"How does a low-level marketing guy afford an apartment in this building?" I ask. Stacy lives in a shit-box. So do I, come to think of it.

"It's a studio, and he rents it from one of his frat buddies who owns it." Stacy holds her arm across me to stop me from walking down the hall. "Richard first."

"You are remembering I have to spend the next two days with this guy, right? He'll hate me on sight if we screw with him."

But it's too late. Richard's knocking. Stacy's grinning. I want to shoot myself.

The door opens, but I can't see Maddox from where we're hiding.

Richard goes from being a weird guy wearing a costume to flamboyant gay in the blink of an eye. "Maddox! Hi, darling. I'm Damon."

I pinch the bridge of my nose. "Richard's right. You are evil."

"Uh … umm …" Maddox's confusion almost makes me feel sorry for him. His voice is deeper than I expected. Even through stuttering, it makes a rich, smooth sound.

"Not what you expected?" Richard asks, putting his hand on his hip which he pops out in the most dramatic way possible.

Oh, geez.

"No. I'm just wondering how much Stacy is paying you to get me to make an ass of myself," Maddox says. He sticks his head out the doorway and glares at Stacy. "Nice try. You're forgetting I know you too well. Also, if you thought I was dumb enough not to stalk your brother on social media, then I've lost all respect for your cunningness. The Stacy I know would've posted this guy's mug on Damon's profile." He points to Richard.

I bark out a laugh. "You're right, Stace. This was fun."

Maddox's blue eyes meet mine. With his square jaw, blondish hair, and young Brad Pitt resemblance, this weekend just became a whole lot more awkward. Of course, the straight guy is gorgeous, because the universe likes to watch me suffer.

Fuck, now he's smiling. "Hey, real Damon. I'm Maddox."

"'Sup." *'Sup? Get it together.*

Stacy drags me toward his outstretched hand for us to shake.

"Uh, is my job done here?" Richard asks.

"Yeah. Thanks," Stacy says. "I'll walk you out. See you on Monday, Maddox. Call you later, Damon."

I watch my sister retreat, half-wishing she wouldn't leave me alone with him. I shouldn't have agreed to this. Not with my track record of falling for straight guys. Well, *guy*. It was only once, and I promised myself I wouldn't do that ever again.

"Ready to head out?" Maddox asks. "I rented a car, and we've got about three hours on the road if traffic isn't shit."

"Yup." I lift my duffel and the bag with my suit. "All set."

"So, uh, I can't thank you enough for doing this," Maddox says as soon as we're out of the city.

The drive so far has consisted of awkward small talk and my brain deciding one-word answers are appropriate.

I nod and stare out my window. I spent four years playing baseball for Newport University, and I never found New Jersey as fascinating as I do now. I didn't realize how awesome the I-80 could be.

"You think I'm an asshole, huh?" he says.

"Little bit."

"At least you're honest."

I shift in my seat. He really wants to go there? Fine. "It's because of guys like you that when I tell a girl I don't date women, they call bullshit."

"Really? They actually call you on it?"

"I've heard '*But you're so masculine*' and '*If you didn't want to date me, then fine, but you don't have to lie.*' My favorite would have to be '*But you're a sports agent.*' I didn't realize liking sports was against the rules. There goes any chance of winning Gay Man of the Year."

"Fuuuuck. Way to make me feel like more of a dick. How did Stacy get you to agree to this?"

"You forgetting your bribe? Be honest, does the hockey guy even exist?"

Maddox's jaw hardens. "Yes. He does. And for what it's worth, I don't like having to go through with this. I swear she's the only girl I've ever pretended to be gay for."

"Whatever," I mumble. "I'm purely here for the opportunity to meet a new client."

"Fair enough."

"We should get our story straight," I say.

"I tried to find out as much as I could from the internet, but you have privacy settings stronger than Fort Knox. All I found out was your name, you go to Columbia, you work for OTS, and your Twitter feed is full of baseball stats and not much else."

"Did you Google me?"

"Uh, no. Just stalked you on Facebook and Twitter." He should've Googled me. It would've given him my whole life story. I made sure to erase my former life as an upcoming baseball player from my social media accounts. "Why, what's there to Google?"

I scoff.

"Damn it, now I'm intrigued. Did you kill a guy?"

"No." Just my career.

"Is it an embarrassing middle name? A boyfriend should know that, right?"

I give him the side-eye. "Are you sure you know what you're getting yourself into? I mean, we're going to have to act like partners. You'll have to hold my hand and touch me like a boyfriend would. Are you going to flinch every time I go near you?"

"Two guys touching doesn't make me uncomfortable."

I want to say being okay with seeing gay guys touch is

different than *being* gay, but I don't. "My middle name is Isaac, after my mother's father."

"Damon Isaac King ... wait, your initials are—"

I grit my teeth. "I know. You don't think Stacy has made that joke to our parents ever since I came out? *'No wonder he likes dick when his initials are DIK.'*"

Maddox bites his lip as if he's trying to hold back.

"You're allowed to laugh," I say.

"I'm Maddox Colin O'Shay. Pretty boring. Sorry my name isn't up to your standards."

"It's very Irish."

"My dad's name is Colin, and his family is Irish. My grandparents moved to the States when Dad was a teenager. He still has the accent and everything."

"Noted."

"What are you studying at Columbia?" Maddox asks.

"I have a degree in sports management from Newport, and I'm about to finish my law degree on top of that."

"Double degree? That means you're smart. What made you want to be an agent?"

I clear my throat and stare out my window again. "It was a backup. The original plan was to become a ball player."

"What held you back?"

"Torn rotator cuff. I was a pitcher."

"Ouch."

I shrug, trying to appear nonchalant, but the loss of baseball is a sore subject—even now, years after my injury. I think it'll always be hard for me to accept it's really over. Nothing has ever made me happier than being on the mound. I still have dreams about pitching no-hitters.

The smell of the grass, the bright stadium lights, the game has always been intoxicating. Now I'm like an alcoholic who's been forced into mandatory rehab, because my addiction is no longer an option for me. But I'm so fucking thirsty for it.

"You need to know anything about me?" Maddox asks.

"Maddox O'Shay. Works at Parsons' Media, went to Olmstead University, and lies to girls about his sexuality." I smirk.

"Girl. One girl. And best not bring that up this weekend. Do you have any allergies? Drink coffee? How do you like your eggs? Isn't this what couples know about each other?"

"No allergies, coffee is essential—and I drink mine black—and if I'm at a restaurant, I'll order my eggs poached, but if I'm cooking, all I can manage is scrambled."

"I'm a sunny-side-up type of guy, I need cream and sugar in my coffee, and I'm allergic to morphine and commitment."

I laugh, and I hate that he's funny.

"But probably shouldn't bring up the commitment phobia this weekend either."

"Smart move," I say.

"So how did we meet?" he asks.

"Can we tell the truth? My sister introduced us. You went to college with her, you work together, and we all live in the same city. It's plausible. It's actually a miracle we haven't met before. Stacy talks about you nonstop."

"The brother and the best friend angle. I like it."

CHAPTER THREE

MADDOX

My boyfriend hates me. Can't say I blame him.

I wasn't sure what to expect when I met Damon. Other than a Facebook profile picture, I didn't have much to go on. I don't even know what color hair he has. In his photo and right now, he's wearing a Columbia ballcap. I could see him as a ball player; he has wide shoulders and biceps I'm jealous of.

When we pull up to my parents' two-story clapboard house and I turn the ignition off, Damon stops me from getting out of the car.

"There's one more important question we should know," he says.

"If it's which one of us bottoms, I'm gonna have to go with you."

Damon laughs so hard he has to hold onto his stomach. At least that's better than the scowl he's been giving me the whole way here. "If someone in your family asks that, I may have to ask them which sexual position they prefer."

"I dare you to," I say.

"My question is more important than that. Who's your team?"

"Uh, as in baseball?"

"Duh."

"Ummm …"

"You do like baseball, right?" Damon looks at me as if I'm about to slaughter a unicorn.

"I'm more of a football kind of guy."

He checks his watch. "Three hours and this fake relationship is already over."

It's my turn to laugh. "How about I go for whichever team you go for. Let me guess, the Yankees."

"Hell no. I'm a Mets guy through and through."

"Good to know. Ready to do this?" I ask.

Damon's eyes travel to the house, and if I'm not mistaken, his skin pales. "I've never met a guy's parents before."

"No need to be nervous. My folks are great and totally fine with the gay thing."

Damon huffs. "Only, you're not gay."

"That doesn't matter. We'll 'break up' in a few months anyway."

He glares at me. "Or you could tell the truth."

I frown. "That's freaky."

"What is?"

"You look exactly like Stacy when you're being judge-y. I would know. She judges me a lot."

He cracks a smile.

"Look, we can sit here and go over the reasons why I should tell my parents the truth, but this weekend isn't the time to do it. We'll have dinner with my folks, attend Chastity's wedding tomorrow, get drunk on free alcohol, crash out, and then head back to the city Sunday morning bright and early."

Damon gives a single nod. "I can handle that."

"Come on, boyfriend," I singsong.

"Are you sure you're not like a little gay?" he asks in a playful tone. "You're way too natural at this."

"Sorry to disappoint." Although, I'm surprised by how easy the word *boyfriend* slips out.

His face falls. "Shit, I didn't mean I'm hitting on you. I—"

"Whoa. It's cool. I knew you were joking." I want to make it as comfortable as possible between us. I've dragged him into my mess, and now he's worried I'm gonna flip out at the fact he's gay or think he's hitting on me when he's not. His downcast expression makes me think he doesn't believe me. I risk reaching for his arm. "Seriously. It's cool."

He stares at my hand with a furrowed brow until I pull it away. Okay, got it. No touching the fake boyfriend. Damon glances out the windshield at the house again. "Uh, I think we've been spotted."

I follow his gaze. "That's my mom. We've been parked out here for too long. She probably thinks you're chickening out."

"That's an option?" Damon asks.

"Too late. Here she comes."

My mother started going grey in her thirties, and instead of dying her long hair, she always said she wants to age gracefully. She's wearing overalls and rain boots and is the perfect picture of a country bumpkin. All that's missing is a piece of straw hanging out her mouth.

"Hi, Mom," I say as we get out of the car.

She approaches and gives me a big bear hug. "My baby."

"I'm twenty-three. I don't think you can call me that anymore."

"You'll always be my baby."

"Cute," Damon quips as he rounds the car. Fuck, he's good-looking when he smiles. So much so, I'm wondering if my family will call bullshit on our little act. Clearly, if I was with Damon for real, I'd be punching above my weight. "Hi, Mrs. O'Shay. It's nice to meet you." He holds out his hand.

"She's a hugger," I warn.

As expected, Mom wraps her arms around him. "And call me Alana."

"Where's Dad?" I ask.

"Inside, carving up the turkey."

I look at Damon. "Did it take us eight months to drive here? I didn't realize it was Thanksgiving already."

"Funny boy," Mom says sarcastically. "You bringing a boyfriend home is a special occasion, so I cooked a turkey. Got a problem with that?"

I throw my hands up in mock defeat. "No problem at all." Only, it turns my stomach sour. This whole fake being gay thing had never been a problem until now, and I never realized how misled my family's been.

We're what I'd call a happy family, but it's not like we're close. I barely see my sister, and I've met my nephew and niece only a handful of times. I see Mom and Dad on holidays and call maybe once every other month and on birthdays.

Mom often asks if I'm seeing anyone, but I always change the subject. I'd do that if she knew I was straight though too. I haven't had a real girlfriend since Chastity.

"Coming, Irish?" Damon asks when he gets halfway up the path and realizes I'm not following.

Mom's already back inside the house.

"Starting with the cutesy nicknames? *Dik?*"

A grin lights up his face. "Well played." He takes off his cap and bows.

Ah, so he's got dark hair. Dark hair and green eyes—probably something I should know about my boyfriend. It's the complete opposite to his sister's blonde locks.

I catch up to him and throw my arm around his shoulder.

Damon stiffens for a fraction of a second before relaxing into it. Leaning in, I say, "I'm sorry for this. Again."

"It's all good." His voice is gruff.

When we enter the house, Mom calls out, "You can put your things in Jacie's room."

"Jacie's room?" I ask. "I figured Damon could take my room and I'll take her room. Don't know if you've noticed, Mom, but we won't fit on a single bed."

Mom appears around the corner from the kitchen. "Didn't we tell you? Last time Jacie visited, we bought a queen for her room and moved the twin beds into your room for the kids. I'm not delusional, Maddy. I know you and your boyfriend sleep together. Take Jacie's room."

Well, fuck.

"And then wash up and come down for dinner."

We march up the stairs, with Damon in front of me, and he pauses at the top. "Which way?"

"Left," I mumble and avoid eye contact. As soon as we're in my sister's room which has been redone into a guest room, I close the door behind us. "I'm so sorry about this. Last time I was home was a while ago."

"It's not a big deal to me, but I understand if it's a problem for you. I don't know if you realize this, but I've shared a bed with a guy a time or two."

"I'm cool with sharing a bed, but I didn't mean to put this on you."

"Don't worry. I'll make sure I stay on my side."

I cock my head. "That's not why I'm worried."

"It's just, I don't know a lot of straight guys who'd be okay with this. If you've got issues, I'll take the floor. I get it."

"If I have issues, then I should be the one to take the floor. But I don't, so I won't."

Damon looks away.

"We should head down to dinner before Mom—"

"Boys!"

"—does that."

"Okay."

The dining room is lit by candlelight, and the feast Mom has cooked makes guilt creep down my neck. Maybe I should make the effort to come home more.

"Da, this is Damon," I say.

Damon towers over Dad who's only five-ten. I have no idea where I get my height or blond hair from. I look nothing like any of my family who are all dark-haired and short.

"Nice to meet you, son," Dad says in his Irish brogue and shakes Damon's hand.

The term of endearment toward Damon eases my mind a bit. I don't want anything to make Damon's weekend any harder than it needs to be, and I know we'll get some type of bigoted comments at this wedding tomorrow.

It's funny, the day I told Chastity I was gay was the same day my parents "found out." Chastity wasted no time playing the martyr and victim over being used as a beard for three years. My parents knew it had ended an hour after it happened. That's Clover Vale connectivity for you. Screw social media; it's got nothing on small towns.

By the time I'd gone home, Mom and Dad were in the living room waiting for me.

"Is there something you need to tell us?" Mom asked quietly. Her tone held sympathy, and I figured she knew Chastity and I broke up.

"Nah. Nothing to talk about," I said. "We're going in different directions."

Dad snorted in amusement. "Or the same direction, really. You know, toward guys."

"Wait, what?"

Mom's eyes watered as she stood and approached me. "You were brave today, honey. I wish you had come to us first, but we want you to know we love you just the way you are."

"What?" I was confused, because I didn't think Chastity would've outed me to the whole town. I would've been pissed had I not been lying about being gay. I guess it was karma's way of getting me back.

Then Dad told me he was proud of me. He hadn't said that when I got into college.

I wanted to tell my parents the truth—that all the other ways I tried breaking up with Chastity didn't work—but I never did. Obviously. Otherwise I wouldn't be sitting here with a fake boyfriend.

Damon elbows me, and I snap out of my trance. "What? Sorry, I spaced."

"How did you meet Damon?" Mom asks.

"I've probably mentioned Stacy before. He's her brother."

"We first met at their graduation ceremony last year but recently ran into each other again," Damon says.

Ooh, that's a good cover.

"And when did you come out?" Mom asks.

"Mom!" I wasn't expecting her to ask that. I get this is all new to her—meeting a "boyfriend" and whatnot—but ... really?

"Sorry, is that inappropriate?"

"It's okay," Damon says. "My story is boring. It was freshman year of college, and I called my parents and told them I was seeing someone. The plan was to take him home and introduce him—come out that way—but Mom said 'Make sure you bring *him* to dinner next time you're home.' I hadn't said it was a guy yet. I didn't have to—they'd figured it out. They didn't treat it like it was a big deal, because they believe coming out shouldn't be a big deal. Straight people don't have to do it, so neither should any orientation."

"That's a nice story," Mom says. "Better than a jilted ex-girlfriend outing Maddy to the entire town."

I tense. "We don't need to talk about her."

"Okay, okay." Mom throws up her hands. "You boys got any other plans while you're here?"

"Nah, just the wedding."

My phone vibrates in my pocket.

Will: Rumor mill has you back in town. You, me, Jared, Rusty's? One hour?

"Unless you want to go for a drink with a couple of guys I went to high school with?"

Damon's smile becomes tight. "Whatever you want."

Me: We're in.
Will: We?
Me: I'm bringing my boyfriend.

The guys will get a kick out of this.

Will: HAHAHAHAHA

CHAPTER FOUR

DAMON

"You sure it's okay if we go out?" Maddox asks me on the way to the car.

Am I that transparent? No, I don't want to go drinking with his friends. The deal was two nights with his parents and a wedding. "It's fine," I lie. "But are you ready to take this act public?"

"We won't have to worry about that tonight."

When we get to the bar, there are two guys outside waiting for us. Maddox rushes over to the dark-haired one and pushes him, hard. When the guy pushes back, Maddox gets him in a headlock.

"Okay, okay, you win," the guy says. "Don't mess the hair."

"And here we thought Maddy was the gay one," the other quips.

Maddox lets his friend go and turns to me. "Damon, come meet two of my best friends from high school. Will"—he points to the one he tackled and then the other guy who's a redhead —"Jared, this is my boyfriend."

"Boyfriend?" Jared asks.

Will laughs.

"Yes, *boyfriend*. Like"—he lifts his hands and uses air quotes—"'boyfriend.'"

"Thought you were serious for a second there," Jared says.

"Wait, they know?" I ask. That'll make things easier.

"You can blame these two," Maddox says. "They're the ones who gave me the idea."

"You know, we tried to convince everyone after you left that you were messing around and it wasn't true. You know what we were told?" Will asks. "That we were being unsupportive bigots."

"So, who are you really?" Jared asks me.

"You know my friend Stacy," Maddox says and then his face lights up. "Jared, you *really* know her. You remember when you came to visit me at school?"

"Oooh, *that* Stacy," Jared says with a stupid grin on his face.

My eyes narrow. "You slept with my little sister?"

Jared's pupils dilate to impossible size. "Oh, shit. Umm, no?"

"I'd love to see my boyfriend beat you senseless," Maddox says.

"Me too," Will says.

"Uh, umm ... well ..."

My glaring makes him uncomfortable? Good.

Maddox pulls on my arm. "Don't make me tell Stacy you're going all crazy older brother for her. You know she'll hate it."

"Do it and I'll tell her everyone back home calls you Maddy," I say.

"You wouldn't."

"Oh, I would."

"Shit."

"Well, you've got the fake couple banter thing straight. Pun intended," Will says. He turns on his heel, and we follow him inside the dive bar called Rusty's. It's a complete hole in the wall.

Maddox buys the first round, and we pile into a booth with ripped vinyl seats and the weird smell of stale beer.

"So, who else is excited for tomorrow?" Will asks sarcastically.

I snigger and turn to Maddox. "When was the last time you saw Chastity?"

"Please, this shithead hasn't been back since he was 'outed,'" Will says.

"Lies," Maddox says. "I've been back."

"For a day or two here and there. Just enough time for word to spread, and then you rush back to New York," Jared says.

"Aww, you guys miss me. I understand. Living without my awesomeness must be tough."

It's easy to see why Maddox gets along with my sister. They're both easygoing, sarcastic ... and full of themselves.

"Actually," Jared says, "since you left, the EPA says we have the freshest air in all of the US. Your ego was suffocating."

Maddox leans back in his seat. "Let's just say you two are lucky I'm gay this weekend. Otherwise, you'd have no chance of hooking up."

I almost choke on my beer, and Maddox pats my back as I cough and splutter. When I glare at him, his eyes glimmer in amusement, and it makes him look adorable.

No. Not adorable. Nope. Not even a little bit. Don't go there, idiot.

"Speaking of hooking up," Jared says and tips his head toward the door of the bar.

Three girls in tight clothing glance around as they enter, and their eyes zero in on us.

"Looks like one of us misses out," Will says.

Maddox laughs. "Pretty sure Damon's okay with that."

"Oh, so you're actually ..." Jared says. "I thought—uh, never mind. How the hell did Maddox get you to agree to this?"

"He's bribing me. I'm a sports agent and he's getting me a meeting with a possible client."

"Oh, his brother-in-law?" Will asks.

I cock my eyebrow at Maddox, but he changes the subject. Guess the hockey player might be real after all.

"One of *them* will miss out." He nods toward the girls who've strategically picked a booth in our line of sight. "I'm not looking for a hookup."

"We're on it," Jared says, and he and Will leave us to go talk to the girls.

"You can go over there if you want," I say. "Wouldn't be the first time I got ditched by guys looking for pussy. You remember I was part of a baseball team, right?"

"Apart from breaking bro-code, it's not smart for me to hook up with a girl here. You're forgetting how small this place is. Driving from my parents' place to here, you basically saw the whole town."

"Bro-code?" I ask.

"Bros before hos. You're here because of me. I'm not gonna ditch you."

Damn. His asshole level keeps dropping, and I have to remind myself why I'm here in the first place. He lied to his high school girlfriend about being *gay*, which makes him an ass, plain and simple.

He also has a fine ass.

Damn it. I shouldn't have checked it out on the way in here, but it was hard not to.

No, Damon. Do not check out your straight, fake boyfriend.

"Want another drink?" Maddox asks.

"Definitely."

"We can leave if you want. We didn't have to come out."

"It's cool. Your friends are great. I was worried they'd be dicks."

"Because I'm one?" Maddox asks incredulously.

"Maybe." It's more like straight guys make me edgy, but I don't want to get into that with Maddox.

"Challenge accepted. I'm gonna have to work harder at proving to you I'm a decent guy."

This should be fun.

At one in the morning, my feet don't want to cooperate as we stumble into Maddox's parents' house. We're both tipsy, but he seems more in control of his motor functions than I am. Maddox bought me round after round, trying to prove that makes him a good guy. Don't know how it worked, but it did. That guy is awesome. And hot.

No, not hot. Maybe I'm more than tipsy.

Jared ended up driving us home in Maddox's rental car, and then Will picked up Jared. They spent half the night trying to get laid instead of drinking. They both struck out, but it was fun to watch and bet on the outcome. Although, I owe Maddox twenty bucks now. I thought for sure Will would've hooked one of them.

"So, *Maddy*, huh?" I joke as we head up to bed. I try not to stare at Maddox's ass two steps ahead of me. When I give in, I stumble and almost fall flat on my face on the stairs. I right myself and keep talking as if I didn't nearly crash land to the ground. "I like Irish better."

Maddox appears to miss my contortionist act of trying to stay upright. "Irish isn't a good nickname in this household. All of us would respond. Well, except Mom."

"Point taken."

"But if you tell Stacy everyone calls me Maddy, I may have to kill you, *Dik*."

As soon as we reach our bedroom, I'm aware of him and every step he takes. I turn my back and try to ignore the urge to check him out when the sound of his belt buckle echoes in my ear.

"It doesn't have to be weird," Maddox says, and clothes hit the ground with a soft thump.

"It's not weird." My voice cracks and I force myself to clear my throat. "Okay, it's a little weird." I stare at him over my shoulder and try to smile, but holy shit, the guy has abs. Quickly, I look away again.

He's straight. He's straight. He's straight.

He hates baseball. He hates baseball. He hates baseball.

I take off my shoes and socks, drop my jeans to the floor, and climb into bed next to him, making sure I face the opposite direction.

"I'm sorry," Maddox says.

"Seriously, stop apologizing. I signed up for this. You didn't sign up for sharing a bed with your gay boyfriend, so it's probably best if I face this way."

"I know this is weird, and I don't know why you think I'm some close-minded asshole, but I honestly don't have issues with you sleeping next to me. And without sounding totally sleazy here, you can get comfortable, and I won't care."

"You know what a lot of guys say when they find out you're gay?" My voice is quiet, and I still refuse to face him.

"I have an idea, yeah. I broke up with Chastity a week before leaving for college. That's a week of small-town opinions being shoved down my throat."

"Nah, I'm not talking about the full-on homophobes. I'm talking about the guys who act like they're totally okay with it, and then throw in a 'so long as you promise to never hit on me.' I got it a lot in college. Locker rooms were a nightmare. My eyes stayed firmly on the ground, because God forbid someone thinks you're checking them out while they're naked."

"Are you saying you never check out straight guys?"

I let out a sad laugh. "You check out girls on the street and in clubs? It's human nature. But when it comes to these types of situations where clothes are … minimal, rest assured, the majority of us won't stare, okay?"

"Okay. I get it, but I want you to know I won't freak out if you look."

I smile.

"Night, Dik."

"Night, Irish."

After a long night of putting up with Maddox snoring, moaning, and talking in his sleep, I wake up alone. I also wake up late. It's ten a.m. according to the bedside clock. In my defense, sleeping next to a hot guy who's moaning is impossible. At one point, I contemplated jerking off in the bathroom to make me pass out but decided against it. I don't want to be *that* guy—jerking off to straight guy moans in his parents' bathroom. That's sadder than I ever want to be.

And yet, you were so close to doing it. Again. Like when Eric—

My conscience likes to remind me of how pathetic I've been in the past, and I'm not going to make the same mistakes with Maddox that I did with Eric. No fucking way.

The smell of coffee wafts up the stairs when I make my way down to find Maddox. I watch him move about the kitchen, cooking bacon and eggs and moving from the stove to the coffee pot and back again with ease. Typical country boy—he knows how to cook. And damn, that's hot too.

Stop it.

"Morning," I say, my voice gruff.

He startles. "Shit. Didn't hear you come down." He continues to rush around the kitchen and never once makes eye contact. Maddox slides a cup of coffee in front of me before he's on the move again, grabbing plates and popping bread in the toaster.

"Thanks," I say and lift the coffee to my mouth. "Where are your folks?"

"Grocery shopping. They wanted us to go out for breakfast, but I didn't want to wake you."

"You should've. Isn't it part of my job to spend time with your family?"

"Nah, you'll spend more than enough time with them this weekend."

Still no eye contact. Not even when he places a plate with hash browns, bacon, and eggs in front of me. *Poached.*

"Thought you were a sunny-side-up type of guy?" I ask.

"Anything for my boyfriend." Even though his voice is light, it sounds forced.

"This is really good," I say with a mouthful of food.

"Thanks," he mumbles.

Why do I get the feeling I've done something wrong?

CHAPTER FIVE

MADDOX

Attraction is a weird beast.

Once Damon loosened up over drinks last night, I began to think we could've come out of this weekend as friends. He's intense but still a decent guy.

For some reason, my subconscious held onto that when I went to sleep and decided to show me exactly how decent—or indecent—he could be. While naked. And begging me to fuck him.

The dream came out of nowhere, but it dredged up shit from college which I thought was long forgotten. Experimenting —that was all it was freshman year. It wasn't like I'd found another guy attractive since then.

Then why are you dreaming of fucking your fake boyfriend?

My dick jumps at the thought.

No. Down, buddy. Not going to happen.

It was only a dream. I once dreamed I was the spider from *Harry Potter*. Doesn't mean I want to fuck a spider.

But you weren't fucking other spiders in that dream.

It was all the alcohol last night. Let's go with that.

The dream is one thing, but when I woke next to him, it

seemed so real, I was harder than I'd ever been, and it wasn't morning wood. I was horny. For Damon.

Shit.

So, yeah, I may be freaking out a little. Or a lot.

"Ready to head out?" I ask as I finish eating. "I haven't bought a wedding gift yet."

Damon downs the rest of his coffee, and I'm mesmerized by his throat as he swallows. I begin to imagine how he'd—

Stop it.

"Ready," he says and stands. "Should we do the dishes?"

"Nah, that's what Mom is for."

"Is that so?" Mom's voice comes from behind us as she trudges in the kitchen door, carrying tote bags full of groceries.

"We can't be late." I feign innocence.

Mom smiles. "Go on, get out of here then."

"Thanks, Mom." I kiss the top of her head.

The awkwardness I'm unwittingly exuding doesn't dissipate as we make our way to the car. I think Damon's picking up on it now too, but if he is, he doesn't acknowledge it aloud.

"You have great parents," he says.

"I know."

"They probably won't care if you told them the truth."

"They won't care that I lied to them for years?" I ask incredulously. "Yeah, okay. They're great but not *that* great."

"The longer you leave it, the worse it'll be. What happens when you find a girl you want to settle down with?"

Pfft, like that's ever going to happen. "I don't plan on doing that."

"You're twenty-three and already resigned yourself to being alone forever?"

"I'm not a relationship type of guy. I learned that after Chastity."

"Because you couldn't break up with her?"

"Because I don't like hurting people. Call me a wimp, call me a pussy, call me whatever you want, but I'd rather not deal with drama. I'm the type of guy who would stay in a relationship for two years too long to avoid confrontation."

"Whoa. It all makes sense now. You think by telling your parents you're straight, it'll hurt them because they've believed the opposite for so long." Damon laughs.

"Laugh it up."

"Sorry," he says, still laughing, "but do you realize how absurd your situation is? Most gay people are scared shitless to come out of the closet. You're scared for your parents to find out that you're straight."

My molars mash together as I grit my teeth.

Out of the corner of my eye, Damon's smile falters as he studies me. "Are we okay? You seem—"

"We're cool," I lie. "I'm just distracted with Chastity getting married today. And we're here." The car's barely in park before I jump out.

Damon slowly gets out of the car, puts his hands in his pockets, and hangs his head.

He probably thinks I'm the biggest asshole. I should say something, but what? *Don't mind me. I had a sex dream about you, and now I can't look you in the eye.*

He follows me into the store, and I pause in my tracks. Damon runs into the back of me, and his hands fly to my waist to steady himself. The commotion attracts the attention of the guy who's getting rung up at the counter.

I know him well. We used to be friends. Teammates, even.

Damon leans in and whispers, "You know that guy?"

"I do. And you need to be extra boyfriendly right now."

His hands tighten on my waist. "This is a boyfriend move. Unless you have a lot of guys holding onto you for dear life."

Right.

Damon releases my waist and grabs my hand, interlacing our fingers as he drags us toward Emmett.

His hand is larger than mine, and it feels weird. Or maybe just different. My palm sweats, and I hope to God Damon can't feel how clammy it is.

Emmett's jaw hardens. "Maddox."

I lift my chin. "Emmett. This is Damon. My boyfriend."

Damon lets go of my hand to stick his out for Emmett to shake. When Emmett stares at it without making a move, Damon drops it.

"Ignore him," I say to Damon.

Emmett's scowl reminds me of why I didn't bother correcting the town when I was *outed*. Most people didn't care. It was a scandal, yes, having been with Chastity for so long, but there was still a lot of support. Then there were the people who decided I wasn't worth their time anymore. I didn't tell them the truth, because if they couldn't accept me for me—which was still the same person whether they thought I liked men or not—then I didn't want to know them anyway.

"Why would you come home for your ex-girlfriend's wedding when you're ..." Emmett starts. I wait for him to say the word *gay* out loud.

He doesn't.

I wrap my arm around Damon's waist. "She invited us."

Mrs. Jones comes out from the back with a giftwrapped box. When she passes it to Emmett, he can't get out of the store fast enough.

"He seems like a stand-up guy," Damon says.

"One good thing about coming out is I learned who my true friends were. Emmett wasn't one of them. Liked to drop the F-bomb a lot. And I'm not talking about the word fuck."

"Maddox," Mrs. Jones says, "I see the big city has done nothing but accentuate your vibrant vocabulary."

I grin. "Of fucking course, Mrs. J. I like to think of the word fuck as a sentence enhancer."

Mrs. Jones approaches and wraps me in a hug. "We miss you 'round these parts. Especially your Mom."

"Aww. You know I was a city boy born in a small town."

"Sounds like a Journey song," Damon says.

"Still, it wouldn't kill you to come home every once in a while," Mrs. Jones says. "New York is not that far away."

Hello, more guilt. I read somewhere too much guilt and stress cause cancer. Guess I'll need a physical by the end of this weekend.

"That's my fault," Damon says. "I don't let him go far."

"And who is this charming young man?" Mrs. Jones asks.

"This is Damon. My boyfriend."

"Well, I assume you're here to buy a gift for Chastity's wedding. There's only a few items left on her registry."

"We'll take the cheapest one," I say, and Damon snorts.

"Of course," Mrs. Jones says with a smile. She reaches for the shelf above her and pulls down glass salt and pepper shakers that are accentuated with gold around the edges. "I'll wrap these up for you."

While she does that, Damon leans in and whispers, "Who the fuck needs glass salt and pepper shakers? Is your ex-girlfriend royalty or something?"

"She wishes," Mrs. Jones mutters, and I can't help laughing.

Once I've paid, and after a "have fun" from Mrs. Jones, we head outside.

"Where to now?" Damon asks.

"Lunch?"

"We just ate breakfast."

I rub my stomach. "I'm a growing boy."

"I could have another coffee. I didn't get much sleep last

night. Someone talks in his sleep." He nudges me with his elbow.

I freeze, and Damon lets out a loud breath.

"Okay, that was a test. What's going on?" he asks.

"You know?" I croak.

"Know what?"

"About my dream. About us."

Damon's eyebrows shoot up in surprise. "I didn't realize it was about me."

And now I'm mortified. "Shiiiiit."

"Wait, you're freaking out about having a sex dream about me? That's why you're acting weird?"

"Maybe."

"You know it doesn't mean anything, right?" Damon says. "We're in an odd situation, we're sharing a bed, and you're facing demons from your past—like your ex-girlfriend who's getting married. Oh, and pretending you have to be gay for a whole town. You're allowed to have weird dreams."

"You think so?" I ask quietly.

"I dreamed I was married to Jennifer Lawrence once. I was totally doing a guy on the side as well, but it counts. Dreaming about me only means you're ten percent gay." He grins.

I laugh, but it's mostly fake. After last night's dream, and the stuff I haven't told him, I wonder if he has a point.

"I'm messing with you," he says, picking up on my vibe.

"I know."

"Let's just get through this wedding, okay?" he says. "Then tomorrow we'll go our separate ways, and we never have to speak of this awkwardness again. It doesn't mean anything."

"I can do that."

"Your tie is uneven," Damon says as we get out of the car at the church.

"Are you going to take my man card?" I force the joke, because the reason my tie is crooked—apart from not knowing how to tie one properly—is because I was too damn distracted by a half-naked Damon when I was trying to tie it. I understand what he meant last night when he said he doesn't look at guys in locker rooms. It seemed wrong to watch him dress, but I couldn't tear my gaze away. He's all muscle and hard edges.

I've looked at other guys before, but I wouldn't have said I've checked them out. Now, I'm not sure that's true. Guys compare themselves to each other all the time ... right?

"Can I fix it?" Damon asks.

"Please."

Damon's hands shake as he loosens the tie around my neck and reties it, and he fumbles with the knot numerous times.

"Thought you said you know what you're doing?" I ask.

"It's harder doing it on someone else."

"That's what he said."

Even though he fights it, Damon breaks out in a smile. "Stacy warned me you'd make those jokes."

"I can't help it. I'm five years old."

"Clearly."

"Speaking of your sister, have you heard from her?"

"I got a call and two texts while we were at lunch," Damon says. "But I haven't opened them. She gets mad when the phone says I've read her texts and I haven't responded."

"I need to try that tactic. I've had three texts—the third one telling me to stop ignoring her. Part of me wants to screw with her and tell her it was love at first sight between us."

His fingers still. "You're as bad as each other."

"Hey, she had a guy turn up in that ridiculous outfit pretending to be you. I need payback."

"That guy borrowed the outfit from me," Damon deadpans.

I pull back and cock my head.

"What? I can't make jokes?"

"I was trying to figure out if you were serious." And trying really hard not to picture it. That image shouldn't be inviting, damn it.

"All done." He pats my tie.

I reach for his bowtie to straighten it. "I don't think I'm doing anything here. I've just seen people do that in movies and shit. How do you even know how to tie one of these things?"

"I have a secret James Bond fetish." When I don't respond, Damon laughs. But when our eyes meet, the light-hearted moment is gone, and it's replaced with tension. "Ready to do this?" he asks, his voice gruff. "This isn't going to be like hanging out with your parents today. You're going to have to touch me."

"I'm okay with that." My feet step forward and my hands run up his chest. For some reason, my brain thinks this is appropriate. Why, I have no fucking clue. I watch my hands as they plant themselves on Damon's shoulders.

He stiffens but doesn't move. I'm pretty sure he's not even breathing.

My gaze moves up to his lips, and I wonder what they taste like. My mouth dries, and my tongue feels thick. The scents of our colognes mix, one woodsy and the other musk, somehow creating a smell that reminds me of sex.

What the fuck?

"Aww, aren't you two cute," Jared says.

Damon and I jump apart. "He was helping me with my tie," I say, probably a little too defensively.

Will eyes me in suspicion. "We should go inside."

I have no idea what just came over me, but it makes me a dick. Chastity's wedding is sending me crazy. Yup, that sounds like a legit reason to think about kissing my fake boyfriend.

As soon as our feet cross the threshold of the church, the walls close in and I begin to sweat.

"You okay?" Damon asks and pulls me back.

Jared and Will take their seats.

"Yeah. It's, uh ... hot in here."

"No, it's not."

I swallow hard. "I may be having a minor panic attack about the fact this was almost me a few years back."

Damon steps forward to speak low. "Repeat after me: it's not my wedding."

"Not my wedding." My voice gets stuck in my throat.

"Say it until you believe it. We should go sit down before you pass out." He drags me over to the pews, and I take the seat next to Jared, but my leg bounces. Damon puts his hand on my thigh to get it to stop.

My brain repeats Damon's mantra. *Not my wedding. Not my wedding. Not my wedding.*

When I can't catch my breath, Damon squeezes my leg and the reassuring touch makes my anxiety disappear.

The ceremony is long and drawn out. I sense the occasional stare from interested parties—the news of me and my boyfriend's appearance already making the rounds. The pastor rambles on about soul mates here, a bond forever there. Add in sappy vows, and bam, it should be over. Why is this taking so long? At one point, Damon leans in and whispers, "I'm falling asleep."

When we're finally released from the torturous ramblings of tying one life to another in the name of God and what-the-fuck-ever, I'm ready for a drink. Or several.

It's a short walk through the cemetery to get to the community center where the reception is being held, and Damon holds my hand the whole way.

I do a quick stop at my grandfather's grave, kiss my hand

and then place it on his headstone, and continue walking. "Is it weird I'm more comfortable here than in there?" I point to the church.

"That you'd rather be dead than married?" Damon asks. "Yeah, it's a bit extreme."

"You have to ignore Maddy," Will says from behind us. "The only type of commitment he can make is a couple of hours."

"Yeah, I've worked that much out already," Damon says and then squeezes my hand.

As soon as we reach the community hall and wade our way through the crowd and over-the-top decorations, we beeline it to the bar. "Scotch," I say at the same time Damon says, "Rum."

"Are you a pirate?"

"Aye. Would you prefer I order a cocktail with an umbrella? Have to give the folks here a nice dose of stereotypical."

"I kinda want a cocktail with froufrou toppings. They're delicious," Jared says beside us.

Damon laughs.

"I'd have to drink about a hundred of them to get drunk enough," I say. "I'll stick with scotch."

"How are we getting home?" Damon asks.

"Cab? Uber? Walk? Don't care."

"Tonight's going to get messy, isn't it?"

"I'm counting on it."

"I'll drink to that," Jared says. "Will and I were hoping to hook up with a bridesmaid or two. Turns out, I've already slept with two of them and Will has the other one, and we're not interested in crossing swords … so to speak."

"So now we're off to find sad cousins and relatives of the bride from out of town," Will says.

"Have fun with your sad women," I say. "I'm ready to be entertained watching you two strike out again like last night."

"Those girls were interested in you two," Jared mumbles. "Targets acquired, Willy Boy." Jared points across the room.

As soon as he and Will are out of sight, Damon slides in closer to me. "Should I be worried that my sister went for a guy like that?"

"I often judge her taste in guys. After all, she rejected me for months, yet that bozo comes to visit and she jumps into his bed a few hours after meeting him."

Damon winces. "That's something I didn't need to know."

"Sorry to tell you that your twenty-three-year-old sister is sexually active and has been since college." I gasp. "Shocking, I know."

We down a few rounds and laugh our asses off at Will and Jared who are trying so damn hard to get laid.

"You wish you could be out there with them?" Damon asks.

"Not in this town." I grab his hand. "Let's go find our table."

When he said we had to be more affectionate, I assumed I was going to have to be conscious of doing it—that I'd need reminding—but it's been natural and reflexive, just as it would if I were on a date with a woman.

I don't know what to make of that, but it also doesn't freak me out like my dream did.

We find our names at the same table as Will and Jared and also a few girls we went to high school with.

"Maddy," Claire exclaims and jumps out of her chair to hug me.

"Hey, Claire. This is my boyfriend, Damon."

"Wow. So you really are gay, huh? We all thought it was your way of breaking up with Chastity."

Damon laughs but recovers by putting his arm around my shoulder and saying, "I thought he was straight when I met him."

Yeah, so did I.

"You still play football?" she asks.

"Not since high school," I admit.

"He's into baseball now," Damon says. "Thanks to me."

"You wish," I say. "You will never convert me."

"Give it time."

"Ooh, there's Chastity and Christopher. I'm gonna go congratulate them," Claire says.

Damon leans in and whispers, "You know, I'm starting to think your town isn't as dumb as I thought they were. I'm wondering if everyone knows you're full of shit."

"I guess they can't exactly say 'you're lying' to my face. It's like one of those pranks where you're sure you're being pranked, but you don't want to call the person on it in case it's not. Like with the dude with the angel wings yesterday. I was ninety-nine percent sure he wasn't you, but I still hesitated because what if it was?"

"That wasn't my idea, by the way."

"Oh, I know. Your sister is pure evil. It's why I love her."

Damon grimaces and changes the subject. "So, you used to play football?"

"I was the punter on my high school team. Nowhere near good enough for Olmstead. Their team's full of NFL-bound players. I like the sport but was never in love with it or anything. Nothing like you and baseball."

"Incoming," Damon says and takes a sip of his drink.

I turn to find my ex approaching.

"Hey, Maddy, so glad you could make it."

"You look beautiful, Chastity." I lean in to kiss her cheek. I'm not lying. She's always been a beautiful girl.

"This is my *husband*, Christopher," she says, pulling the guy forward. He's a balding guy in his late twenties.

I shake his hand. "Congratulations."

"Thank you."

"Uh, this is Damon. My boyfriend."

"Ah, this is the boyfriend," she says. "I thought he was making you up. Couldn't even tell me your name last week."

"I was a wee bit drunk," I say.

"Are you ..." Christopher narrows his eyes at Damon. "No, wait, are you ... Damon King?"

Damon stiffens.

"Holy shit. I can't believe Damon 'The Lion' King is at my wedding."

"Lion King?" I ask.

Damon rubs the back of his neck. "I didn't realize I'd be famous in these parts."

"I'm a Newport alum," Christopher says. "I played for the Lions, and then the year after I graduate, in comes freshman Damon King and takes the team on to win the fucking College World Series three years in a row. Almost made it four until—" Christopher's mouth slams shut. "Oh. Sorry. That last game was brutal."

"Don't sweat it," Damon says, but I think I can hear his molars grinding. "It was a few years ago."

"Are you okay now? All healed?" Christopher asks.

"All healed. Never playing ball again though."

I think I see the actual moment Christopher's heart breaks. I'd find it funny if Damon didn't look like he was about to vomit.

Chastity's gaze ping-pongs between me and Damon. "Christopher's running for mayor. He's going to be a politician." I don't know if she can sense Damon's discomfort too or if she's trying to one up me on the whole *my new partner is better than yours*.

"Local government is a long step from the White House, honey," Christopher says.

"Chris and Chas, come over here," a woman calls from the table next to ours.

"Better make the rounds," Chastity says. "Thank you for coming, Maddy." She hugs me. "You were an important person in my life for so long, and—"

My throat does that constricting thing again. "You should get to your guests. Congrats again."

She smiles a classic Chastity smile, and I have to admit a part of me—way, way, way deep down—has missed her, but as soon as she walks off, I sag in relief.

"Chris and Chas? Could they get any more sickeningly cutesy?" Damon says.

I turn to my pretend boyfriend who has obviously been keeping a huge secret from me. "So, S*imba*—"

"Fuck me," Damon mumbles.

"You didn't tell me you were famous."

"Because I knew you'd call me fucking Simba."

I laugh. "You must've been a big deal for someone who didn't go to school with you to recognize you."

Damon sighs. "I was a gay ball player with rumors of becoming the number one pick in the draft. It was big news, so I was everywhere for a while. Especially in baseball."

"I was wondering why you went to Newport instead of Olmstead like Stacy. I mean, Jersey versus New York? No contest."

"Newport was better for baseball back then. I wanted to get the attention of agents, but you know that saying *be careful what you wish for*? I didn't get just agents' attention. When the media caught wind that I was an openly gay player headed for the big leagues, everything exploded. More media and sporting journalists went to Newport's games than any other school. I had people recognizing me on the street. I felt like a celebrity."

"That's a lot of pressure."

"Right? It was the pressure that made me push through the pain. I never told my coaches my arm was pinching. Then a few weeks after the pain starts, I'm on the mound during the championship game for our conference." He gulps down a mouthful of rum, and his knuckles turn white holding the glass. "We're up by one, it's bottom of the seventh, bases are loaded, and I just need one out. I'd kept them from scoring the whole game. The coach tries to take me out of the game and put a closer in, but I'm determined to finish the inning." Damon's voice cracks.

"You don't have to tell me if it's too hard."

"It's not that. I just ... fuck, I'm still mad at myself for not paying attention to the signs. I threw a fastball, and then *bam*, I was on the ground trying not to pass out from the pain. The fucker from UMass hit it deep left field, and two of those assholes crossed home plate by the time the ball was back in our catcher's mitt."

"Farrrrk," I say.

"The closer couldn't turn it around, and we lost the game. There was pain in my shoulder, and I ignored it. The doctors say I probably had a small tear, and I kept playing on it and did more damage. Career suicide."

"Athletes are taught to play through the pain, though."

"Exactly. I told myself to suck it up, because I was worried I'd be benched if they found out. And I often wonder if it would've been different if I was closeted. If I was the number one draft pick as a straight guy, I doubt the media would've jumped on it so hard."

"Let's drink more," I say. "Because that's depressing."

"Welcome to my life."

After we get new drinks, the mood is somber when we get back to the table. Damon's dream was shattered in mere seconds, but he went and moved on and had made a life becoming a sports agent. Something he loves ... probably. It's a logical step. Ballplayer turned sports agent. My only goal was to get out of this town, and I did that. Now what?

"You know," Damon says and leans forward. "Your ex isn't the ball-busting girl I thought she was going to be. I don't get it."

"Don't get what?"

"Your aversion to all this and your ex-girlfriend. I'm missing part of the story."

I hate that this guy who I've known for all of twenty-four hours can read me. He stares right into me, leaving me vulnerable but not entirely uncomfortable. Confusion clouds my head again for the sixtieth time in the last twenty-four hours.

"Why are you looking at me like that?" Damon asks.

"No one—not even Stacy—has asked me why I am the way I am."

"So, why are you?"

"You ask me for my deepest and darkest secrets so casually as if it's not a big deal."

Damon runs his hand over his jaw, as if he's trying not to smile. "Unless you've killed a guy, been abused, or belong to ISIS, your deepest and darkest secrets can't be too scary."

I blow out a loud breath. I don't talk about this stuff—to anyone. "This town was my home for eighteen years, but I don't belong here, and I never have. Can't tell you why because I couldn't work it out. I lived here, I had fun here, I was a normal kid, but the idea of living here my entire life made me break out in hives. And with Chastity ..."

"You would've been trapped here."

"Exactly. My parents are great, but I've never been close to them. Or my sister. I look nothing like them, act nothing like them. My whole life has been one big game of *one of these things is not like the other*."

"Maybe you were switched at birth," Damon jokes.

"You'd be surprised how many times I asked myself that growing up, but it's not just them. Or here, for that matter. I've never belonged anywhere. Even in New York. I almost transferred junior year because I was bored out of my brain. Now I've graduated and been in my job for a year, it's like I'm on that never-ending conveyer belt I left here to get away from. I wanted to travel and explore. I've done none of that."

I could keep talking. I could ramble all I want about seeing the world and not being tied down, living a life trying new things, doing new people, but I don't say those things aloud. I can't explain why being stuck in the one spot for the rest of my life scares the shit out of me.

"What keeps you in New York?" Damon asks.

That's easy to answer. "Your sister."

He screws up his face as if he's tasting something sour.

"Nah, man, not like that. I had a thing for Stacy freshman year, but after I gave up trying to get her into bed, we became actual friends. I'm glad she stood her ground, because if she hadn't, I wouldn't have her now. Does that make any sense or is the scotch already affecting my speech?"

Damon's face remains stoic. "It makes sense."

"When I told her I wanted to transfer out of OU, she asked me to stay, so I did."

"Because you couldn't man up and do what you wanted? I'm starting to sense a theme. Chastity wouldn't let you go to New York; Stacy won't let you leave."

"It's not like that with Stacy. When she asked me to stay, I realized she's the closest thing to home I've ever had."

Damon takes a swig of his drink. "Okay, I'm going to ask this once, and whatever you say, I'll accept as the truth. Are you sure you don't still have a thing for my sister?"

I burst out laughing. "No way. And if I did, Jared's done her, so she's off limits. I'm not into crossing swords either. She's honestly more of a sister to me than Jacie is."

Damon leans back in his chair and finally looks satisfied that there is absolutely nothing between me and Stacy. "Okay.

Should we dance? You need to make a choice, because I'm fairly certain everyone here knows we aren't together and that you're not really gay. You either double down on this lie of yours or come clean. I vote for the latter but will support you if you choose option A."

"Guess you need to show me your dance moves then."

Damon shakes his head in disappointment. "'Kay. I'm gonna hit the head and then drag you onto the dance floor."

While Damon walks away, my eyes gravitate to his ass. The one he was begging me to fuck last night in my dream.

I shift uncomfortably in my seat.

"What's the story?" Will asks, taking the chair next to me.

"What story?"

"You say this is all fake, but is it?"

"And here Damon thinks we're not convincing enough." Yeah, I'm deflecting. "He's a cool guy. I think we'll be friends after this."

"You keep staring at his ass."

"Jealous? Want me to stare at your ass instead?"

"Well, shit, I'm sorry for being concerned for my friend after you came home freshman year and—"

"This is nothing like that." Only, it's a hell of a lot like that.

Will is the one person in the world who knows what happened between me and my roommate freshman year of college, but I wasn't expecting him to throw it back in my face.

"What ended up happening with that, anyway?"

I crack my neck and breathe deep, because I don't want to get into it right now. I'm already confused enough as it is.

"Ready?" The rumble of Damon's voice brings me out of my murderous mood. Will's a lucky man, then.

I stand. "Ready."

Damon leads me to the dance floor and pulls me close.

"I'm not gonna be the chick," I say when we fumble with where to put our hands.

He rolls his eyes and grabs me around my waist, and with his free hand, clasps our hands together out to our side. Damon mumbles something that sounds like "God forbid a straight man do anything that resembles a feminine trait."

Eyes from everywhere around the room land on us. I don't need to glance around to know the burning sensation at the back of my head is from the stares of both curious and disgusted spectators. Emmett wasn't the only person to cut me out when Chastity told everyone I was gay.

"Might wanna look like you're enjoying this," Damon says at my frown. "We have an audience."

"I hate dancing."

"Of course, you do."

I'm lying. I don't mind dancing, but the truth is, I hate dancing right now. I hate that we're on display and that everyone is passing some form of judgment. They're wondering why I came home, why I'm at Chastity's wedding, and some are probably even wondering what I'm doing here with Damon. But what I hate more than that is the fact I like being pressed against him a hell of a lot more than a straight guy should.

My gaze wanders around the room and lands anywhere but on Damon. It's not the stares that are getting to me—it's *him*.

"Aren't you in marketing?" he taunts. "That's selling, right? You're not selling this very well." He cups my head, forcing my eyes to meet his. I beg him silently to let me out of whatever invisible hold he has on me, because his piercing green eyes make me think about things that I shouldn't.

Like my dream.

His strong arms and how good his hard body feels against me.

And his lips. Those damn lips I can't stop looking at.

"It's a short song," Damon says. "You only have to pretend to like me for a little longer."

Pretending certainly isn't the problem. Pretending I'm not drawn to him is.

My eyes go to his mouth again, but when Damon's brow drops, he catches me in his confused gaze.

"Maddox—"

I don't know I'm moving closer until my mouth meets his, and I swallow his gasp. My name on his lips breaks the fraying cord attached to my denial.

And when he kisses me back? I'm completely lost.

CHAPTER SIX

DAMON

His mouth is domineering and forceful. And damn, if it doesn't send a shock straight to my groin. His tongue forces my lips to part, and a moan gets stuck in the back of my throat. Our bodies continue to sway to the slow Ed Sheeran song as I get lost in a kiss that's fake.

This whole thing is fake.

I need to keep reminding myself of that, because this feels so good. Fuck, too good. Maddox no doubt can feel my cock growing against his hip. Trying to step back—because *awkward*—I realize I'm not the only one who's too into this. The hardness between us definitely isn't just me.

The exact moment Maddox's brain catches up with his dick, he pulls away. His eyes widen in shock, but his lips are parted in want. He shakes off his dazed expression. "You were right. Everyone was staring, so I thought I'd give them what they were waiting for."

I nod and take a step back.

"Do you wanna get out of here?" he asks. "I have absolutely no reason to be here anymore. I've filled my obligation."

Again with a nod. Apparently when he kissed me, he took my ability to talk.

Maddox heads straight for the exit, without so much as a goodbye to the bride. Or his friends. I don't think he's aware everyone's staring at us. My eyes catch Will's right before I slip out the door, and he's scowling. Don't know what that's about.

"Maddy, wait up," I say as I try to catch up to him. If anything, his feet move faster.

He gets to his car and pauses. "Shit, I'll be over the limit. Guess I'm calling a cab." He refuses to look at me, and nothing I say or do will change that, so I awkwardly stand a few feet away from him with my hands in my pockets and my eyes looking anywhere but Maddox.

"Uber will be here in a few minutes," Maddox says and throws himself on the curb next to his car.

"Okay."

"Fuck, I'm sorry."

"For what?" I take the spot next to him but make sure to keep my distance.

"For kissing you."

"Part of the charade. Although, I'm not sure the tongue was necessary." My attempt at a joke falls flat. "Probably didn't help you ran out of there immediately after."

"It wasn't part—" He shakes his head. "Sorry, yeah, you're right. All part of the charade."

We sit in silence, and I stare out at the street. What should I do? Say *"Hey, it's okay you were turned on while making out with a guy. Happens all the time. Doesn't mean anything."* Yeah, I don't think that'll work this time. The dream he had about us is one thing. This ...

"Sorry," Maddox says again. "Chastity getting married has messed with my head. Coming back here—"

"You don't have to explain." I want him to, but it's not my business, and I have no idea what to say to comfort or reassure him if that's what he needs.

"You're gonna go home and tell Stacy I'm a complete head case, aren't you?"

"She already knows that. She warned me about it."

He scoffs. "Figures. Look, the dream, the kiss ... it's—"

The sound of a car horn makes both of us jump. "Car's here," I say.

"Of course, it is," he mutters.

Our poor Uber driver tries to talk and be friendly, but Maddox and I keep giving one-word answers. When we pull up to the house, Maddox jumps out and arrives at his front door before I've scrambled out of the car.

Maddox pauses in the doorway. "It's still early," he whispers. "My parents are probably awake, so—"

"Need to pretend you're not being weird. Got it."

We don't get two feet in the door before his mom comes in from the kitchen. "You boys are home early."

"Uh, yeah," Maddox says, "said our congratulations and then got out of there."

"Come join us in the back for a bonfire and beers."

"Coolest parents ever," I say.

Maddox hesitates. "We'll just go get changed out of our suits first."

He heads for the stairs, but his mom whispers, "Damon." When I turn to her, she's waggling her finger at me to come closer.

"What's up?" I ask quietly while simultaneously watching Maddox climb the stairs. He doesn't look back at us.

"Is he okay? He looks ... down. Did something happen? There's a few in this town who still live in the stone ages. I mean, for a small town, we're pretty accepting. There's just a handful of them who aren't."

Well, your son kissed me, which you wouldn't find weird because you think he's gay, but he's not. Although, he's definitely freaking out about kissing me. Okay, so I can't say that. "There were a few, uh, stares. Nothing major."

"Did you have a fight?"

Not really. Maybe? I have no idea what's going on in his head. Apart from freaking out. But maybe he blames me for the kiss. "No."

I don't think she believes me.

"Okay, well, make sure you boys join us outside, okay? Don't let him wallow about whatever's bothering him in his room. That's his MO."

"We'll be right down."

When I reach the bedroom, Maddox is rummaging in his suitcase for warm clothes. Even though he stiffens at my presence, he pretends he doesn't know I'm in here.

Wordlessly, I grab my own bag and pull out sweats and a long-sleeved Henley.

"We don't need to go down there if you don't want to," Maddox says.

I laugh. "Yeah, we do. Your mother's spidey senses are tingling, telling her something's up with us. She told me not to let you stay up here and wallow."

"How does she do that? She has like a sixth sense or something."

"To be fair, you're wigging out."

"I'm not wigging out. I'm ... okay, fine, I'm wigging out. I'm confused as fuck right now."

"Kissing a guy might do that to a straight dude."

Maddox bursts out laughing. "I don't think it's the kiss. It's

..." His eyes meet mine, and his laughter dies. "We should get down there—before Mom gets impatient."

When we dress and go downstairs, Maddox's parents have set out two more folding chairs opposite theirs and brought out extra blankets for us.

Maddox hands me a warm beer and then holds my free hand as we take our seats. I'm confused by the move. He's freaking out about kissing me, but now his fingers are relaxed and warm, intertwined with mine. He could use the argument that we're in front of his parents and it's part of the act, but we haven't shown much affection in front of them all weekend, so there's no real need to do it now. Unless he wants to ease his mother's mind, in which case, makes sense. But—

"You thinking deep thoughts over there?" Maddox asks quietly.

I shake my head and mumble, "Confusing thoughts."

"Welcome to my world." His smile is easy and his panic from earlier gone.

I wonder if he's suffering some sort of PTKD—post-traumatic kissing disorder—and has blocked it out already.

The fire barely does anything to keep us warm in the late February cold, but the blanket draped over us is thick and does the job.

My lungs fill with fresh air and smoke. The sky looks as it should outside of the city. I grew up on Long Island, so I'm not used to seeing so many stars. I went camping upstate once when I was thirteen with my best friend, Eric, and his family. Staring up at the sky, I try to spot the constellation that looks like a dick. I couldn't see it when I was a kid, and I guess I won't find it now. Maybe Eric was messing with me. He's a pro at that.

"Your aunt Cheri called while you were at the wedding," Maddox's mom says.

"How is crazy Aunt Cheri?" Maddox asks and then turns to

me. "She's seriously a nut. You know how people say they're gonna run off and join the circus? Mom's sister did it."

"She does not travel with a circus," Alana says, her tone exasperated. "She's a psychic. She travels with others and does astrology readings and all that stuff."

"Exactly. Circus," Maddox says. "She dresses like a hippie and calls herself a free spirit."

"You might not believe in all that mumbo jumbo, but how do you explain the fact she hasn't called in months and calls tonight looking for you?" The light flickering across Alana's face from the fire makes her look smug.

Maddox rolls his eyes. "Coincidence. Why was she looking for me?"

"She's coming into town next month and she wants to see you. Talk to you about … some things."

Maddox is too busy looking at his mom to notice his dad tense beside her. Guess he's not a fan of his crazy sister-in-law.

"What things?" Maddox asks.

"I don't know, Maddy, why don't you come home and ask her yourself next month?"

He leans forward. "Can't she come to New York?"

"Is it really that hard to come home again?" Alana's words hold mother's guilt—something my own mother has perfected over the years. A woman's brain must change after giving birth, or their guilt gene kicks in, because mothers have it down to an art.

My mom pulled the guilt card last year when I ditched Stacy's graduation ceremony to hang out with Eric. She didn't understand I was in a bad place with him because of stupid, stupid shit that wasn't worth losing a twenty-year friendship over, but I couldn't come out and tell her that's why I skipped out. And to think, if I had gone to Stacy's graduation, I would've met Maddox then. Would've been better than what I ended up doing that night.

"I'll try." Maddox sips his beer.

Mother's guilt wins again.

"It's a shame Tommy had a home game this weekend," Alana says. "If he was away, Jacie and the kids could've come to see you. He's gone so much during the season; they need family time when he's home."

"Tommy?" I ask. Boston player named Tommy ... Holy fucking shit. "Your brother-in-law is Tomik 'Tommy' Novak? No fucking way." My eyes widen. "Sorry for swearing, Mr. and Mrs. O'Shay, but that is seriously cool."

"We're fucking Irish, we don't care about swearing," Colin says.

"How did you not know about Tommy?" his mom asks.

Oops.

"I didn't tell him," Maddox says. "Maybe I didn't want Damon to use me to get to Tommy."

Yet, he offered him up anyway. My meeting is with Tommy Novak? There's no way he'd dump his agent for a newbie like me ...

I let out an exasperated grunt when I work it out. Maddox never told me who it was because he knew I wouldn't have accepted the terms. Meeting with Tommy would be a complete waste of time at this stage of my career. When Maddox said high profile, I thought he was overselling and possibly knew someone on the farm team for Boston. I didn't realize he was underselling. He should've said *hockey god*.

"Tommy-fucking-Novak," I mumble. "He's like the biggest player in the NHL this season. Superstar forward for Boston. Traded from New York a few years back. He's scored more goals this year than any other player. He—"

Maddox puts his hand on mine to make me stop talking. "I

get it. You're a fan." He leans in and whispers, "Don't worry. I'll keep my side of the bargain."

I slink back in my seat. "Don't worry about it. I mean, hell yeah, I'd want to meet him, but there's no way someone like Tommy will sign with a green agent like me." I should be pissed, because this has been a waste of my time, but I'm not. Perhaps it's because I actually like Maddox. Had I known him before all of this, I would've volunteered to come back with him without the incentive.

"I still can't believe you didn't tell him," Alana says.

"I would have eventually," Maddox says.

I shrug. "It's not like it's baseball. Had you been related to Zach Pritchett and not told me, I would've broken up with him."

His mom eyes us warily, so I wrap my arm around Maddox and pull him closer. His breath hitches when my mouth lands near his ear. "Your mom's suspicious," I whisper as if I'm telling him sweet nothings. "Smile as if I'm being romantic."

Instead, he laughs. With a quick kiss to his temple, I pull away but keep my arm around him. He tenses briefly when my lips land on him, but he relaxes again just as fast. Rubbing a soothing hand over his shoulder probably isn't a good idea, so I keep as awkwardly still as possible.

His parents ask me question after question about my family, and they're shocked when they find out I grew up in New York and I'm not a thug. Or that I've never been mugged. I have to bite back a laugh. There's more small talk, but every time there's a lull in conversation, his mom glances between the two of us again and her face takes on an analytical expression. She looks like me when I'm trying to do algebra. I'm all right with math until the alphabet gets involved.

The cold air gets colder somehow, and I move in closer to Maddox to block some of the breeze.

"I know what you're doing, dickhead," he mutters with a

smile. "We should swap places. You're wider than me."

"Then I'll be cold," I complain.

"But I won't be."

Maddox's dad gets out of his seat and throws another log on the fire. "That should be good for another two hours, boys. We're heading to bed."

"We are?" Alana asks. He walks over to her and offers his hand and then leads her toward the house. "Okay, I guess we are."

"They're so cute," I say.

"If you say so. I'm worried about the glimmer in Dad's eye." Maddox shudders. "Parents aren't supposed to get freaky. Especially when their son is visiting." He shudders some more. "You, ah, can let go of me now. They're gone."

"But I'm not holding onto you for show. I'm freezing my nuts off."

Maddox laughs. "We can go inside if you want."

"Nah, if your parents are going at it, I don't want to be hearing that."

"Dude. No. I can't un-see those thoughts." He leans forward and hangs his head in his hands.

My arm drops, and I pull it under the blanket to keep it warm now it's not being heated by Maddox's body.

"About our deal ..." I say. "As much as I'd love a chance at representing someone like Tommy-fucking-Novak—"

"He's still a human being, you know."

"Nah, he's a hockey god. But it's all good. You don't have to introduce us. I'm officially taking back our deal."

"Nope. Consider it done. It's the least I can do after what I've put you through this weekend." Maddox sits up straighter. "I guess now would be when to say—"

"If you apologize one more time, I may have to kick your ass. I've never been in a physical fight in my entire life—got into a few yelling matches with an umpire during a game—but I've got muscles. I'm sure they could do some damage."

Maddox's smile has a dimple appearing in his chiseled face. "I was going to say I should give you an explanation."

"Not my place. You don't owe me anything. We kissed. You liked it. Now you're confused. It's got nothing to do with me." I don't want to shut him out, but the needy side of me wants him to say he wants more, and I can't be that guy. I don't want to be Maddox's sexual guinea pig, and I already have a tiny crush on the guy, so he needs to work this out on his own. Harsh, maybe, but I can't go through this again.

"How do you know I liked it?" he asks defensively.

I cock my eyebrow at him, because we both know I felt how hard he was when his tongue was in my mouth.

"Okay fine, I more than liked it. Which ... okay ... so ... and—"

"You do know you're not constructing a sentence right now? Scotch make speech good?"

"There's no more scotch in me." Maddox's knee bounces. "I wish there was, because this is hard to say. The only person I ever told was Will."

"Is that why he was scowling at me at the wedding?"

"Probably. He thinks I'm going to get all fucked up over you like I did with ..." He draws in a deep breath. "Like I did with my roommate in college."

My ears—and shamefully, my cock—prick up at that.

"You know how I said I had a thing for your sister freshman year?"

"Yeah ..."

"One of the nights I struck out with her, I went back to the frat house and my roommate was asleep. Or, I thought he was. I ..." He takes in another deep breath. "You know that unspoken rule where if your roommate's jerking off, you pretend it's not happening?"

My eyes narrow. "You were jerking off in your room, while your roommate was asleep but not?"

"Right. Anyway, he asked if I needed a hand, and—"

"Smooth."

"I thought it was his way of being all 'Stop whacking off, I'm awake over here.' So I stopped. But it was his way of ..."

"Actually asking if you wanted a hand?"

"Right. Well, a mouth." Maddox shifts in his seat, and the light from the fire shows off his flushed cheeks. "At first, I was all 'What the fuck, I'm not gay.' And he said he wasn't either. He said he and his high school buddy used to give each other brojobs all the time."

"Brojobs," I repeat like a moron. I hate that term—always have. "Okay, so your roommate gave you a blowjob?"

"Sort of, umm ... yeah. Uh, multiple, actually. It kind of became a running joke between us that he'd only do it on weekends."

"Did you ... enjoy it?" Why am I asking that? It doesn't matter whether he did or not. I shouldn't care.

"The first few times I closed my eyes and pretended he was a chick. But, really, it was a wet, hot mouth on a horny eighteen-year-old's cock. What do you think?"

I chuckle but it comes out as a harsh breath. "Right. Of course, what was I thinking? Maybe that straight guys generally don't like gay guys manipulating them into fooling around, but whatever."

Maddox's brow furrows. "Matt's not gay. It wasn't like that. He gave me plenty of chances to say no and constantly asked if I was okay with it. There was no manipulation on his part. And I never touched him. I didn't offer to return the favor, and he never asked."

"Matt? Matty and Maddy? How cute." Why am I getting defensive and tight-chested, and—oh, fuck no. I can't be ... *jealous*. I was literally just thinking I can't be Maddox's sexual experiment, and now I'm pissed he's been with another guy before.

"Matt claims to be heteroflexible."

I scoff. "Right. Only gay on weekends. Got it."

"What's with the pissed-off tone?" Now *he's* getting defensive, but he's right. I have to tone down the attitude.

I try to tame my irrational side and go for the coverup excuse. "First off, *heteroflexible* is a term someone uses when they don't want to admit they're bi. If you're sexually attracted to both males and females, even if you'll only have relationships with one gender, congratulations, you're still bi. Pretty simple philosophy. But do you know a lot of straight guys who'll willingly give blowjobs for nothing in return? *Your* man is gay."

Maddox's mouth drops open but nothing comes out.

"Sorry if that bursts some kind of bubble you were living in."

"Well, fuck."

CHAPTER SEVEN

MADDOX

Damon psychoanalyzed Matt in a few mere sentences and reached a conclusion that made so much more sense than what Will and I could figure out. That's where I went wrong. I went to a straight dude for advice when it all happened.

The thing is, I'm downplaying what Matt and I had. The first few times, I did pretend he was a girl. Perhaps it was easier for me to handle that way. But then it started happening regularly, and I loved watching him as he went down on me. I loved gripping his short hair while I thrust into his mouth which was rough against my skin because of his stubble. And *maybe*, I chased after Stacy for longer than I would have any other girl because every time I was rejected, my consolation prize was a blowjob from my roommate. Part of me wonders if I was even trying with Stacy in the end.

I looked forward to my nights with Matt, but I never found it in me to take it further or ask him for more.

The closest I got was asking him to visit me in summer housing while I interned at a marketing firm over the break. He flat-out said no. Said we had fun, I was a great roommate, and he'd miss me the next year. It was like we broke up, even though we weren't in a relationship. It was weird but not as confusing as the disappointment I had over him ending it.

Before I started my internship in the city, I went home for two nights and ended up spilling everything to Will.

A bottle of tequila later, we decided to test a theory. We went to a bar, and I watched every guy that entered. I wasn't attracted to any of them. But every time I thought of Matt, my cock hardened in response.

Will, the rationalizing genius he is, came to the conclusion that it was something about my conscience not wanting to have been a complete jerk to Chastity and my explorations with a guy was my way of making my lie a half-truth. I thought that was bullshit, but it made for an excuse to dismiss the Matt situation. I chalked it up to college experimenting and let it go.

This weekend has brought it all back—how I wanted to ask Matt for more but didn't have the courage. I want to ask Damon for more.

I didn't think I'd be attracted to my fake boyfriend. I haven't thought about Matt or another guy this way since junior year when he was drafted to the NFL.

"You okay?" Damon asks. "You've gone silent on me."

"Just thinking," I murmured.

"What happened with the roommate in the end?"

"Sophomore year, he moved out of the frat house and into the dorms, so I barely saw him. He was around campus occasionally, but we weren't friends. I was half-convinced he hid from me for a year."

"Wait, he was in a frat? That'd be enough for any guy to stay closeted. I had a hard enough time coming out to my teammates. They ended up being cool with it, but I wouldn't have liked to have thrown in a frat on top of that."

"My point in telling you all this is I put it down to experimenting, because since then, I haven't been attracted to another guy." I suck in a sharp breath. "Until you."

Damon stares at me, his green eyes seeing through me, and that vulnerability I have around him seeps back in. "So, you're bi."

I pull back. "Huh?"

"Did you not hear my defining criteria? Attracted to both male and females. And I'm pretty sure I'm still a guy. I can go check in case it's changed in the last few hours, but—"

I shove him. "Shut up. I've been attracted to two guys but countless women, so—"

"It's not a fifty-fifty thing. I know a heap of people who have mostly hetero relationships but identify as bi. For some, it's easy to meet others of the opposite sex. A friend from college only hooks up with men because he says it's easier than having to woo a woman. Those are his words, by the way, not mine. I have no idea what it would take to get a woman into bed. I've never tried."

I purse my lips. "Okay, so I'm bi." It doesn't sound right on my tongue. "But I've kissed one guy and gotten blowjobs from another. I kinda feel unqualified for the label."

"What are straight people labeled as if they've never kissed another person? They're still straight."

I've never thought about it that way. "Interesting."

Damon continues to study me, as if waiting for me to break down over it. "You okay?"

I have to think about it, because I don't think it's sunk in. Am I supposed to feel different?

"I think so. But I want to kiss you again." I hold my breath. When he doesn't reply immediately, I joke, "You know ... for scientific purposes."

Damon breaks his gaze and stares at the fire. That can't be good. "Sorry, man. Don't think that's gonna happen."

"Why not?" I frown.

"Not into being used as an experimental thing. Been there, done that, have the broken heart to show for it. Not to get all emo on you or anything."

"It's not entirely about experimenting—I ... I think I actually like you." God, I sound twelve years old. "But it's cool. I'm used to being rejected by you Kings." I smile to cover my slightly dented ego.

Damon winces. "Can you please stop bringing up your crush on my sister? It weirds me out that the guy I kissed a few hours ago had a thing for her. I don't share guys with Stacy. When I came out, she was worried I'd cut in on her action. I tried to explain to her that wouldn't happen because, generally, guys who are interested in me wouldn't be interested in her, but you've proved me wrong. So, thanks for that. No way in hell am I going to tell her she was right."

I can't hold in my laugh. "If it makes you feel any better, I've gone further with you than I ever did with her."

"No. It really doesn't."

"You wanna tell me about the guy?"

"Nope."

"Come on. I'm sitting over here going through an existential crisis—"

Damon snorts. "Yeah, you seem to be really suffering. You're taking this whole thing better than I did when I first admitted to myself I liked guys. And that's saying something, because I always knew—on some level."

I shrug. "I guess I'm not all that shocked. I dunno, it makes ... sense. The label doesn't feel right, but the definition of it does. It certainly explains some shit I've been confused about since college. But I've shared, and now it's your turn. Don't make me feel like a loser on my own."

Damon sips his warm beer. "This story is going to make you

feel so much better about yourself. You know how every family has that other family they grow up with?"

"Like me and Will, you mean? Our parents are friends, we've been friends since grade school, and—"

"Exactly like that. My best friend, Eric, we did everything together as kids. He was the first person I came out to."

"So exactly like me and Will."

Damon shakes his head. "Nah. From the sound of it, Will didn't give a shit you were hooking up with a guy."

That's true. I didn't even second-guess telling him about it. I knew he wouldn't care.

"I came out to Eric senior year of high school. He, uh … was one of those straight guys I told you about. The ones where they act cool but stiffen at the same time and tell you not to hit on them."

"Is he why you've tensed every time this weekend when I've joked around?"

Damon nods and takes another sip of beer. "Thing is? With any other guy, had he said that, I would've told him to go fuck himself. Just because I'm gay doesn't mean I want to hump the entire male population. And homophobia certainly isn't a turn-on."

"But it was different with Eric?"

Damon hangs his head. "Yeah. Had a huge crush on him since we hit puberty. Real Callum Scott 'Dancing on My Own' shit. I watched him go through girlfriends, have prom dates, homecoming dates—all that fun stuff I never took a date to because I wasn't out and didn't want to pretend with a girl. I never acted on my crush, never hinted, and made damn sure I didn't make jokes about it, because I was terrified of him figuring it out. Eric was straight, and I told myself to forget about him. After I came out to him and we left high school, we drifted apart. He went to Yale, and I did my thing at Newport, but our families still got together over the holidays, so we still saw each other. Hell, his family came to my graduation ceremony, and mine to his. For the most part, it was the same between us, but he always acted ... straighter around me."

"What do you mean, *straighter*?"

"He emphasized his sex life whenever I saw him. Talked about his hookups nonstop, even though I kept my mouth shut about mine. When he moved back to the city, we started to hang out again, and I thought I was over him. I had countless boyfriends during college."

"Manwhore," I mutter to try to break the tension. I don't like where this story is going.

Damon laughs. "Hey, Stacy's told me plenty about your manwhorish ways. I'm a saint in comparison."

"Fair enough."

"Last year, he broke up with his long-term girlfriend, and we went out drinking." Damon's lips turn down as his face fills with regret. "We ended up kissing."

"Did you make the first move or did he?"

"I've gone over that night so many times in my head, because I wasn't sure. But you know how I said in certain situations I've always made sure to protect myself? Like in locker rooms and that? It was the same with Eric. I don't know if he knew about my crush, or it was that I was gay and ... there. But that night was all him. I'd gone years without kissing him, so I know it definitely wouldn't have been me. I've overthought it so much I think my memories are starting to warp. Though, I remember him saying he wanted to kiss me because if I was a chick, I'd be the perfect person for him. I should've pushed him away, but I'd wanted it for so long. And then we wake up next to each other in the same bed, and he suddenly lets his homophobic freak fly."

"Shit."

"Everything he said was in the heat of the moment, but it made me feel like the shittiest person in the world."

"What did he say?"

He swallows so hard I can see his Adam's apple bounce. "That I manipulated him. That I took advantage while he was drunk. He said I knew he was straight, so it was up to me to put a stop to him. All we did was make out a little and some hand stuff, but it didn't go any further than that. As drunk as we both were, I knew deep down it wasn't going to end well. What we did was enough to freak him out."

"I completely fucked up by kissing you, didn't I?"

"It's cool you're discovering this new side to you, and that you're not freaking out about it, but I can't be the one to—"

"I'm sorry your friend is a dick." And I'm pissed this Eric guy has ruined any chance I had to hook up with Damon, because now I've kissed him, I really want to do it again.

"I wish the story was done," Damon says with a groan. "A few weeks after the incident, I get a phone call from him. Then a text. Like a good little puppy, I went to him and ditched out on my sister's graduation. For *him*. He knew it was Stacy's graduation, and then when I get there, he's drunk and apologizing profusely and wants to go back to the way things were. Said he missed my friendship. I figured we've been friends our entire lives, right? Hooking up wasn't worth losing him, so I forgave him." The laugh that comes out of Damon is humorless. "Then he said he forgives me too. For letting it go that far."

"He still blames you?"

"Yup."

"Please tell me you're not still friends with him?"

"Our families are friends. We spend Christmases together. It is what it is. We're not as close as we once were, and I'm always making excuses to blow him off ... wait, wrong choice of words. We're friends, but if I didn't have to see him and be civil,

I'd cut him off. I don't have feelings for him after what he did, but I can't hate him."

"I hate him for you."

"Hey, Stacy doesn't know—"

"She doesn't know about me and Matt either. Prefer to keep it that way."

"Deal. Are you going to tell her about your ... uh, discovery?"

I have no idea. "Eventually, yeah. If I do it as soon as we get home, she'll think I'm messing with her. Which reminds me, we're soooo going home and telling her we're in love."

"Do I get a say in this idea?"

"Nope. All you have to do is stand there and look pretty."

"God, I'm Switzerland. I don't want to get in the middle of you two. But this trip has definitely been a confidence boost. I mean, if I'm so fucking hot that Maddox O'Shay, manwhore of OU, finds me attractive, what does that say about my sex appeal?"

"Hmm, not so attractive now your head is suddenly ten times bigger than it was an hour ago."

Damon laughs and downs the rest of his beer. "Think your parents are done?"

I wince. "Eww. Now we're stuck out here all night, because the risk of overhearing that is not worth it."

"Come on, boyfriend. If my balls shrivel up any more, I really could become a woman."

Pulling up to Damon's apartment has me torn in two. On one hand, I'm glad that disaster of a weekend is over. On the other, I'm not ready for my relationship with him—fake or otherwise—to be finished.

"Thanks for the ride. Would've been better without all the Lady Gaga, but I guess you had to get it out of your system because you're 'allowed to listen to it now.'" He uses air quotes, and I'm trying so damn hard not to laugh.

"Baby, I was born this way."

Damon's lips twitch but he refuses to let himself break out into a smile.

"Come on, I'm messing with you, and it's a little upsetting it's taken this long for you to realize that. Are you sure you're related to Stacy?"

"So this was all just to torture me?" Damon asks.

"How else am I going to annoy the guy who refuses to fool around with me?"

"So glad we're joking about this already," he says.

"Have to admit, it was a weird weekend."

"*Awkward*. I would call it awkward. After two nights, you know more about me than my own family does."

"I won't tell a soul. Although, would you object if I track down this Eric guy and punch him? Because that sounds fun." I wouldn't, because I avoid conflict at all costs, but I'd like to.

Damon grins. "Thanks for the offer, but I've moved past it. Really. And your secret is safe with me too."

I want to yell at him that he hasn't moved past it, because Eric obviously fucked him up enough to not trust I wouldn't do the same thing. But I understand his hesitance. I can't be one hundred percent sure I'd still be interested if we hooked up. No girl has ever been able to keep my attention, and now that I think about it, apart from Chastity, the one person I stayed with for longer than a weekend hookup was Matt. Yet, I had no idea I was bi until this weekend. One thing's for sure, Mensa isn't going to be knocking on my door any time soon. I wonder if they have an award for the most oblivious person in the world. I'd win, hands down.

"We're cool, right?" I sound like a moron. "Like, can we hang out sometime?"

"Of course. I can introduce you to some guys if you like? Give me your phone." Damon taps in his number and gives it back. "I usually catch up with my friends once a month or so. I can already see a few of them drooling over you. If you're cool with me telling them about you, that is. I won't out you to them if you're not ready."

My stomach plummets to the floor. I don't want his friends. I want to do this with *him*. I force myself to not say that aloud though. He's made it clear where he stands on the subject. "I don't mind if you tell them. Although, I don't know if I'm going to pursue this thing."

"This *thing*?"

"The label still feels weird to me." Logically, I know the bi label fits. But it's just like going home to PA. My family's there, I have friends there, being in Pennsylvania makes *sense*, but that doesn't mean I fit in there. I wonder if it's normal to not feel connected to your orientation. It doesn't freak me out or worry me. It's just not something I'm comfortable with yet. It doesn't feel ... real.

"Sorry. I've gone and pushed you into trying to define it," Damon says. "When it comes to sexual orientation, to me, it's either gay, bi, or straight. But not everybody thinks that way, and they don't have to. That's *my* opinion on it. I like being straightforward and fitting into a box, but you should do your own research and identify with whatever feels right. Tell everyone else to fuck off if they don't like it. Even me."

I nod. "I'll work it out."

"My friends are cool, and we've all been through what's going on in your head. So even if you're not ready to *pursue this thing*—as you put it—you can never have too many friends, right?"

"Right. Better than asking Will for advice."

Damon's smile lights up his face until a knock at his window almost makes him shit himself. "What the hell?"

Stacy's grinning face stares down on us. Using the buttons in the center console, I lower Damon's window.

"Hey, guys," she says, dragging out her words.

"You're too happy," I grumble. "Stop looking at us like that."

"How did it go?"

With a sigh, I turn off the ignition and exit the car with Damon and then sling my arm around him. "The weekend went *extremely* well."

"What, you guys got a bromance going on now?" Stacy asks.

Damon remains stoic, but I can practically feel his internal eye roll.

"Well ... actually ..." I pull Damon closer.

Stacy's eyes dart to my hand on Damon's shoulder and then to my face and back again. I see the exact moment it clicks. I wait for the smile and *"Nice try, asshole."* What I don't expect is—

"Oh shit, are you crying?" I ask. I hate tears. I don't do tears.

"Is this for real?" Her voice is uncharacteristically quiet, and I have to ask myself if this prank is worth it.

I step forward, about to reassure her, when she flinches back.

"Are you kidding me?" she suddenly yells. "What the hell, Maddox? That's my brother!" She takes on her high-pitched screech she does when she's mad.

"Stace—" I start.

But now she's crying again, and I have no idea what's going on. Damon stands frozen, and I assume he's as confused as I am.

"We were ... and ..." She sucks in a shallow breath as if she's hyperventilating.

I take her in my arms and hug her, but she doesn't hug me back. "I'm sorry. I didn't think you'd react this way."

She pushes me off her. "I've been in love with you since college, you idiot. I've been waiting and waiting for you to want to settle down, and then you hook up with my *brother*?"

"No. I mean—wait, what?" I stumble back and hit a hard wall of muscle. Damon grabs my arms to prevent me from falling over my own feet. "You're ... what? You've never seen me that way. I don't ..." *What the fuck is going on right now?*

Stacy sniffles and wipes her nose with the sleeve of her jacket. "The reason I didn't hook up with you during college is because I knew you'd lose interest as soon as we did. I figured being your friend, when you were ready to take that next step, I'd be the first person you thought of. But I can't ... not if you've been with my brother." Her cries become sobs, and she hangs her head in her hands.

Well, shit. I had no idea she felt that way. We're friends. We're awesome friends. I haven't looked at her like that since we were eighteen. I have no idea how to handle this.

"Stacy," Damon says through gritted teeth. "Enough."

Stacy's shoulders shake, and at first, I think she's still crying, but then she looks up at me through her lashes, and her mouth turns up at the edges. Then she glances at Damon. "You're the meanest brother ever. You couldn't let me have more fun? Maddox looks like he's going to puke."

The fog and freaking out over my best friend having a thing for me clears, and I realize— "You traitor." I turn to Damon. "You ratted me out."

Damon holds up his hands in surrender. "I'm sorry. But the way you guys talk about each other, I wasn't entirely sure Stacy didn't have a thing for you, and finding out you hooked up with me would've crushed her, and she's my baby sister. I messaged her this morning before we left and begged her to let it go, but you know her."

"So much for being Switzerland," I mumble.

"Bros before hos," Stacy says.

"You're not his bro. And I'm not a ho."

Stacy's *I call bullshit* face has me backing down.

"Okay, fine, I am."

"Besides, I needed payback for Friday," Stacy says. "That guy in a costume cost me two hundred bucks, and you didn't fall for it."

"So, this was all bullshit?" I ask.

She wipes fake tears from her eyes. Or maybe they're real tears from laughing so hard. "Definitely. I love you, Maddox, but not in that way. I couldn't care less if you hooked up with my brother."

My eyes find Damon's, and his brows go up in encouragement. He wants me to tell her, and I should. Knowing her, she'll laugh at me, say *"Oh, Maddox"* and then try to set me up with a guy.

"Just so you know, I hate both of you," I grumble instead.

"No, you love me," Stacy says and snakes her arms around my waist.

"Fine. But uh ..." I swallow the lump in my throat. "You busy right now? Maybe you could come with me to return the car and I'll walk you home?"

"Sure. You have to fill me in on your ex's wedding. I should've made Damon wear a GoPro."

"Yeah, because that's inconspicuous," Damon says.

"I want to hear all the wedding drama. I want a story," Stacy says.

Yeah, she's going to get a story, all right.

"Be a good fake boyfriend and help me with my bag, Madd—ox."

I glare at Damon, because he almost called me Maddy. It's funny—my whole hometown calls me that name, and I've hated it forever. But out of Damon's mouth, it sounds like a term of endearment. Stacy can't start calling me that. No way.

"I'll be in the car," Stacy says.

When we get to the stoop of Damon's apartment, he puts his hand on my shoulder. "She'll be cool with it. Apart from my parents, she's my number one supporter. Sometimes so supportive it crosses boundaries."

"Yeah, I can see her being like that. I don't know why I'm nervous."

"Not used to admitting it aloud is my guess. And if you're not ready, you don't have to. I just know she's not someone you have to worry about telling. It's your call."

"Thanks for this weekend. It didn't exactly turn out how I'd planned."

Damon grins. "That might be understating it."

"I'll text you later."

"See ya, Irish."

I tip my head. "Dik."

Stacy's analytical green eyes appear even more intimidating than usual as I get in the car, but I don't let it get to me. I can do this. Even if I hurl while doing it.

"So tell me everything. What did the bride wear, what did she say, did anyone call bullshit on yours and Damon's fake relationship?"

"A gigantic white dress, she said a lot of things, and no one called bullshit." I take a deep breath. "Probably helped that we made out on the dance floor."

"You what? How the hell did Damon convince you to do that?"

Another deep breath. "He didn't. I kissed him."

"For show?"

Here we go. "For ... for real. I, uh, kinda really like your brother."

She blinks at me, stupefied. "Is this still part of the fucking with me shtick?"

"I wish I was fucking with you, because that would mean I wouldn't have made a fool of myself by kissing Damon and him rejecting me." I wait for the shock, the disbelief, maybe even betrayal—like I've been lying to her for years, but instead, she's silent.

Her mouth drops open, and she blinks a few times, but before I can ask her if she's stroking out, she recovers. "He rejected you?"

"*That's* what you ask? Not, holy shit, Maddox is gay?"

She scoffs. "You're so not gay."

"I know I'm not, but I thought that's what you'd assume."

"So you're bi-curious. Not shocking."

My brow furrows. "What do you mean?"

"Well, you had to run out of women sometime." Her smile does me in, and I burst into laughter. "I'm more interested in why Damon didn't go for you."

I get why he's reluctant, and I can't tell her the truth, but Eric's not the only reason Damon turned me down. "He thinks I'm confused and doesn't want to be my 'experiment.'"

"Are you confused?" Straight to the point, as always with her.

"Nah. I never told you, but freshman year, I had this ... thing. With ... this guy."

"Who?"

"Oh, hell no. I'm not telling you who." I don't think Matt and Stacy had any classes together, and Stacy barely hung out in our room, but I won't risk it. Matt and I swore we'd never tell anyone.

She slinks back in her seat. "Huh."

"That's all you have to say? *Huh?*"

"What, you want me to throw you a pride parade for figuring out you like dudes? I don't give a shit who you fuck, so long as it's not me."

Another laugh. This is why I love Stacy.

CHAPTER EIGHT

DAMON

I haven't even dumped the clothes from my duffel into the washing machine when my phone vibrates in my pocket.

Smiling, I figure the message is from Maddox already telling me Stacy took his news well. My face falls when I see it's from Eric.

Eric: You around?

"Not for you," I mutter to myself.

I throw my phone on my bed and go for a shower. As much as I try to not think about Maddox while I'm naked, I've been hard up for two days—ever since I laid eyes on him standing in the doorway to his apartment with that confused look on his face as he stared at the half-naked guy in front of him.

His blond hair and blue eyes ... damn it, now I'm painfully hard.

Taking myself in my hand, I close my eyes and picture a different set of piercing blue eyes—the ones that belong to my future husband: Matt Bomer. It works for all of two strokes, until the name Matt makes me think of Maddox's Matt, which makes me jealous as I picture some frat guy going down on him. Then the faceless guy morphs in my mind, and I'm the one on my knees, giving Maddox what he wants.

No matter how many times I try to stop picturing Maddox, my brain has other ideas. And because my hand is attached to my brain, it pumps my cock in hard and fast pulls.

My spine tingles, and my orgasm slams into me. "Fuck," I grunt when the guilt comes before I've even washed the evidence away.

I may not have done anything wrong, and it's not the same as when I was a teenager jerking off to the thought of Eric, but it feels exactly the same. I'm thinking of a guy I can't have, which is going to screw me up. Even though Maddox wants us to … fool around or whatever he wants, I can't be the one.

That doesn't stop the smile when I towel off and check my phone again.

Unknown number: You were right. She's cool with it. Offered to set me up with a guy named George. Then we got into an argument about not knowing any sexy Georges. George is not a hot name.
Damon: Let me guess, she argued that Prince George will be a heartbreaker when he grows up. She has a weird obsession with Britain's royal family.
Maddy: I know. She literally cried on my shoulder when Prince Harry got engaged. I freaked her out today by saying I'd do Harry. This whole being bi thing could be a new fun way to fuck with her.
Damon: Play nice, children.

I wait for him to respond longer than would be considered normal. My fingers itch to keep talking—maybe even flirt a little.

And that's exactly why I need to stop. When I realize how sad that is, I finish dressing and get stuck into studying. Three more months until I'm done with my law degree—another reason I shouldn't hook up with Maddox. I need to focus on finals and my career. I also need to come up with a game plan for getting myself some clients.

The last thing I want to do right now is stick my head in a textbook, but I need a distraction. I get lost in the words but am pretty sure none of it's sinking in. Two hours later when my phone plays the rap version of "Take Me Out to the Ballgame," I sigh at my sister's name lighting up the screen.

"What?" I answer.

"Why won't you hook up with Maddox?"

"Jesus H. Christ."

"He said you're not into noobs."

I laugh. "Pretty much. I don't want to be that guy for him."

"Too late. One kiss and you turned him gay."

I stiffen. "Stacy, don't say that shit."

"Why not? You know I'm joking."

"Just don't, okay?" I can't tell her the real reason I hate that attitude, and it's probably thrown her off because she's always saying un-PC shit to me and I don't usually care. I have to say something, or she'll know something's up. "I had a guy accuse me of trying to do that. It's a touchy subject for me."

"What the fuck? Who?"

"That doesn't matter."

"Yes, it does. I want to punch him. Whoever he is."

"As much as I appreciate the sentiment, the last thing I need is my little sister fighting my battles. Besides, it was a while ago. All water under the bridge ... or whatever."

"I'd like to push him off a bridge," she says.

"So, you're okay with the Maddox thing?" I ask.

"Okay, honestly, I was shocked, but I think I covered it well.

I feel bad for him in a way. Like, it'd be weird for me if I suddenly found a girl attractive and didn't know what it meant."

"I'm gonna introduce him to a few of my friends. That'll help."

"Don't introduce him to Noah. He thinks he's God's gift and comes across as selfish and stuck on himself. Maddox deserves better than that for his first time with a guy."

I run my hand over my face. "I can't believe I'm having this conversation," I mutter. Not only that, but I've already decided not to introduce Maddox to Noah because Stacy's one hundred percent right about him. Great guy, but not the type you'd set a friend up with. "Don't get all overprotective on him. He's a big boy. Do you get this way over the girls he dates?"

"Well, no, but he's the selfish manwhore in that situation. He seemed ... vulnerable when he was talking about you. I don't want him to get hurt."

Neither do I. Would it be better for him if I was his first? No, I don't want to put myself in a position to get screwed over again. "That's why I don't want to go there with him. I've got to get back to studying."

"Of course, you do. Oh, before you go, have you spoken to Eric?"

"Nope. Why?" I don't mention he texted me and I refuse to reply.

"I was talking to Julian, and he said Eric needs to talk to you about something."

Julian is Eric's younger brother and kinda what Eric was to me for Stacy. Although, they aren't as close as Eric and I were. And I'm sure Julian never kissed Stacy and then accused her of manipulating him into it.

"I'll call him when I have time."

Stacy goes silent on the other end.

"I really have to go, Stace."

"What happened between you and Eric? You used to be inseparable."

"College happened. Speaking of college, Maddox's friend Jared said to say hi."

He didn't actually, but I need a subject change.

"J-Jared? You met Jared?"

"Mom would be so proud of you. Jumping into his bed after only knowing him a few hours. Not to mention, he's a ginger. He could've stolen your soul, Stacy. Was your Prince Harry fantasy worth it?"

"Don't you have studying to do?"

"Bye, sis." *Worked like a charm.*

CHAPTER NINE

MADDOX

Stacy's knocking echoes through my apartment. "I bring gifts in the form of margarita mix."

Ugh. "Tequila and I aren't on speaking terms."

"All the more for me."

When I open the door, she helps herself to my kitchen as she always does.

"Your brother is ignoring me," I say. It's only been two weeks and a couple of texts, but still. I told myself not to bring it up too, and look at that, she's been in my apartment for three whole seconds. Yay, willpower.

"Don't be offended. He's always insanely busy with school and work. Tonight's the first night he's taken a break since the weekend he spent with you. If it wasn't for Eric, he'd probably be holed up in his apartment with his face in a textbook."

I tense. "Eric?"

"Yeah, his best friend. Eric's getting married, and he's going to ask Damon to be his best man tonight. It's been hard to keep it a secret, but Eric wanted to be the one to tell him, and Damon's been too busy. So, you're not the only one he's been ignoring."

What. The. Fuck.

The tension in my spine shoots up my neck, making it twinge. The last thing Damon needs is to hear Eric's getting married, let alone get asked to be his best man. What the hell is wrong with this Eric guy that he thinks that's okay?

"Don't suppose you know where they were going tonight?" I ask.

She eyes me warily, and perhaps I should try to be more discreet, but it's kinda hard to be when I know what Damon's walking into.

"That hole in the wall pizza place in SoHo. Why?"

"Okay, please don't think I'm stalking your brother, but I have to go."

"What? Why?"

"I need to talk to him about all this same-sex stuff, and he's been ignoring me. You stay here, get loaded on margaritas, and by the time I come back, you'll be loveable Stacy."

"Hey, I'm always loveable."

"I know, but you're a lot nicer to me when you've been drinking. I'll be back soon."

"Want me to come with you?"

"No," I snap. "I mean … no offense. I don't … uh … it's a guy thing."

"That's sexist."

I step forward and kiss her forehead. "I'm not going to dignify that with a response."

"And now you're being condescending."

"For fuck's sake, woman, have some tequila." Before she stops me again, I grab my phone, keys, jacket, and scarf and leave her in my apartment.

What am I doing? Last thing Damon probably wants is to see me right now. Do I go in and hide and wait until Damon's alone to make sure he's okay? Do I pretend to bump into him?

As soon as I step over the threshold into the restaurant, my eyes find him at a table near the back. Eric has his back to me, but he brought his fiancée.

Holy douche-canoe, I already know he's a dick, and I haven't seen his face yet.

Damon looks miserable even with his forced smile as he downs the rest of his beer. He hasn't shaved for days, and his fledging dark beard makes him look even hotter than the clean-shaven jock I met a few weeks ago. I don't know what it is about this guy that draws me to him, but all I know is I want to be near him. Even if it's just as friends.

He hasn't spotted me yet, but I know a way I could rescue him. It's time for me to repay the favor he did me.

Eric's telling some story when I approach, his voice all douchey and frat boy like. No wait, that's an insult to me and my brothers. Damon's eyes widen when he sees me. There's a half-eaten pizza in front of them, so Damon's already had to endure this a while.

"Maddy—"

"Hey, sorry I'm late." God, I hope he hasn't told Eric he's not seeing anyone or this will totally backfire. I squeeze in next to him in the booth.

He remains silently stunned until I lean in and kiss his cheek. His woodsy aftershave smells familiar—like I've already memorized his scent.

And my brain has officially gone into creepy territory. I follow this guy to a restaurant and then smell him? Suddenly, coming here doesn't seem like a bright idea.

"Thought you said you couldn't make it," Damon says.

Phew. Thought I lost him for a second there.

"My other plans fell through." I turn to fuckhead and don't like what I see. Blond hair, blue eyes, just like me. Guess

Damon can't use the argument I'm not his type, because clearly, I am. "I'm Maddox."

Eric frowns. "You didn't tell me you were seeing someone, D."

D. Ugh.

"Can say the same about you," Damon says. "Turns out you're engaged." His tone is light but there's aggression underneath it. "Maddy and I are new."

"I'm Kristy," the blonde woman says to me.

"Getting married, huh?" I ask. "Congratulations. You're going to make very blond children."

Eric's still glaring. "How did you two meet?" He slings his arm around his fiancée. God, could he be any more obvious about what he's doing? We get it, you're straighter than a fucking ruler.

"I'm best friends with Stacy," I say.

"Wait, you're *that* Maddox?" Eric asks and then smiles. "You've hung out with my brother, Julian, a few times. He, uh, says you're a great wingman. You know, and great at picking up *women*."

Well, shit. I do know Stacy's friend Julian, and yes, I've hooked up in front of him a few times.

"What are you getting at?" I ask.

Eric turns to Damon. "Really? Resorting to getting a straight guy to pretend to be your boyfriend? That's sad."

"Who says I'm straight?"

Damon grabs my hand on top of the table. "You'll have to excuse my friend. It's all gay or straight to Eric. He doesn't like the grey area in between."

Ooh, burn.

Eric turns a shade of tomato. "Bisexuality is the middle step to gaytown."

Damon's grip on my hand becomes deathly.

"That's classic bi-erasure shit," I say. I may've Googled a lot these past two weeks. Definitely learned some new terms. "I'm here, I'm bi, and I like guys … and girls." I turn to Damon. "Hmm, not as catchy as *We're here, we're queer, get used to it*, is it?"

"Not so much," Damon says with the biggest smile.

"When my boyfriend asked me to meet his best friend, I wasn't aware I'd have to defend my sexuality. Sorry, *D*, but your friend is a dick." I have to give Damon credit; he holds in his laugh well.

Kristy's gaze ping-pongs between the three of us. It's not clear if she's confused or entertained.

Eric turns to his fiancée. "Can you go get me another beer from the bar, hon?"

"But—"

"Now," he barks at her, and she obeys. They're in for a great marriage.

As soon as she's out of earshot, Damon slumps in his seat. "What are we doing here, Eric?"

"You know our families will expect you to be the best man at my wedding."

"Can't you tell them you're all bromanced up with someone from college? Or ask your brother. Friends drift apart, and they know we haven't been as close since college. They don't have to know how much of a homophobe you've become. Or always were."

"Just fucking do it, okay?" Eric says.

I scoff. "Well, when you ask him so nicely."

Eric's glare turns to me. "Did we ask for your opinion? Damon knows it'll be easier this way. Our moms won't get involved and become nosy."

"Can't have them knowing the truth, can we?" Damon says. "If I say yes, can we leave?"

"It's not like it's hard to stand up there and pretend to be happy for me."

"I'll do it, but I'm not giving a speech or organizing a bachelor party. Get someone else to do that shit. I'll put up appearances, but don't think this means we're okay or whatever."

"Fine. Deal."

"Let's go," I say to Damon. "Your sister's currently getting loaded at my apartment, and I think we should join her." I practically drag him out of his seat, but as we pass Eric, he reaches out and grabs Damon's arm. He mumbles something I can't hear, and then Damon and I are out the door.

"How did you know where I was?" Damon asks on the walk to the subway.

"Tracking app I installed on your phone while we were at my parents' place."

He stops walking, and under the dim light of the street, his face pales.

"You should so see your face right now." I laugh. "Stacy told me, you dumbass. She said you were out with Eric and that he was getting married. Figured you might've wanted some backup. Sorry if I crossed some sort of line back there, but that guy pisses me off."

"You and me both. And considering you're someone who hates confrontation, is it weird I'm proud of you right now?"

"Proud? Of what? All I did was defend you."

Damon smiles. "Actually, you defended *you*."

Oh. Right. "I guess I did, huh? Didn't feel like it as the words were coming out. It wasn't about me personally, even though it was about me." I shake my head. "Sorry. It's still weird."

"Thank you for showing up. I enjoyed you putting Eric in his place a little too much."

"You should've said no to being his best man," I say.

"Like he said, it's easier this way."

"What did he say when we left?"

Damon blows out a loud breath. "It doesn't matter."

"It does matter."

"It's the same old shit he's said since we kissed. If our families find out, who do I think they'll believe?"

"That's bullshit." I've never been a violent guy, but right now I want to march back in there and throat-punch the guy. I'd probably break my hand, but whatever.

"Did you say something about Stacy and alcohol?" Damon asks.

"Yup."

"Let's go."

We head down to the subway and jump on the first train. It's busy for a Saturday night, so Damon and I are practically pushed together as we stand near the doors.

"So ... you've been avoiding me," I say.

"You waited until we were in small confines before you asked that, didn't you? I can't get away."

"Precisely."

"I got your texts, and I'm not lying when I say I've been busy, but yeah, I have been avoiding you a little bit."

The train car shudders and pushes me into him so we're chest to chest. "Why?" I croak.

Damon takes a small step back. "Honestly? I'm waiting for the memory of you kissing me to go away so I'm not tempted to do it again."

CHAPTER TEN

DAMON

Damn it. I was doing so well. I've been preoccupied and distracted with work and study, so I've barely had time to think about Maddox. Then he goes and swoops in and saves me from the most awkward night of my life. And that's saying something considering a few weekends ago I traveled interstate with a straight guy I didn't know and pretended to be his boyfriend.

Maddox takes a step back, but on the crowded subway, he doesn't get far. He hasn't said anything to my admission, and I don't want him to. I don't want him to ask me to kiss him again, because I know I'll do it, but I also don't want to hear that he's over whatever attraction he had to me.

The train car comes to a stop and the doors open. "This is us," he says and walks off. His steps are fast, and I have to scramble to keep up, pushing my way through the crowd.

"Maddy, wait up."

"Can't. If I stop moving, I'm going to do something you don't want, so I'm going to walk as fast as I can to burn off this excess energy."

He couldn't have answered more perfectly.

His East Village apartment isn't far from the subway, and I

practically have to chase him the whole way because his feet don't slow down. As we enter his building, I can't get over how he could afford this place.

"Are you fucking your landlord?"

Maddox stops dead in his tracks, and I don't have time to slow down, so I run into the back of him. "Did you just ask what I think you asked?"

"How can you afford a place in this building?"

"You a real estate agent now? One of my frat brother's parents own it, and they gave me a good deal."

"I pay over two grand where I am. It's not a studio, but it's a fucking dump."

"The joys of living in New York."

"Just tell me one thing. The guy isn't ..." Matt's name gets stuck in my throat.

"No. It's not my freshman year hookup." He turns and cocks his head. "Would it be a problem for you if it was?"

Busted. "Nope. Just ... curious."

My sister is already halfway drunk when we enter Maddox's apartment. She's lying on the small couch that's in front of a queen bed, watching *Sex and the City* reruns. She's been obsessed with the show since before she was even old enough to watch it. "What's my brother doing here?"

"Love you too," I say.

Jealousy over Maddox's apartment rears its ugly head. Yeah, it's small, but the countertop in the kitchen—which is bigger than mine—is granite, the floorboards are a sleek oak color, and if there was to be a wall that divided his sitting area from the bed, it'd basically be the same size as my one-bedroom apartment but fancier.

This is why I should be nicer to people. They could give me an apartment, damn it. Maybe I'll tell Noah he's slacking in the friend department. He's like a kazillionaire. He lives in a four-bedroom brownstone. I could totally move in—no, wait, then I'd have to be Noah's roommate, and I don't think there's anyone alive who could deal with his ego twenty-four hours a day.

Stacy wobbles as she stands from the couch. "Why aren't you out celebrating with Eric?"

An excuse would be a good thing to come up with right now, but I've got nothing.

"His fiancée was there," Maddox says. "She had a headache so they left early. I invited Damon back here for drinks."

Stacy screws up her face. "Is drinks a euphemism for something else? I'm all for you two doing the nasty, but not while I'm here, 'kay?"

"Yay, loose-lipped drunk Stacy has arrived," I say sarcastically.

Maddox snorts. "Nope. Not gonna happen between me and your brother, Stace. He's made that perfectly clear."

And now I feel like an asshole. "Mad—"

"Tequila me." Maddox cuts me off which is for the best because I have no idea what I was going to say.

"Come and get it." Stacy pours a shot, licks her hand and shakes salt on it, and then shoves a lemon wedge in her mouth, facing outward.

"Oh, geez, shots?" I ask.

Maddox doesn't hesitate. He licks the salt off Stacy's hand, takes the shot, and then leans in to take the lemon wedge out of her mouth. And fuck, if I don't hate my sister right now.

That's when he turns his sights on me. Shit. I watch as he licks his hand and gets a shot set up for me. "I haven't done shots since I was like nineteen," I say.

"Stace, I think your brother is calling us immature."

"No," I say, "I'm pointing out that I chugged three beers at dinner, and if I do this, I probably won't be able to walk."

Stacy coughs in between saying "Lightweight."

"I'm sorry I grew out of the binge-drinking phase sophomore year of college and applied myself to get a usable degree."

"Oooh, they're fighting words," Maddox says.

"Marketing is usable. I'm employed, aren't I?" Stacy says.

"You're smart, Stacy. You could've been anything you wanted, and you chose a highly unstable industry—"

Stacy throws her head back. "You sound like Mom. Besides, kettle meet pot. How is marketing more unstable than sports agenting ... agentry? Is agenting a word?"

Maddox ignores my sister's ramblings and places the lemon in between his lips as his eyes bore into mine.

"Guess I'm doing this then." I step forward and lick salt off Maddox's hand—ignoring his sharp intake of breath—and throw back the tequila. My heart pounds in my chest as I move in to take the lemon. A small piece of fruit separates our mouths, and my head chants for him to "accidentally" drop the lemon wedge. He doesn't.

When I pull back and am done screwing up my face at the taste, Maddox grins. He looks innocent and adorable as fuck.

Our eyes lock and I can't tear my gaze away even if I want to.

"Ugh," Stacy whines, breaking Maddox and me apart. "Big is such an asshole." She plucks a tissue from the box on the coffee table and throws it at the TV.

"What have I told you about watching that shit here?" Maddox says. "Last time, you threw a coaster at my TV."

"You love it, and now you're riding the rainbow train ... oh, wait, the bi train is blue, purple, and pink, isn't it? Either way, you're allowed to admit your love for *Sex and the City* now."

My sister, ladies and gentlemen—saying the shit that could get her bitch slapped if she said it to anyone but me. And now Maddox, I guess.

"You don't like it because Big is your spirit animal," she says.

I rub my temples. "How is a character from a shitty TV show a spirit animal?"

Stacy waves her hand dismissively. "You know what I mean. They're both commitment-phobic manwhores."

I nudge Maddox with my elbow. "There's a hockey game on. You should be a supportive brother-in-law and watch it."

Maddox sighs. "I don't know what's worse—*Sex and the City* or hockey."

"Ooh, sexy hockey players with missing teeth. I'm sold." Stacy grabs the remote and flicks it over.

Maddox throws himself on the couch and puts my sister's feet in his lap. He gestures for me to take the single armchair, but I can't stop staring at his hands on Stacy's feet.

"Another shot?" Maddox asks me.

Definitely. "Sure. Studying hungover is always fun. Getting back to SoHo tonight will be interesting."

"Crash here," Stacy says. "I sleep on Maddox's couch all the time."

"She's right. And it's not like we haven't shared a bed before," Maddox says and hands over the shot glass.

I forgo the salt and lemon this time and throw it back. Then Maddox fills the same glass and slams it down his throat.

"I thought you were making margaritas," Maddox says through a wince at the afterburn.

"Effort," Stacy says. "Shots were easier."

Despite Maddox's protest of hockey, that doesn't stop him from yelling "That's my brother" every time Tommy's on screen. And every time Tommy takes a shot on goal, Maddox pours us a shot each.

I tell him that the game is to drink when they actually score a goal, but he argues that will take way too long and hockey is a lot more fun when he's buzzed.

Stacy bows out in the third period and falls asleep, which means I have to keep my yelling at the TV to a minimum.

Maddox and I watch as Detroit tries to take down Boston, but the game ends up tied and heads into overtime.

"Oh my God, there's more of this?" Maddox whines.

"We can watch something else." Totally empty gesture. The game is tied 2 – 2 and all that's left is for one team to score. He won't really make me change it, right?

"It's cool. I can see how into it you are. I'm gonna head to bed, but as I said earlier, you're welcome to stay."

My cock likes that idea, but I don't think I can handle being in a bed with him without touching him. I've tried not to think about him for the last two weeks, but my distractions have only taken the edge off.

While Maddox goes into the bathroom to brush his teeth, Tommy sinks one and the lamp lights up. I can't even get excited about it, because I'm freaking out about staying.

My brain goes from telling me to go for it and forget about Eric to getting angry at myself for letting Eric affect my decision at all. But if I were to start something with Maddox, I'd always wonder if I was manipulating him somehow. I have a theory that homophobia stems from two things—guys who are confused about their own sexuality and are afraid of it or people who are literally dicks for the sake of being a dick. In the beginning, I believed Eric was the second type, but after he kissed me, I realized it's because he doesn't want to admit that a part of him—even if it's a small part—is attracted to males. What happened between us not only ruined our friendship but also made his attitude drop the *passive* from passive-aggressive. And while Maddox seems fine with his realization, I don't want to screw him over. Not that I plan to. But I never planned to screw over Eric either. I don't want to pressure him or push him into something he's not ready for and then have him freak out on me.

"You okay?" Maddox asks, reappearing from the bathroom. Guess I was staring into space.

"I should go. I'll catch a cab home." I stand to leave.

Maddox's face falls, but he tries to hide his disappointment. "I'll walk you out."

"It's not like it's far to the door."

His lips quirk. "True. Are you sure you're going to be okay getting home? How drunk are you?" He gives me a playful shove, but I don't budge. "Okay, not that drunk."

"I'm sure I can handle fifteen minutes in a cab."

"Okay." He looks at his feet and leans back on his heels.

"What?" I stupidly ask. *Leave already.*

"You going to go back to ignoring me?"

I rub the back of my neck. "No. I don't think I can anymore." *Shit, not what I should be saying.*

Maddox steps toward me, and I stumble backward.

"But, uh, I ... umm." Great time to forget how to talk.

By the smug smile on his face, I'd say he's enjoying me fumbling over myself. He closes the gap between us, his chest against mine. The urge to reach up and pull on his blond hair has my fingers twitching.

"Dik ..."

My gaze falls to his mouth, and there's no doubt that I want him, but I won't be that guy for him. "I can't," I whisper and step back.

"You can. I'm not Eric."

My eyes dart to Stacy who's still passed out on the couch. My family can't know what happened. Ever. "As much as I want to kiss you again ..." I force myself to spit out a lie. "I'm not into the whole inexperienced guy in the bedroom thing. But I know a heap of guys who'll jump at the chance to help you out."

My feet shuffle toward the door, walking backward. "I'll, uh, text you. I'm catching up with the guys next weekend."

Maddox puts his hands in his pockets. "Yeah ... uh, sounds good."

I mentally check off a list of all my friends who would be into Maddox. And then I make a note not to invite them next weekend. Because even though I can't be his experiment, I don't want them to go for him either.

Asshole level achieved: expert.

CHAPTER ELEVEN

MADDOX

What am I doing here?

Since Damon made his escape from my apartment last weekend, I've been telling myself to let it go. He doesn't trust me not to freak out on him. End of story. I need to move on.

So now I'm standing outside the bar where he told me I could meet his friends—friends who could "help me out." Damon doesn't understand this isn't about experimenting but wanting to go out with *him*. If I was looking for a hookup, I'd go out and do what I've always done.

Why is it that the one person I've genuinely liked in years—the one person I could see myself having more than one date with—doesn't want to go out with me because I've never been with another guy before? And that's a technicality because I'm not sure what my thing with Matt would be classified as.

A guy passes me, and his piercing blue-green eyes roam over me. When his lips quirk, I realize he's checking me out. Do I have a sign on my forehead now? Or am I only noticing it now?

When his lips turn into a full-blown smile, I swallow hard

and turn away from the bar. I swear I hear the guy chuckle, but it might be my imagination.

I only get a few steps when I stop and turn back. Then I change my mind and go to leave again.

I get seven steps this time before I pause.

Just do it. Enter the bar.

When I turn this time, I almost run into Damon.

"When Noah said there was a hot, freaked-out guy out here, I thought it might've been you."

"Noah?"

"The annoyingly attractive black guy with blue eyes who eye-fucked you until you got weirded out and left."

At that, the tension in my gut eases. "Oh. *That* guy."

"In my defense, Noah wasn't supposed to be here tonight. Wyatt invited him. I didn't want Noah to … uh, scare you off. Apparently, he doesn't even need to open his mouth anymore before people run the other way."

"It wasn't him that scared me off. I-I don't know what I'm doing here." I mean, I do. I'm here for Damon, but I can't say that aloud. This isn't supposed to be about that.

"Come in and meet everyone, have a drink, and then you can go. This was to make you more comfortable, not intimidate the hell out of you."

I manage a nod, and he leads me inside to a table with four other people—including the guy who checked me out—and their conversation doesn't stop at our arrival.

"How can you say that?" a skinny guy says. He looks like he could be a surfer with his sun-kissed, long blond hair. "It's the most offensive thing to ever come out of your mouth."

A girl with long, wavy brown hair throws her arm around a chick with a short, black bob haircut. "Stop being so dramatic. Skylar's trying to get a rise out of you."

I look at Damon for any type of explanation. He shakes his head with a smile.

"But she ... and ..." The guy's voice goes high-pitched. "There are lines, Rebecca. Your girlfriend crossed a major one. No one can say things that offensive without being ridiculed."

In my experience, only three things can create this type of argument: politics, religion, and—

"All I'm saying is," the girl with black hair says, "*The Phantom Menace* was so much better than *Empire*. Get over it."

"Agreed," Damon says.

Star Wars it is. This shouldn't need debating. I turn to Damon. "I'm sorry, but I *can't* be friends with someone who thinks *Episode One* was better than the originals." Then I face the rest of the group. "And if any of you say *The Force Awakens* was even better, I'm going to walk out. Right now."

"Well, you passed the nerd test," Noah says.

The surfer guy leans in. "Ignore him. He's a closet Trekkie."

Damon points as he goes along. "That's Rebecca, Skylar, Wyatt, and Noah. Everyone, Maddox."

Staring at the group, I can't help noticing how mismatched they all are.

"Damon, I think we broke your friend," Noah says. "He's staring at us weird."

"Sorry," I say. "Just ... odd dynamic."

"Think you have us figured out already, huh?" Damon asks. "By all means, tell us how we're *odd*."

I'm worried I'm about to offend a table of people I've just met. "Uh ..." I clear my throat. "Wyatt surfs. Skylar's in a band or is an artist, and Rebecca looks like she'd be a nurse or in childcare."

Noah leans in, resting his elbows on the table and his blue eyes shining. "And me?"

"I could see you as an athlete. Basketball or track, maybe."

"Congratulations," Damon says, "You got none of them right." Everyone at the table snickers. "Although, you came close with one. Skylar's the nurse, not Rebecca."

The black-haired punk smiles at me. "Pediatric nurse to be exact." My eyes fall to her tatts. "I wear long sleeves at work and take out the nose ring."

"Rebecca's in some of my law classes, and she's going to be a killer litigator," Damon says. "Don't let the sweet appearance fool you. She's a shark. Wyatt's an analyst—"

"I'm not an analyst. I'm a data manager for a start-up."

Damon shrugs. "Same thing. And then we have Noah. Noah is, uh ..."

"Go on, Damon, you can say it. I'm a trust-fund baby and haven't worked a day in my life." Noah turns to me. "But if I hadn't been so terrified about my team beating me shitless, I would've played basketball. So you were close."

"You're forgetting you lack a thing called ball skills," Damon says.

Noah flips him off.

"That was a fun lesson to not judge those by how they look," I say.

"We all found each other in college," Damon says.

"And now that you've had your fun," Noah says, "we get to have ours and guess who you are."

"Frat boy," Rebecca says.

"Marketing major," Wyatt says next.

"Total manwhore when it comes to the opposite sex," Skylar adds.

"He may be a manwhore when it comes to women, but we know he's only recently realized he's into guys," Noah says.

Meanwhile, I sit here with my mouth hanging open. "How did you—"

Damon nudges me. "They're not psychic, just assholes. I

already told them about you. I also told them to be nice, but they're ignoring me."

"Nothing wrong with a little hazing," Noah says.

"I made it through Alpha Phi rush week, so hazing doesn't scare me," I say.

Noah grins. "Want a drink, newbie?"

"Yeah, I'll take a cocktail. Because, you know, I have to order those now."

Four pairs of eyes blink at me.

Damon laughs at me and mutters, "Now you're the asshole." He turns to his friends. "He's fucking with you. He's best friends with my sister, so do you expect any less?"

"Ooh, we love Stacy," Rebecca says.

Damon gestures to me. "Meet male Stacy."

Eww. Damon sees me as the male version of his sister? No wonder he doesn't want to hook up.

"So, that drink?" Noah asks.

My phone dings in my pocket. "Sorry, I thought it was off—" I go to turn it to silent but see it's a text from Stacy.

STACY: It was Matt Jackson you hooked up with, wasn't it!?!?

Panic has my fingers flying across my screen.

MADDOX: How did you find that out?

I glare at Damon, but it's premature.

STACY: Check the news.

"What is it?" Damon asks at my furrowed brow.

"Nothing good," I murmur.

Stacy attached a link, and when I click on it, photos of Matt in a compromising position with another guy pop up on screen. From what I can tell of the dark images, he's in a club.

The headline reads *NFL Star Matt Jackson Spotted at Gay Nightclub.*

"Ah, shit," I mumble.

"What?" Damon asks.

I shove my phone at him. "Guess you were right."

"Matt Jackson is your ex-hookup?" Damon asks incredulously.

"*The* Matt Jackson?" Noah asks.

"Who?" Wyatt asks.

"Geez, Wyatt," Skylar says. "Even I know he's a tight end for the Pennsylvania Bulldogs."

Damon scrolls through the article. "This is bad."

"What is?" Noah asks.

"This article outed him," Damon says. "There's definitely no denying it's him in the photos."

Noah holds his hand out for the phone. "Damn." He pinches the screen and zooms in. Matt's holding up his shirt, showing off the lower part of his abs, while a guy's on his knees in front of him. "Can't see any of the good stuff." Noah gives me my phone back. "Although, you'd think they'd come up with a better headline. How did they miss a pun about being a gay tight end?"

"At least he isn't a wide receiver," Skylar jokes.

Normally, I'd laugh with them, but I can't help wondering how Matt's dealing with this.

"This isn't a professional press release or tasteful at all," Damon says. "His contract is up, there's been no public announcement of renewal yet, and the season's over. I hope he has good representation."

Maybe I should call him. Or Facebook him. Although, what would I say? *Hey, we haven't spoken since the last time you blew me, but sorry someone outed you?* Yeah, maybe I won't contact him.

"I could go for that drink now," I say.

Noah buys me a beer and moves to the stool next to mine. I'm aware of Damon's scowl, but I tell myself not to read into it. Maybe Noah's a dick, and Damon's looking out for me. Then again, he said he'd introduce me to his friends who'd want to hook up with me, and between Noah and Wyatt, Noah is closer to my type. At least, I think he is. Considering the two guys I've been attracted to are athletic guys, I guess I have a type.

Damon's friends are great, and minus the initial screwing with me, they accept me. I understand what Damon means now about being around people who have gone through the same thing. Just knowing they get it without having to talk about it makes me comfortable around them.

That is, until I go to leave and Noah says he'll walk me out.

My eyes find Damon, and he frowns, but then he mouths "Go for it."

Right. Guess I know where I still stand. Guess I also know I should stop trying to change it.

Noah follows me out, and as the cold, frigid air hits me, I try to come up with an excuse to leave Noah on the curbside.

"Where you headed?" he asks.

"Subway."

"Want a ride? I have my car." The lights on a Beemer nearby flash. Of course, he drives a BMW. A luxury one by the look of it.

"I'm fine with the subway. Thanks." Shit, I'm usually not this rude. Or blunt. But dating a woman is easy. Flirting with a guy? Shit, pass me a manual. Plus, I don't even know if I want to flirt with Noah. Since realizing I also like guys, I'm more confused than ever. Noah is hot, there's no doubt about that, but do I think he's hot because I'm attracted to him, or do I merely see that the guy looks like a model and could be an actor. He's generically good-looking. That doesn't mean I want to bone him. Or does it?

I have no idea anymore.

Noah leans against his car. "What's the deal with you and Damon?"

"There is no deal."

"Okay, I'll rephrase. What's Damon's deal with you?"

"I don't know what you mean."

Noah rubs his chin in thought. "Well, let's see. He didn't tell me about tonight, and Aron isn't here either. Not to mention, the 'hands off' warning Wyatt gave me when Damon came out to greet you. It's ... odd. I haven't seen Damon interested in anyone for a long while, but he's definitely showing possessive tendencies over you."

"Nah, it's not like that. I'm his sister's best friend. He doesn't want me to get screwed over because he'll have to answer to Stacy."

"Stacy is pretty scary," Noah says with a small smile, "but I think it's more than that. And I think you have a thing for him too. Otherwise, why else wouldn't you get in my car? Free ride with a hot guy versus the subway when it's still freezing. I'd think that'd be no contest."

"Well, when you're so modest and all ..."

Noah chuckles. "I'm a realist. I'm hot and have money—I'm the perfect catch."

"If I wanted a sugar daddy. Which I don't."

His smile doesn't waver as he eyes me up and down. "I'm too young to be a sugar daddy. I promise not to hit on you if you let me drive you home. It's obvious you've got something going with Damon, and while you're definitely my type, I'm not into guys who are into other guys. Unless it's a three-way type situation, and then—"

"Okay, okay. You can drive me home."

He needs to stop talking about me and Damon and three-ways. It's making my brain explode with images that could make a long trip home uncomfortable.

Noah gestures to his car. Guess I'm doing this then.

CHAPTER TWELVE

DAMON

Damon: Don't hook up with Noah.

I stare at the text I sent an hour ago. Maddox doesn't have that feature enabled that lets me know if it's been read or not, and I resent him a little for being smart. Then I realize it's my own fault, because I told him that's how to trick Stacy into thinking you haven't read her messages.

Let me stalk you, damn it.

And now I'm being neurotic. *Fun.*

A crappy shower later, I'm climbing into bed and telling myself not to check my phone like some desperate loser. And look at that, my hand reaches for it. I have no willpower when it comes to Maddox, and I'm sure my mixed signals are giving him whiplash.

Maddox: Why not? Isn't that what you wanted?

Shit. I get the feeling he's pissed. Or fishing. I wish I could talk to him instead of having this conversation via text, because tone is impossible to read. No way in hell I'm calling him though.

Damon: He's not good enough.
Maddox: He's hot and rich and doesn't want anything serious. Isn't that what you wanted for me? To "experiment"??? Why isn't that good enough?
Damon: He's an asshole. And a manwhore.

This is not exactly true. He can be an asshole, and he has acted like a manwhore in the past, but he's actually a bit of a loner.

Maddox: You and Stacy call me a manwhore.
Damon: Maddy ... Just please tell me you didn't.
Maddox: I dunno. I'm liking this. Although, it'd be better if I could see you squirm in person instead.
Damon: Asshole.
Maddox: :) I didn't hook up with him.
Damon: Not many people turn Noah down.
Maddox: I got that. Thanks for introducing me to everyone. Skylar's already Facebook friended me, so I guess I didn't make too much of an ass out of myself.
Damon: In front of them? It's not possible.

I hesitate before sending another message through.

Damon: What are the chances of you getting out of work on Tuesday afternoon? I have to go to OU to scout a baseball player. I figure you could show me around campus.

It's a horrible excuse. I visited Stacy a few times when she went there, so I know my way around, but apparently, I can't help myself anymore. Wonderful.

There's too long a gap in between messages, and by the time my phone vibrates, I've chewed my thumbnail down as far as I physically can.

Maddox: Sure.

⚾

A nervous ball sits in my stomach as I wait for Maddox at the east entrance to his alma mater.

"Hey," Maddox says behind me.

I turn and try to smile, but by the concerned expression on his face, I'm clearly not pulling it off.

"You okay?" he asks.

"Yeah ... fine. Uh, you?"

"I'm good." His eyes travel over me. "Where's your suit?"

I stare down at my jeans and T-shirt. "I didn't want to stand out. If people find out you're with an agency, they'll pounce and start rambling about their son who's the best at everything. I should know—my parents did it back when I was playing. They'd randomly go up to people wearing suits asking who they worked for."

Maddox laughs. "Baseball field is through here."

Numerous people stop and say hello to him, and he greets them all as if they're long-lost friends. His easygoing nature is only one of the things I admire about Maddox, but it also means it takes twice as long to get to the field than it should.

"So, are we being spies right now?" he asks as we finally step through the stadium gates.

"Spies?"

"Yeah. Does your subject know you're scouting him, or are we supposed to be stealthy?"

"Is it possible for you to be stealthy? Everyone seems to know you."

"I was loved at this school. No, I was a god."

I snort. "Okay then."

"Fine. Most of the people who stopped us were in my class when I was a TA last year. They only love me because I graded their papers generously."

"You were a TA?"

"You say that as if you're surprised I was smart enough."

"Not at all. I just figured you were like Stacy—skating by on average grades because you were too hungover to put in the effort."

"I was here on a partial academic scholarship. I needed to keep a three-point-five GPA to qualify for it. I partied hard while I was here, but I was better at studying and working hungover than Stacy was. Poor city girl couldn't keep up with me. I'd been drinking moonshine out the back of Will's family's farm since I was fourteen."

"You really are a country boy, aren't you?"

Maddox shrugs and looks away. "Not really. I just grew up there. So, who are we scouting?" He leads us to a set of bleachers to the right of home plate. "And is here okay?"

The stands aren't overflowing with people, but there's a decent crowd.

I nod toward two free seats farther along. I should be able to check out this guy's talent from there.

"It's the pitcher," I say to Maddox. "Some kid named Logan."

Maddox leans back in his seat. "So, this is your homeland, huh? Your mothership."

"Yup."

"Are you sure you're okay? You're being all ... first-day Damon-like."

"First-day Damon-like?" I ask.

"Standoffish and grunty. Makes me think I've done something wrong or you're in a shitty mood, like the first day I met you. Do you need to get drunk? Because that worked last time. They might sell beer at the concession stand."

I rub the back of my neck. "I'm fine."

"Why ..." he starts.

"Why what?"

"Why did you ask me here?"

Fuck, why did I ask him here? Showing me around campus was just an excuse. I made him take time off work to be here, and all I'm doing is giving him one-word answers.

I shrug. "To hang out."

"Okay." Maddox gives up and turns his attention to the game.

It's already the third inning, but I made sure to come late. I want to see what this guy can do when he's tired.

So far, OU is up by one, but that doesn't mean shit this early in the game.

Logan's form, from the windup to follow through, is anything but textbook, but he's got a powerful arm. Too bad he doesn't know how to use it.

"That was a strike, right?" Maddox asks.

I shake my head. "It was a ball. Missed the strike zone, and the batter didn't try to hit it."

"Wait, baseball has rules? Isn't it all, hit the ball and run?"

I'd cry if Maddox wasn't so damn cute. "Uh, no. There's a lot more to it than that."

"Okay, then teach me, Coach."

I'm not sure if he's doing it to try to break my weird mood, but it works. I go into the specifics of the game and get lost in my old world. And fuck, I miss it. Each play, I explain to Maddox what's happening—stealing bases, fake outs, and the different types of pitches Logan tries. The kid's only successful in about half of what he delivers. He's nowhere near ready for representation yet, and with every slow or misaimed pitch, the more irritated I become that I've been sent here to scout him. When I was playing, this guy wouldn't even get a look in.

"Wait, so you can legally fake out someone by pretending to throw the ball but still have it in your hand?" Maddox asks. "Isn't that cheating?"

"It's misdirection. Trickery. Kinda like the beginning of our relation—uh, friendship." *Not relationship. There is no relationship.* I wish I had the ability to put words back in my mouth.

"True, I guess."

We only get two innings before Logan is taken off and replaced with a reliever. It's too early in the game to be pulling the starting pitcher, so he must be having an off day. Knowing he's not on top of his game makes me feel a little better about coming out here to watch him.

"What do you think?" Maddox asks.

"Honestly? He's got talent, but he's too green right now. He needs more control and stamina. He looked wrecked when we showed up. I have to go talk to him, but we can head out afterwards. Go grab coffee, maybe?"

Did I just ask him out on a date? Shit.

"Sure."

"Meet you out front? I have to deliver the news that OTS isn't interested."

Maddox pales as if he's the one about to endure a confrontation. "Good luck with that one. I might stay here and finish watching this period."

I cringe. "*Inning.*"

The fucker smirks. "I know. I really like seeing you squirm."

With a shake of my head, I make my way to the back of the dugout and mentally prepare to give the rehearsed speech I heard myself a few times. *You show potential, but we're not ready to represent you at this time. Keep at it, and we can reevaluate. Good job out there today.* When I knock on the door, one of the other guys answers. "I'm Damon King from OTS. I'm looking for Logan."

Logan comes to the door wearing his jacket only on his pitching arm to keep it warm. His blond hair is a sweaty mess now his cap's off.

"I'm—"

"Damon King. Holy shit," he exclaims.

Ooh, boy. "Can we talk?" I tip my head behind me.

"You know who I am?"

"I work for OTS. I'm here to—"

His face falls. "Oh, damn. If I'd known that, I wouldn't have signed with Hewitt and Locke last night."

"I'm sorry, you what now?" I ask. He got a fucking contract already? What am I even doing here?

"Yeah, my father was supposed to call you guys. He wanted me to go with Hewitt. They're bigger, you know? But shit, being represented by Damon 'The Lion' King? I'm kicking myself for listening to my old man. And, damn, you were watching today? I was throwing shit. Me and the boys got fucked up last night, celebrating."

This kid is talking a million miles a minute. Someone get him some Adderall, stat.

This whole thing is bullshit. I wish I could say it wasn't pure jealousy filling my veins with anger, but I know it is. This guy, who has the same amount of talent that my little finger did when I was top of my game, has an agent. He has the fucking idiocy and disrespect of going out the night before a game, but he has a future in baseball. What do I have? I have to sit back and watch others—others who don't deserve it—succeed where I failed.

I grit my teeth and force myself to stay professional and calm. "Well, congrats on the contract. I need to get back to the office and inform my bosses you're already taken."

"Wait. Can I get a selfie?"

Jesus Christ on a cracker.

"Sure."

He takes his phone out of his pants—geez, if either me or my teammates had our phones on us in the dugout, it was immediate one-game suspension. Guess Newport has higher standards than OU. Logan snaps the shot, and my feet practically make divots with each hard step I take from the dugout to the field entrance.

It's not until Maddox catches up to me I even remember he's here.

"Didn't go well?" he asks.

"You could say that."

Maddox grabs my arm to stop me from walking so fast. "What happened?"

"He signed with another agency."

"Isn't that a good thing? You didn't want him."

I shake my head and walk off again. Maddox doesn't get it. He won't ever understand it.

"Damon—"

I spin on my heel. "How is it fair? That kid has my future, and he's half the pitcher I was. After my injury, I became kryptonite. No one wanted me. Even if I'd pushed hard and risked further injury to get back to where I was, all the agents had disappeared." I don't realize I'm yelling until I notice the people around us are staring.

"Come with me." Maddox grabs my arm and pulls me down the path that runs behind the bleachers.

"Bet you spent a lot of time back here," I grumble.

Maddox laughs. "I was a bleachers type of guy in high school. In college, I had class. Used to fuck behind the stacks in the library."

"Much classier."

Maddox pulls me down to the ground, and we sit with our backs against a concrete pillar. His arm is flush up against mine, and I like it way more than I should.

"Was this the first baseball scout you've done?" he asks.

I nod and stare into the distance.

"Okay, so that's going to be hard no matter what. Now the first one is over, the next one will be easier."

"I was fine until he told me he's already got an agent when nothing here today showed me he was ready for it. Kinda lost my shit."

Maddox laughs. "Just a bit, and can I just say, I'm liking this freaked-out Damon more than I should."

"You what?"

"You always seem so together and in control. You have direction and drive. You're like ... a grownup."

"Hate to break it to you, but so are you."

"Nah, I float by on life and run away from my problems. I have a job I'm good at—and don't get me wrong, I love it—but I had plans when I went off to college to travel and see the world once I was done. But I went straight into my job, and even though I have the funds, I haven't done anything about going anywhere. I graduated almost a year ago now. It's like I'm content to always think about what I want without acting on it. What made you decide to become an agent?"

"It was always my backup. I knew the chance of playing ball professionally was small, but I was so close. The first year of law school was the hardest, because I was still dealing with the fact I was never going to play again. Not at a competitive level. And then I was angry at everyone who abandoned me. My agent, the millions of offers from other places. I understand why they did it, but it made me want to be better than them. I wanted to become the agent those guys weren't." I haven't told anyone about this shit. There's something about Maddox that makes me lay it all out there.

"Since I met you, I've had this weird awe-slash-jealousy thing toward you," he says. "Until now, the most I've seen you close to losing it was when I cornered you in my apartment and you fled like your ass was on fire. Even then, you were still in control of that whole situation. So, yeah, as mean as it is, I like seeing you ruffled. Makes you more human."

"Don't put me on a pedestal I don't belong on, Maddy. I may act like I have my shit together, but I'm faking it. I think most adulting is faking it."

Maddox grins.

"And I think you should just do it," I say. "Plan a trip somewhere. Anywhere. Go to Niagara so you can say you've been to a different country, at least."

"Canada doesn't count, but you're right. I should just do it. Maybe Stacy will come with me."

I almost blurt out I'd go, but that's not going to happen. I don't have time to go away. Then there's the long list of other reasons like being around Maddox drives me crazy, I want him, and it's still a bad idea to be with him.

"As far as baseball goes," Maddox says, "it sucks you can't be the one on the other side of the contract. But look at it this way, when you find that ballplayer who's great—who's even better than you were—you're going to do everything in your power to give that guy what you couldn't have. His success will be your success, and you get to be by his side when he makes it big. It won't be the same, but it's the closest you're going to get. And not everyone has that opportunity."

I turn my head to find his blue eyes piercing mine. "I see it now. The TA thing. I can see why they all loved you."

His gaze drops to my lips. I want to kiss him, and it's getting harder and harder to remember why I shouldn't. But when he shifts, my immediate reflex is to break the connection and turn away.

"What are you doing on the weekend?" Did I swallow a chunk of dirt in the last five seconds? My mouth is dry and my voice comes out rough.

He sighs, probably because I've rejected him again. "Have to head back to PA. Crazy aunt's visiting."

"Right. You said that. Need your fake boyfriend to tag along?" What am I doing? I can't survive another weekend with him.

"You've got finals coming up. You need to study."

The disappointment is heavier than I expect. I do need to study, but I can't make myself care about it. I'd rather be in Pennsylvania, pretending to be Maddox's boyfriend.

"I can study anywhere, but if you don't want me to go—"

"Thanks. I'll let you know if I change my mind."

He doesn't.

CHAPTER THIRTEEN

MADDOX

Philadelphia is out of my way, but I figure I'm already making the long-ass trip to see my parents, and a small detour won't hurt.

I catch the train, but when I arrive in Philly, I wonder if I'm making a huge mistake. Against my better judgment, I messaged Matt the night his news leaked. The way he was outed was harsh, and I wanted him to know he wasn't alone. Or something. I don't know. My gut told me to message him. Now I'm wondering if this is a dumb idea. He gave me his address when I told him I'm coming home this weekend and said we should catch up.

My GPS app on my phone says Matt's place is around this corner, and for some reason, I feel sick. And when I see the media circus outside his building, my gut churns more.

The news broke six days ago, and they're still camped outside. I'd hate to be Matt right now.

Matt's doorman stops me and asks my name and who I'm there to see. When I mumble it so the vultures behind me can't hear, he repeats it into a two-way loud enough for the whole building to hear.

Thanks, dude.

That's when I realize he's not a doorman but hired security. For Matt.

The back of my neck burns as cameras go off behind me. My ass might be in some tabloids tomorrow, but I refuse to turn around and give them a money shot of my face. I'm not ashamed to be here, or for them to speculate who I am or what I'm doing, but I don't want to bring more shit to Matt's life. And considering I'm holding my duffel bag for the weekend, they might print Matt and I are getting married. Because duffel bag equals serious relationship in the tabloid world.

The security guy waves me through, and I head up to Matt's apartment on the top floor. When he opens the door, the late afternoon sun pours into his huge-ass loft. His brown hair sticks up at all angles as if he just crawled out of bed. He hasn't shaved in God knows how long, and his tight wife-beater and sweats are dirty.

We stare each other down, and then wordlessly, he steps aside to let me in. His apartment is the size of my entire floor which has nine studio apartments on it.

"Damn. The NFL must pay the big bucks, huh?"

"Something like that. What are you doing here, Maddox? Are you here to yell at me too? I actually deserve it coming from you, so go ahead and get it out of your system and then leave."

"What the fuck are you talking about? I'm here to make sure you're okay. Who yelled at you?"

"Let's just say not all of my teammates were happy when the news broke last week."

"Are you serious? Like ... serious, serious? Who was it? That's not okay."

"Doesn't matter now. It's done. My career is done. They win."

"Why is your career done?"

Matt stares in disbelief and he asks again, "Why are you here?"

"Because we were roommates? Because of ... what happened between us? Getting outed the way you did, it's got to suck."

"But I—but we—and ... you don't hate me for misleading you years ago?"

"Did you do it on purpose?"

"I-I ... Shit, I don't know. I think I was in denial when you and I hooked up, even though I did mess around with a high school buddy too—I didn't lie about that. I wanted to be straight but I just ... wasn't."

"So how was I to know if you didn't know?"

"I've always felt guilty. Like I took advantage or—"

"Uh, pretty sure I never told you stop. Or returned the favor. If anyone was taking advantage, it was me. I enjoyed myself. *A lot.*"

Matt grins.

"And the joke's on both of us, because even after what happened between us, I thought I was still straight. Turns out, not so much."

"You're—"

"Bi. Apparently. It's a new revelation. Still seems fake when I say it aloud, but I'm slowly getting there." It's rolling off my tongue easier now. My head knows it to be true, but I don't know why it's hard to admit it aloud. There's a small part of me that worries how people will react, but I don't know why. When I was outed back home, I didn't give a shit what people thought. Maybe that's because I thought it was fake. This is real. And the threat of someone reacting violently is real, even if the world is getting better. Slowly. Really fucking slowly.

The smile on Matt's face falls. "Wait, is that why you're

here? So we could …" He waves a finger between us. "Because I don't think that's a good—"

"No. I'm not here for that. It's a long story, but my hometown thinks I'm gay, so I guess, technically, I'm already out. I haven't had a massive struggle with this. But the thought of going through what you are right now …"

"Oh, so this visit is out of pity? Thanks, but I don't need it. I'll be fine on my own."

"No. It's not pity. I'm screwing this up. I'm here as a friend, letting you know you don't have to do this on your own if you don't want to."

Matt's eyes glisten but he shakes it off to hide it. "Want coffee?"

"Sure." I dump my bag on his couch and follow him into the kitchen.

"Plan on staying?" He tips his head toward my bag.

"Nah, heading home after here to see my parents and aunt who's visiting."

"And everyone at home thinks you're gay?"

"It's not an interesting story. Trust me. It also makes me out to be an asshole, so I'm not going to share it right now."

"What's the fun in being losers if we can't make fun of ourselves while doing it?"

"Matt, you're not a loser."

He lets out a sad laugh. "My contract, which was in the middle of negotiations, isn't up for renewal anymore. Funny how it disappeared when the photos were leaked. I can't leave my apartment without being stalked by paparazzi, and my management team has told me there's nothing they can do in terms of getting me a new contract. No one wants to invite this circus to their club. And to top it off, my endorsements are gone. If that doesn't tell you I'm a loser, then maybe you're not as smart as I thought you were."

"You haven't left your apartment in a week?" I realize he spat a whole lot of other important shit at me, but that's the thing I get stuck on.

Matt shakes his head.

"Want to come home with me for the weekend? No one's going to be looking for you in the sticks."

"Really?"

I shrug. "Sure. Last month I brought home a baseball player. This month a football player—a *famous* football player. That's one way to keep the gay rumors afloat."

"Okay, please tell me that story."

"I will on the long-ass drive. We can take your car, right? Otherwise, you might be spotted on the train."

"No problem. I'll go pack a bag."

Getting out of Philly proves more difficult than we expect. Those fuckers with cameras follow us in their vans. Doesn't help Matt drives a Lamborghini. Way to be inconspicuous.

We think we lose the vultures around the exit for Red Hill but can't be sure. It takes half as long to spill my story to Matt than it does to lose the people chasing him.

"Wait, wait, wait. Your ex told your entire town you were gay, you never bothered correcting them, and it turns out you do like guys?"

"Yup."

At least my story puts a smile on his face. I get the feeling he hasn't smiled that wide in a long time.

When he pulls up to my parents' driveway, he makes no move to turn the car off. "I'll leave you to your family thing if you point me in the direction of the nearest hotel."

"The best you'll do in these parts is a motel, back on the

main strip. You have a choice of one. Told you we're small town."

"Better than the four walls of my apartment."

"I was in your apartment, and I guarantee you, there's way more walls than four."

He waves me off. "You know what I mean."

"Okay, well, I'll have dinner with the folks and message you later. Maybe we can hit a bar tonight or something."

"Uh, dunno if that's a good idea."

"Right. Public. We can hang out in your room. Might be an idea to book the room under my name. We may be small town, but we are connected to the internet, and news of a celebrity will spread."

"Thanks, I'll do that."

Mom's already waiting for me curbside when I get out of the car. "Who's your friend?" She ducks her head to peek through the windshield.

Matt gives an awkward wave before he drives off.

"Friend from Philly. He needed to get away for a few days so he's staying at the motel in town."

"Where's Damon?"

"He had to study. He's got less than eight weeks of graduate school left, Mom. He can't drop everything to come home with me every time I need to."

"Your … friend …" She points toward the direction Matt went. "He's just a friend, right? Because we love Damon."

I roll my eyes. Hard. "Just a friend."

"Okay, well, Aunt Cheri hasn't arrived yet, but she should be here soon."

"Why does she want to see me anyway?" I ask as I follow her into the house.

"You'll have to ask her that."

Dad hands me a beer as soon as I walk in and tells me to

take a seat in the living room. Seeing as I was here a month ago, we don't have much to talk about. We rarely have anything to talk about normally, but the silence is familiar—comforting, even.

When the telltale sound of a car idling in the driveway comes, Mom and Dad rise to meet Aunt Cheri at the door.

"Do you have any cash?" she asks. "I've only got my credit card and I have to pay for the cab. Sorry, I'll pay you back."

"I've got it," Dad says and heads outside.

This whole visit is odd to me. As Jacie and I grew up, we'd see Aunt Cheri sporadically, but she never once asked to see me that I know of, so I don't know why she wants to now. The last time I saw her, I was a teenager, and I can't remember the exact specifics. I could've been fifteen or seventeen for all I know.

She's a vision of perfect hippiness. When she takes off her coat, her long white dress flows over her thin frame, and her long blonde hair falls down her back. The only thing missing is a halo of flowers on her head.

"Maddox," she says, her voice melodic.

I hold my arms out, because Aunt Cheri has always been a hugger like most of that side of the family. She's nearly as tall as me and double the height of Mom.

"Dinner's almost ready," Mom says. Aunt Cheri stares at Mom in silent question. "I have a vegan option for you," she adds.

Still a nutcase. Vegetarians, I can forgive. Vegans? Are they even real humans?

Aunt Cheri drags me over to the couch and sits next to me while Mom and Dad putter around in the kitchen. "So, tell me about your life."

"Uh ... well ... I work for Parsons' Media."

"What's that?"

"It's an advertising firm."

"Does that pay well? Living in the big city, it's exciting but expensive, right?" And this just got weirder. She's never been interested in my life as far back as I can remember.

Her hand lands on top of mine, and my eyes focus on the millions of silvery rings she has. She has about three on each finger.

Yup. Nutcase.

"It pays enough."

"Your mom tells me you're seeing a nice boy."

Right. "Yeah. His name is Damon." I wonder when I should tell them all we "broke up." I would've done it already had I not been keeping hope. He didn't want me to hook up with Noah last week. No matter how many times I tell myself not to read into that, I can't help wondering. Although at the baseball game, I thought we were about to kiss, and he pulled back. *Again.*

Women are right; guys are so much harder to understand.

"As long as he's taking care of you."

"He's great." I'm not lying. Damon *is* great, but the words feel thick on my tongue.

"You're probably wondering why I've come to see you."

"Little bit." Or a lot. Whatever.

"Dinner's ready," Mom calls out from the kitchen.

Aunt Cheri smiles. "Better get to it then."

Mom and Dad are already sitting at the dining table when we walk in, each of them staring at Cheri with an intensity I can't decipher.

"Okay, can someone please tell me what's going on?" I ask, taking my seat.

"Maybe Cheri can explain," Dad says.

"Well," Aunt Cheri says. She takes a napkin and lays it on her lap. "I have some news. Some not great news. And I wanted … I mean, I think it's time to …"

Dad's fork clatters to his plate. "I was worried you'd try to pull something like this. Calling us out of the blue to let us know you need to speak to Maddox."

"I'm still lost over here," I say. Something like knowing ticks in the back of my brain, but I think—no, I hope—I'm jumping to the wrong conclusion.

"Maybe it's time," Mom whispers. "We always planned to tell him eventually. But then we kept putting it off and putting it off."

"Putting what off?" I ask, more convinced I know what's coming. I stare at my mother, her grey hair that was once dark. My dad's dark eyes, and then Cheri's blue eyes staring at me ... *Oh, fuck.*

"There's no easy way to say this," Aunt Cheri says, "but, I'm your mother."

"*Biological* mother," Mom corrects.

You'd think with that type of bombshell my mind would be racing. I wait for the irrationality to hit me, but it doesn't come. All I can think about is all those times I felt like I didn't belong. Or how I look nothing like my family. I thought of ridiculous theories like being switched at birth, but being adopted? Never even crossed my mind.

I begin to wonder if I'm completely oblivious or just a dumbass. Maybe both. An oblivious dumbass.

Yup, that's me.

"Who's my father?" my mouth asks. I didn't realize my brain was heading in that direction.

Aunt ... *Mom* Cheri? Nope, too weird. I don't care if I carry her DNA, she's not my mom. My mom's my mom ... No. My aunt's my mom? Fuck, I need another beer. Or a drawing of my family tree, because I'm confused.

Cheri avoids eye contact as she answers, "I don't know. It was a one-night stand at a rave."

Classy, my birth mother.

Jesus Christ. *Birth* mother.

"Maddy, are you okay?" Mom asks.

I nod but stare at the plate of food in front of me. My appetite's gone, and my throat is dry.

"Life is a bit shit right now," Aunt Cheri says, "and I realized I don't want to leave this Earth without knowing the boy I gave birth to. I don't want to—"

"Leave this Earth?" I ask.

She sighs. "A few years ago, I was diagnosed with MS."

Mom gasps. "Why didn't you say anything?"

"I was barely symptomatic," Cheri says. "I thought if I ignored it I wouldn't have to face it. But now …" She stares down at her hand which shakes with a small tremor. "It's advanced far in a few short years—faster than average—and I don't know how long I have before it takes away my ability to do the things I want. I want …" She breathes deep. "My highest priority is to get to know Maddox."

"I-I … uh, umm …" I stutter.

"You don't have to agree to anything right now," Mom says. "You've been hit with some big news."

"Is this something I could inherit?" Again, my mouth asks questions I don't realize I'm contemplating. At least some part of my brain is functioning.

"It's not a hereditary disease," Cheri says. "Although, you are at a higher risk of developing it because of me."

"Is there a test or something I could get?"

"No. They can test your probability of developing it, but it's invasive and the results aren't conclusive. MS isn't caused by a single gene. It's got a lot of factors to it."

"Maddy," Mom says, "You might want to look at the bigger picture. Do you have any questions for us? About why—"

I shake my head. "Crazy Aunt Cheri didn't want to keep me, and you guys took me in. Not much to say, is there?"

Cheri frowns. "It wasn't like that. I knew you would be better off with your mom and dad. They already had Jacie, and they're great parents, and—"

"I know they're great parents," I say through gritted teeth. "But that doesn't mean I haven't known something was missing. I don't belong here. I never did. Now, what, you suddenly care and have a conscience because you're sick? I'm twenty-three years old. Where were you when I was growing up when I could've used the truth about who I am and where I come from?"

"Maddy," Mom says, her voice full of sadness.

"Sorry." Only, I'm not sorry. "This is a lot to handle right now. I need to ..." I stand. "I need to go. I'm sorry."

Footsteps trail after me as I storm through the house to the front door. I expect it to be Mom or Cheri, but a firm hand lands on my shoulder.

"Let me drive you," Dad says.

I look into his brown eyes and don't like what I see. Fear. "I'm not going back to New York, Da. I just need some space. A friend of mine is staying at the motel. I'll go there and cool off— come back in the morning."

"Still let me drive you."

All I can do is nod and pick up my bag as I follow him out to the garage.

The drive is literally ten minutes long, so Dad doesn't waste time getting to the point. "We did plan to tell you, but we didn't know how."

The laugh that escapes me is almost hysterical. "I understand. More than you know. I'm ... uh ... I'm not gay."

I don't know what possesses me to come clean now. Some act of childish revenge maybe? They lied to me for twenty-three years, so they deserve the same? I probably shouldn't have said it, but it's out there now.

Dad slams on the brakes. "You're not what?"

"I said it to break up with Chastity, and then suddenly the whole town knew. I didn't mean for it to get that far, but I didn't correct anyone. I had to decide between letting the town think I was gay or an asshole. And to be honest, I never cared people thought I was gay."

It's Dad's turn to laugh manically. "Oh my God, that's gold. You're straight? But Damon ..."

"Ah, no, not entirely straight, but I'm not gay. Definitely not gay. College was—"

"Don't need to tell your old man the details."

I laugh. "Well, up until I met Damon, I was ninety-nine percent sure I was straight. He came home with me as a favor, because both Chastity and Mom were on my case about my boyfriend who didn't exist."

"Well, I'm not going to be the one to tell your mother. She loves Damon. Wouldn't shut up about him for a week after you left."

"I thought you'd be pissed I lied to you guys."

"I don't like that you thought you couldn't come to us, but, well, we don't have the option of being hypocrites here. And you know us—we love you no matter what. We didn't care when we found out you were into lads, and I don't care now. No matter who you end up with. Man, woman, woman who used to be a man ..."

I chuckle. "Could happen."

"We just want you to be happy. It's all any parent wants." Dad pulls up to the motel. "And that's what we are. We're still your parents. Take all the time you need but try not to let your mother worry too much. We barely see you as it is; I don't want this to come between us and you more."

"Wait, you think I needed to get out of there because of you? Fuck no. Da, I'm confused and feel rejected but not by you or Mom. I wish you told me sooner, but you couldn't know how I'd react. Can you tell Mom I'm not mad at her? I just …"

"Need to process everything. That's the reason we kept putting off telling you. We didn't want to put you out or confuse you. We almost told you when you were eighteen, but then you came out, and we figured it wasn't the time. Don't exactly want your kid to say "I'm gay" and then turn around and tell him he's adopted. From there, it was never the right time. Maybe we should've ripped the Band-Aid off when you were a teenager."

"Maybe Cheri should have realized being sick isn't an excuse to finally face a responsibility she should've dealt with ages ago."

Dad opens his mouth to say something but I cut him off.

"I'm not saying I hated the way you raised me or you're bad parents, but this revelation gives me answers to questions I've been asking myself for years. And now it's convenient for her, she wants to get to know me? It leaves a bitter taste in my mouth."

Dad purses his lips. "Take your time in dealing with this, but we don't know how advanced her condition is, so keep in mind you don't want to become Cheri. Don't leave it until it's too late."

"I'll literally be back in the morning, Da."

He nods, but I don't think he believes me. "I'll see you in the morning then."

Matt's Lambo is the only car in the parking lot of the motel, so I head straight to the room it's outside of.

Matt peers through the thin curtain to check who's knocking before he opens the door. "That was fast."

"You have no idea. I'm crashing with you tonight." I push my way into his room. "Sweet, two beds."

"What am I missing?"

"My family dropped a pretty big bombshell on me, and I don't want to deal with it."

"There's a minibar if you need it."

"I think I need to be sober to deal with this one. You know how growing up the ultimate sibling insult was 'You're adopted'?"

"I may've said that a lot to my younger brothers and sisters."

"My sister never made that joke. She's eight years older than me. Turns out, she couldn't throw that in my face, because it's actually true."

Matt's eyes widen. "Oh shit. You just found out?"

"My aunt is my mother and my mother is my aunt."

"Fuck that."

Yeah. He said it.

CHAPTER FOURTEEN

DAMON

My head slumps on my desk. Criminal adjudication will be the death of my degree. All I need is a pass, but it's not sinking in. It's not even a subject I'll use, but I need it to graduate.

Seven weeks. S*even*.

My phone dings, and I've never been happier for the interruption. Only, when I see it's a text from Stacy with the thumbnail of an article about Matt Jackson, my heart sinks. Something tells me I don't want to open that link.

Another message comes through.

STACY: YOU FUCKED IT UP.

Yeah, I did. Like a masochist, I click on what she sent me, and sure enough, photos of Maddox shirtless and opening the door to a shitty roadside motel are splashed all over the same rag site that outed Matt. Maddox is with Matt. In his hometown.

"Guess I know why he didn't want me to come home with him this weekend," I mutter to myself.

And the thing is, I can't even hate him for it. Or blame him.

I had my chance, and I pushed him away. We aren't together; he can do whatever he wants. I told him to go experiment with guys, so I can't be pissed that he's doing it.

But I *am* pissed, even if I don't have the right to be.

My fingers hover over his name in the texting app. I shouldn't text. I should leave him alone. Freakishly, with his text window open, he messages me.

Maddox: Can we set up a time this week to meet? I have something I need to talk to you about.

And just like that, I squash the masochist in me. I don't want to meet up with Maddox so he can tell me he's with Matt. Seen the photos, thanks.

Damon: Finals are kicking my ass. Sorry.
Maddox: It's important.
Damon: So are finals.

I try to tell myself the photos might not mean what I think they mean, but Maddox half-naked in a motel room with his ex? Pretty sure it's exactly what it looks like.

○

Another week of school over, six more to go, but I'm burned out on studying. So when Noah sends a text with an invite to have a pizza and beer night at his house, I only hesitate for a few minutes before agreeing.

I need a break. If I try to memorize anything else for my upcoming exams, I think I'll be pushing old information out. Like how to walk and talk properly. I'm at serious risk of turning into a bumbling crazy person who talks in nothing but legislative laws.

I find Wyatt and Noah in Noah's living room, drinking and playing video games. I have no idea which game, but they're shooting people; *COD*, *WOW*, OMG—who knows. I wasn't born with the gamer gene.

"Thank fuck," I say when my friend Aron appears with a beer for me.

"Hi to you too," he says. "First, you don't invite me to meet your boy toy, and now you don't even say hi?"

Aron's one of the guys I purposefully didn't invite a few weekends ago because he's way too hot with his killer smile and would love Maddox.

"Maddox isn't my boy toy," I grumble. That honor belongs to Matt-fucking-Jackson. They've been in more tabloids this week. Apparently, Matt's in New York now. Not that I've been stalking them in the news or anything …

"Maddox wouldn't hook up with me because of Damon," Noah says without taking his eyes off the screen. "Yet, Damon still found a way to fuck it up."

"Well done, man." Aron claps me on the back.

"Fuck you very much."

When Skylar walks through the entrance and our eyes lock, she bites her lip and looks away. I'm about to ask if she's okay when Maddox trails in behind her. With *him*.

Great. Just great.

Matt's got his head down, but he's wearing a Bulldogs cap. Way to stay incognito, man.

Skylar approaches and hugs me hello, so I lower my head and whisper in her ear. "Traitor."

"You told me to be friends with him, and that's what I'm doing."

Maddox approaches and playfully shoves me. "You've been avoiding me again, Dik."

I wonder if he's using my nickname or actually calling me a dick. I'll pretend it's the former, but I can't be sure. "Busy." More beer goes down my throat, and then I watch my bottle intently.

Interesting, it's a brew from Staten Island. Good to know.

Out of the corner of my eye, Maddox frowns. "Uh, well, are you too busy to meet Matt?" He pulls Matt forward. "I brought him here specifically to meet *you*."

Huh? "*Why?*" I scowl.

"I told you this was a bad idea," Matt says to Maddox. "Just drop it, okay? I should go back to the hotel."

Yeah, you should. I suppose I should feel sympathy toward him with what he's going through, but oops, can't find any fucks to give.

"No," Maddox says. He turns to the group. "Everyone, this is Matt. Be nice." Then his blue eyes bore into me. Their usual crystal clarity is dulled by a stormy grey. "Damon, can I talk to you for a minute?"

"Nah, I'm cool here." Being an asshole sucks.

"I'm sorry," Maddox says sarcastically, "that wasn't a request."

"Oooh, someone's in trouble," Noah singsongs. "Take him upstairs. First door on your right."

"Thanks," Maddox says and grabs my forearm. I hand off my beer to Aron as I'm dragged into Noah's guestroom—a room I've crashed in many times when I couldn't be bothered going home. "What the fuck is wrong with you?" Maddox yelling. This is new.

"Nothing."

"Really? So, you're sticking to the you've been busy lie? At least when you were avoiding me a few weeks ago, you gave excuses. This past week has been radio silence."

I fold my arms across my chest. "Surprised you've noticed with all the time you've been spending with Matt. The tabloids love you guys. You're going to be the *it* couple of football."

"What has Matt got to do with it?" His eyes widen. "Wait, are you *jealous*? Mr. You-Should-Hook-Up-With-Everyone-Except-Me doesn't like that I'm spending time with another guy?" He breaks into a smile, and it pisses me off.

"No. I'm wondering why you're bothering with me when you have Matt."

Maddox shakes his head. "Skylar's right. You *are* an idiot."

"Huh?"

"Matt and I are just friends, you jackass. Last weekend, I went to visit him because the way he was outed was so fucking wrong I wanted to make sure he was okay. He was a wreck, so I invited him home for the weekend to get away from the vultures circling him. I had my own family drama going on, which if you'd answered any of my texts, I would've told you about, and so we stayed in a motel room—with two beds—under my name so Matt wouldn't be followed. But when I visited him in Philly, I had to give my name, and someone leaked it to the tabloids or the paparazzi overheard; I'm not entirely sure. They found out where I was from and tracked us to the motel. *Nothing* happened."

"Oh."

"Yeah. *Oh*. Then Matt came to New York to talk to *you*, because his current management team is screwing him over in contract negotiations. I thought you could use a client considering you don't have any."

"Oh." Apparently, my whole vocabulary consists of only this word now.

"I recommended you because you're not a dick. Guess that was a wrong assessment, huh?"

Yep.

"You want to act all jealous when you've made it clear nothing can happen between us, that's okay. But don't be an idiot. There's a high-profile client within your grasp. Don't let me be the reason you don't pursue it."

I stand completely stunned and unmoving, barely even blinking. Maddox scoffs and pushes past me. My head screams at me to stop him, but my body doesn't move. Only when he reaches the door, do I find the courage to get my feet going in his direction.

"Maddy." My hand goes over his head, pushing the door closed so he can't escape, and he turns to face me.

This close, we share the same breath, and we're both breathing hard. His eyes are either hooded or narrowed; I can't tell if he's angry or turned on, but I don't give him a chance to let me know which, because I move in and fuse my mouth to his. He accepts it willingly—eagerly.

Resisting him has made the buildup to this more explosive. His tongue, his lips, his mouth seeking mine, it's as natural and inevitable as magnets finding each other.

I tried to be strong, I tried to hold back, but I know now it would've been impossible to keep up forever.

His back hits the door. Our tongues tangle, and there's no hesitance on his part. He dives in fully, and he tastes the same as I remember but better. He's either recently cleaned his teeth or chewed on gum, because his mouth is minty.

With my hips pushed up against his, I can feel him hardening. My body instinctively rocks into him, and I'm hard as an iron bar. All he's done is kiss me.

Weeks of thinking about doing this again has my hands shamelessly wandering all over him. I grip his hair and tilt his head back while my lips trail down his neck. My free hand finds its way to the button and zipper of his jeans.

"Damon—"

"Can't talk now." We need to, but I can't.

"Okay." He clears his throat. "But I was going to warn you that I've been fantasizing about this since I met you. I'm already close to coming."

A growl gets stuck in the back of my throat. I kiss him again and pull him off the door. Without breaking our lips apart, I drag him over to the bed. The voice yelling at me to slow down gets pushed away by my needy cock. The rational side—or maybe it's my horny side—reassures me this isn't like what happened with Eric. Maddox is sober. He's been interested for over a month; this isn't a fleeting experiment ... At least, I hope it's not.

But the biggest thing that keeps running through my head is what he told me in his apartment: *he's not Eric*.

I push him down and land on top of him, our mouths moving in sync. It's been so long since I've been with anyone I've forgotten how awesome kissing is, but it's not nearly enough. Not with Maddox.

His stomach muscles contract as I move my hand between us. I grip his cock through his jeans, and he throws his head back on the mattress. We're hanging half off the bed, but I can't bring myself to pull off him and move us farther up.

His moans are intoxicating, and I'm lost in everything Maddox.

Instead of pulling away like I should, I move down his body, slinking to the floor on my knees. I've barely got his jeans and boxers down his thick thighs before I'm engulfing his cock with my mouth, taking him to the back of my throat. My deep-throating skills are rusty, and it doesn't help Maddox is hung.

"Fuck!" he hisses.

I pull off him. "We have to use our inside voices. There are people downstairs."

He leans up on his elbows. "If you're going to do that again and need me to be quiet, you're going to have to gag me."

"That can be arranged." I slap my hand over his mouth. He mumbles something against my hand. "What was that? I can't hear you."

He shakes my hand off. "You're enjoying this way too much."

"Yeah, I am. Now, shh." I cover his mouth again.

He chuckles, but it dies when my tongue lands on him and circles around the tip of his cock. I'd love to take my time, savor his taste and the soft moans coming from him, but there are people downstairs, and if I'm completely honest, I'm scared he's going to freak out any moment.

It doesn't take long for the doubt to seep back in now I'm actually doing this.

Logically, he shouldn't—this isn't his first blowjob from a guy—but it doesn't stop the nagging feeling in the back of my mind that this could be a one-time deal. That maybe he's pretending I'm a girl like he said he used to do when he was with Matt.

The insecurity and vulnerability trying to distract me evaporate when I lift my gaze and his eyes are on me. He says something against my hand that sounds like "Damon" ... or maybe it was "don't." *Shit.*

I pull off him again. "Please tell me this is okay."

His eyes soften. He knows exactly why I'm asking that. When I pull my hand away from his mouth, he reaches for my cheek, and his thumb runs across the stubble there. With a warm smile, he gently says, "If you stop, I'm going to kick your ass."

I can't stop the laugh.

"I'm so close. Need you."

No way am I stopping now.

When I take him back in my mouth again, I relax my jaw and breathe through my nose. His hips buck, sending him deeper to the back of my throat, and I moan around his cock. It's enough to make him crazy. He mutters incoherently, but when the first spurts hit my tongue, I realize his babble was trying to warn me. I suck him down, taking every last drop until his body melts into the mattress.

"So good," he murmurs.

I climb up his body until we're face to face, me pinning him to the bed and our legs hanging off the end. "I'm sorry," I say.

His hands go to my hips. "What for?"

"For being a dick. I do want you, Maddy. I've wanted you since the weekend I met you. But—"

"You're scared shitless. If Eric hadn't fucked you over, or even if I realized I was bi back in college, maybe you wouldn't have this hang-up about me being new to all this. I don't know what I can say to make you understand you're the one I want. This isn't about sex or experimenting, and I don't care that you're a guy. You're the only *person* I've wanted to date since high school. Ask Stacy, that's a big step for me."

I lean in and kiss him softly. His mouth moves lazily against mine, and I have to force myself to pull away. "I want that too, but maybe we should take it slow."

His lips curve up at the edges. "Should've thought of that before you sucked me off."

My head falls to the crook of his shoulder. "You're right, but I couldn't help myself. I've been fantasizing about doing that for a month." I pull up off him and stand.

Maddox sits up and reaches for my belt, bringing me back to him. His hand rubs the hard length in my jeans. "I need to return the favor," he says, and I'm so tempted to let him, but I'm still hesitant. If there wasn't a room full of people downstairs, I'd probably feel differently. There's no clean escape route if this goes wrong.

"Maybe later. We should get back downstairs before they come looking for us."

His eyes flick up to mine. "You'll come home with me?"

Despite my reservations, there's no way I can go back to denying I want him. "You won't be able to keep me away now."

Maddox grins. "Good."

CHAPTER FIFTEEN

MADDOX

While I pull my pants up and tuck myself away, Damon watches me with a satisfied smile on his face even though he's not the one who got off. "What?" I ask.

"They're gonna know. Your cheeks are flushed, and you're all loose. Dead giveaway."

"Well, coming hard does that to a guy. Why are you smiling wider?"

He steps forward. "Because I like that I'm the one who did it to you." When his lips find mine, they're soft and tentative, so I force my tongue into his mouth to harden the kiss, but he groans and pulls away. "Don't start or we won't be leaving this room."

"I'm totally okay with that."

"We should make sure my friends aren't grilling Matt."

"Oh shit. I kinda forgot I dragged him here."

When I head for the door, Damon stops me. "I really am sorry. I saw the tabloid photos, and it drove me crazy."

"I'm not the one you should apologize to. If you and Matt are going to work together—"

"I'll go apologize now." Damon kisses me one more time,

and instead of the cringing, itchy feeling I normally get after a hookup—not in the STD way but the I-need-to-get-out-of-here way—all I want is more. All I want to do is go downstairs, say goodbye to everyone, and take him home.

Our fingers intertwine, but as soon as we reach the stairs, he lets go. "We don't need to give them any ammunition."

Even though we aren't touching, that doesn't stop the intrigued and smug looks we get from everyone when we rejoin them. I try to ignore them and not give anything away, but my cheeks still have that post-orgasmic burn, and I worry they're fucking glowing.

"Okay, let's try this again now someone's not a cranky asshole," I say and approach Matt and Noah where they're talking in the living room nook. "Damon, this is Matt. Matt, Damon. Hey, Matt Damon. That's funny."

Damon manages a smile and holds his hand out for Matt. "Hey. Sorry about earlier. As Maddy said, I was a cranky asshole."

"Maddy, huh?" Noah taunts. Damon ignores him.

Matt gives Damon a chin lift and shakes his hand. "Maddox has told me about you, so I get it. The tabloids have made us out to be a couple, and it's kinda shitty considering all Maddox is doing is trying to help me."

"Yeah, you're having issues with your current management team?" Damon asks.

Matt looks from Noah to Damon and then stares at his shoes. "Uh, yeah. Ever since my ... news broke."

"On that note," I say, "Noah and I are going to get a beer while you guys talk shop. Lead me to your kitchen."

I follow Noah, and he hands me a beer from his fridge.

"You found a way to make Damon apologize?" he asks.

Why, yes, I put my cock in his mouth. "Uh ..."

"You might have to tell me your tricks, because he's a stubborn son of a bitch usually."

Yeah, I won't be telling Noah to do it my way. I shrug. "I explained the situation and told him he was wrong."

"And that worked? Damn, my friend has it bad." Noah corners me against the bench, crossing way too many human decency boundaries, and I'm about to push him off me when he speaks low. "I'll lie if you ever repeat I said this. As you've probably been told, I don't have many friends, but Damon's one of the few good ones. So, treat him right, okay? Be upfront with him if you're ... having doubts."

My eyes narrow, and I take a stab that he knows about Damon's hang-ups. "I'm not ashamed to say I want him."

Noah steps back. The intimidation is gone as he says, "You a *Call of Duty* man?"

"Uh ..." I take a second to recover from my interrogation. "I'm in."

We kick off Wyatt and another guy from the game, and Noah sends them on a beer run seeing as I'm apparently drinking the last one. Damon and Matt stay in the corner, talking in harsh whispers. The concentration line on Damon's face is hot as fuck. It's weird to think ten minutes ago that same guy had his mouth wrapped around my dick, but staring at Damon from afar, one thing is clear. I want more. A lot more. I don't think I've come that hard since ... probably since I lost my virginity to Chastity and blew in like twenty seconds flat.

"Concentrate." Noah's voice snaps me to attention.

I don't know how long Noah and I play, but people come and go behind us. I'm vaguely aware of greetings and goodbyes.

"I'm out," another voice says behind us. Don't know who it is, and I don't bother looking. Noah and I are too busy commandeering a chopper and killing bad guys, because we're motherfucking badasses.

"Go, go, go," Noah yells at me.

"I am!"

"Kill faster, noob."

I don't know if he's calling me that because he knows I'm a same-sex virgin or if he's mocking my *COD* skills, but I can't smack talk him back because a loud booming voice snaps us to attention.

"*Babe.*"

I turn to Damon. Did he just call me—

"You weren't answering to your name. Matt's gone. You wanna ...?" He tips his head in the direction of Noah's front door.

I scramble to my feet so fast everyone finds it comical, but I don't care. Damon and I will be back at my apartment in twenty minutes—tops.

"Practice safe sex," Noah calls after us.

Damon flips him off, but not for long, because I grab his hand and drag him out the door.

For all the eagerness I had to leave Noah's place and get back to my place, my hands tremble as I try to unlock my door. It doesn't help that Damon's pushed up against my back and his lips are on my neck. The sensation sends a jolt straight to my cock.

When I drop the keys to the floor, I let out a curse, and Damon chuckles against my skin.

"I've got it," he says and dips to pick up my keys.

I stand completely still, staring at my door like a moron.

Damon's hand clamps down on my shoulder. "You okay?"

"Is it stupid that I'm legit nervous right now?"

He drops his hand and steps away. "We don't have to do anything you're not ready for."

"Oh, I'm ready ... for, uh ... stuff. Maybe not ... uh ..."

"Ass stuff?" he says with a laugh. "Got it. I probably shouldn't mention the fact I usually like to top, right?" His easy smile relaxes me.

"Of course, you do. And ..." I run a hand through my hair. "I'm not exactly against ... err, ass stuff, as you call it. Best feeling ever is a finger up there while getting a blowjob."

A throat clears, and Damon can't contain his amusement as his eyes lock on someone behind me. He tries to hide his smile by rubbing his jaw.

I turn to face my neighbor—my elderly neighbor. "Hey, Mrs. Jacobs." Mortification doesn't begin to describe this moment.

Mrs. Jacobs grumbles something about the youth of today and pushes past us in the narrow hallway.

"How about we finish this conversation inside your apartment?" Damon asks. As soon as we're inside and we've taken off our jackets, he's back onto my now least favorite topic in the world. "So, you've been holding out on me. You could've said something while I was blowing you."

"I couldn't remember my name, let alone think to give you instructions." I step closer. "You definitely didn't need any guidance." When I try to close the distance, he steps back.

"Who was it? Was it M—"

I sigh. "No, Matt didn't play with my ass. Funnily enough, he never went near it in the four—no, five—months we fooled around. And speaking of fooling around, can we please get to it already?"

"Wait, I want to hear more."

I groan. "*Why?*"

"It has to do with your ass, so I'm interested." He hasn't lost his damn smirk.

"I don't know if I like playful Damon. Where's the serious and uptight guy who's hotter than fuck when he loses control and blows a guy in his friend's guest bedroom?"

Damon's green eyes darken and fill with lust.

"There he is," I taunt and move closer again. This time, he lets me get within a foot before he stops me.

His hands go to my hips. "Maddy." His voice—so tortured. "Are you sure?" He winces. "Sorry, I don't mean to be insecure and annoying. I never used to need this much reassurance." He lets out a sad laugh. "And you thought you were the head case."

I swallow my irritation, because it's not at Damon. It's at the shithead who messed with him. "I have an idea." Grabbing his hand, I drag him over to my bed and push him down on his back, but I don't join him. Not yet.

My tiny closet is full from top to bottom and left to right. I push aside my work shirts, but they don't go far. I have to pull off some impressive contortionist moves to reach into the back for my ties. I'm lucky enough to work for a laid-back firm that I don't have to wear them in the office.

"What are you doing?" Damon asks.

I almost get swallowed whole by the closet. "Aha."

Damon's eyes narrow when I pull out a tie.

Cautiously, I approach him and reach for the hem of his shirt to take it off. Then I nudge him. "Move up the bed." He wiggles his way up so his head hits the pillow, and I climb on top of him, straddling his hips. I have to close my eyes and fight the urge not to rut against the hardness beneath me. "Hands above your head."

"I'm not really into kink." That doesn't stop him from lifting his hands or me from tying him to my headboard.

"Calm down. It's just a little bondage. I promise not to spank you or make you call me sir."

He snorts.

"It's loose so you can easily get out if you want to. It's more a mind over matter thing. You're not the one who's going to be doing the touching, so anything that happens here will be all on me. It'll be everything I want to do."

My eyes meet his, and I freeze. It's an odd moment to have an epiphany-like event. But being this close, me on top of a half-naked Damon, our mouths inches apart, and sharing the same breath, I finally *get* it. I don't give a shit about labels, because I don't need to. All I need to care about is making this guy mine.

The possessiveness takes me off guard, because I've never had that with anyone. I don't even know if the feeling is temporary or long-term. The only thing keeping my mouth glued shut is the fear it will go away. I don't want it to. All I know is, I've never wanted anyone more, and if he makes me chase him for months like his sister did, I'd do it. And I wouldn't give up this time, because it's different with Damon. This isn't about sex. If it was, I would've ditched Damon as soon as I found out about his issues and hooked up with Noah instead. Or a chick. I wouldn't be willing to tie Damon to a bed just so he'd let me touch him. I wouldn't care to work through the shit going on in his head.

My epiphany might be insignificant to most people, but Maddox O'Shay realizing he wants to try a *relationship*? Better call NASA, because I'm sure an asteroid is headed for Earth.

"You okay?" Damon whispers.

I'm frozen on top of him. "I don't know," I say truthfully. I'm not going to start spouting random I-want-you-so-fucking-bad speeches.

When he struggles against his restraints, I reach up and

wrap my hand around his wrists to stop him before he freaks out.

"Let me finish. I don't know, because I have no fucking clue where to start. There are so many dirty images running through my head right now, and I want to do all of them."

He relaxes and that easy grin of his takes over. "That's simple. I want you to kiss me. So start there."

Our mouths come together, and even though I'm the one on top, and he's tied to the bed, Damon's the one in control.

The kiss we shared at Chastity's wedding is a blur now. I don't remember if he tasted like he does now—warm with a hint of beer on his breath. I don't remember the stubble around his lips. The adrenaline pumping through me wore off and took my exact memories with it. And earlier tonight was frantic—the pent-up tension from the last month releasing itself in the moment. This time, I'm going to savor it.

Damon has other ideas. His hips roll and lift off the bed, grinding against me.

"Someone's impatient," I say.

"Yeah, well, *someone else* has already gotten off tonight. Maybe he's not impatient because he hasn't been hard for hours."

"Hours ... really? It's been like two. There are starving kids in Africa."

"What does that have to do with anything?" Damon asks.

"Isn't that what you measure everything against? It was my sister's comeback for everything. If I complained of being cold, she'd say—yeah, well, there are starving kids in Africa. Meaning, there are always people worse off than you."

"I dunno. Pretty sure you can die from blue balls."

"Pretty sure you're lying," I say.

"Fine. It just feels like I'm dying." He rolls his hips again.

His cock rubs against mine, and fuck, he is hard. Impossibly hard.

"Guess I have some work to do then." My lips drop to his shoulder, and I pepper light kisses down his chest.

Foreplay for me has always been just that—a way to get a girl ready so I could fuck her. And as selfish as it is, if she got off while I went down on her, it meant I didn't have to work as hard while fucking her. Yeah, I'm a real catch. It's not that I didn't enjoy the foreplay, but more it was a means to get to where I needed to go. With Damon, I *want* this. I'm enjoying his shortness of breath and his moans as I kiss his skin. I like exploring his hardened body, because I've never experienced it before. It's new and exciting and hotter than I ever anticipated.

The only downside to this is I feel like a teenager again. My hands tremble, and insecurities about not knowing what the fuck I'm doing seep in.

But then I gaze at Damon and take in his slightly parted mouth and his flushed cheeks and think *I've so got this.*

I move agonizingly slow on purpose, not only because it seems to frustrate him, which turns me on, but because it gives me time to work through the nerves. I need to get over them soon because I won't be able to keep this level of control for long. I want him under me. On top of me. All over me.

My mouth traces his hairless chest, and I love the smooth, flat skin of his pecs under my tongue. I moan around his nipple, and he hisses. As I move farther down, a small trail of dark hair leads from his belly button to my end goal.

He lets out an impatient grunt when my hands fumble with his belt and zipper. I glance up at him, and his biceps bulge as he holds onto the headboard he's strapped to. I already know Damon doesn't like giving up control. Having me take the lead has to be hard for him, but for me, seeing him on the last thread of his restraint, I've never seen anything sexier.

I'm the one in charge, and the power trip goes straight to my head.

Leaning back on my heels and kneeling in front of him, I reach back and take my shirt off. I want skin on skin. I want *everything*.

Damon watches me as I climb off the bed and stand. His eyes follow my hand as I drop my pants and kick them off with my shoes and socks. He helps me by toeing off his own shoes, and then I'm reaching for his jeans.

He sucks his bottom lip into his mouth. "Do you know how hard it is not to boss you around right now?"

"Yup. And I love it. This is my show."

Damon throws his head back. "Can you at least go a bit faster?"

What do I do? I take off his pants and boxers so slow I'm sure it's some kind of record for the slowest undressing in history.

"Just so you know, I hate you," he grumbles.

"You won't in a minute." I blanket his body, our cocks lining up perfectly. The smallest roll of my hips has me panting. "God, this feels good," I say as our bodies move against one another.

"Take us both in your hand," he orders.

"My show," I remind him. "Or do I need to gag you like you did to me?"

"You can stop me from talking by kissing me." Damon loves my mouth, I'm finding out. And I'm one hundred percent cool with that.

I put all my weight on my left side as I kiss him, and move my right hand down and in between us. It's hard to get my fist around us both, but I slick us with precum from ... I don't know which one of us it's from. Probably both.

I'm painfully hard, my balls heavy and my cock ready to explode. I give us a hard pump, and the air turns serious. Gone are the jokes, the teasing, the going slow. My wrist is at an odd angle, but the pain isn't enough to take away from the pleasure zinging through my body. All that's left between us is the need to come.

It takes all my strength to hold off. I don't want Damon to come in my hand—I want my mouth on him—but I'm reluctant to pull away.

Damon rips his mouth away from mine and grunts.

"Not yet," I say and frantically release us both. "Come in my mouth." I don't know where my boldness has come from, and after my nerves, part of me thinks I would be a little hesitant to do this, but I'm not. I want it. I want it all. In an instant, I'm sliding down him so I'm eye-level with his impressive cock. Its velvety skin is pulled tight, ready for release.

"You don't have to."

"I know I don't have to. I want to. Fucking duh."

I never understood when girls say they love giving head because it means they're in control. I'm always like *Yeah, okay, you're the one with my cock in your mouth. Pretty sure fucking your face means I hold all the cards.* But as my mouth wraps around Damon, and he squirms underneath me, I understand it completely. *I'm* in charge of when he comes. *I'm* the one driving him crazy. His salty skin tastes so fucking good I could do this forever. Or until my jaw locks up—one or the other.

And okay, yeah, relaxing my throat is difficult at first because my gag reflex is telling me I can't take much more, but I'm determined to be awesome at this. Except, when I push through it, I push too far, and a weird snorting choking sound comes out of my nose, because I refuse to clamp down on Damon's dick.

"You don't have to take it all," Damon says, his voice breathless. "Do what you like being done to you. You'll know if I like it."

In that case, I grip the base of him with my hand, and the heel of my palm makes circles on his balls.

"Fuck yes," he hisses.

I continue to pump my hand while I suck the tip of him in my mouth and slowly move down his shaft. My tongue finds that sensitive vein on the underside of his dick, and if the *oh fuck, oh fuck, oh fuck* that comes out of his mouth has anything to say, I guess he likes that.

His encouragement turns me on the most, and my dick leaks. I need to touch myself. My spare hand reaches between my legs, and Damon's "Ughnamlgh" has our eyes locking.

"So hot watching you touch yourself. I'm gonna ..."

I suck harder with my mouth. He comes on a strangled cry, and he fills my mouth. I'm hit with more of his saltiness, and the taste has me shooting all over my hand and on his thigh. The orgasm makes my brain short-circuit, and I'm cut off from the rest of my body.

I can't even bring myself to climb up next to him right now. Flopping onto the mattress, I roll onto my side, my face right next to his crotch.

"A-plus for effort," Damon pants. "B-minus for technique. We'll work on it."

I try to slap his ass, but my arms are lead, and I can only reach his leg. "Ass."

"I'm kidding, I swear. That was ..."

"Awesome?"

"Yeah. That. Come up here." His hand runs through my hair.

"Hey, you're supposed to be tied up."

"Like you said, it was loose. Come. Up. Here."

I wiggle my way up next to him, and he wraps an arm around my shoulders and brings me into his side.

"Regrets?" he asks quietly, as if expecting me to say yes and kick him out.

"Can't regret coming like a motherfucker twice in one night."

"Do you want me to get out? I know how you manwhores hate when a hookup outstays their welcome."

I pull back. "You think this was a hookup? After I told you I want to *date* you?"

Damon shrugs. "I thought the dating was going to be separate to ... uh ..."—he waves his hand around—"this."

"Granted, I haven't dated a lot of people—okay, no one—but isn't it all the same? I want you to stay the night."

"Can we at least clean up before we pass out?"

I roll on top of him and cover more of him in my cum. "Can't move."

"We'll have a quick shower. Together."

"Sold." I jump out of bed and practically race him to my bathroom.

CHAPTER SIXTEEN

DAMON

It's been too long since I woke up next to someone. I'm not including the weekend I spent at Maddox's parents' house, because that's not like this. Not with my dick resting in the cleft of his bare ass while I spoon him.

I wasn't lying last night when I said I usually like to top, and being this close to his ass is making morning wood more than uncomfortable. But with Maddox, if he rolled over right now and told me he wanted to fuck me, I wouldn't hesitate. In fact, the thought of it alone has me groaning into the back of his neck as I try to wake him with kisses.

His hand swats my head. "It's not morning yet."

"Yeah, it is."

He reaches for his phone on the nightstand, and the screen lights up. "It's already nine? My—" There's a knock at the door. "Right on time."

"Who's that?" I ask.

"My birth mother."

"Your what?" I exclaim.

"You see what you miss when you avoid me? Get up and get dressed. I'll explain later."

Maddox mentioned something last night about family drama, but then we got too distracted to get into it. I jump up and dress as fast as I can, just in time for Maddox to let the blonde woman into his apartment. She drags a suitcase behind her.

"Aunt Cheri, this is Damon," Maddox says.

"Ah, the boyfriend," she says, her voice warm and smile-friendly.

"Ah, the birth mother …" My voice goes up at the end as if it's a question. Maddox's aunt is his mother?

Maddox turns to his aunt … mother … person. "Sorry, I kinda just sprung this on him. He's been busy lately, and we haven't spent any time together. Not exactly the type of conversation you have over the phone."

Cheri nods. "Of course. How are you doing with it all now? I know it was a shock, but—"

"Mom and Dad will always be my parents, but I'm glad to get the answers to questions I've had forever. And I want to help you any way I can."

"Help?" I ask, even though I probably shouldn't. It's not my business.

"Aunt Cheri needs a place to crash for a few days while she undergoes experimental treatment here in the city. She has MS."

Damn. "I'm sorry to hear that."

Cheri waves us off. "It's okay, and I promise I won't stay long. I'm fine with sleeping on the couch."

"You can take my bed. I'll take the couch," Maddox says.

My eyes go to his couch which is lucky to fit my sister on it who's a short-ass. No way Maddox would be comfortable there. "You could stay with me," I find myself saying.

So much for going slow. The words fall out of my mouth without thought, but I don't like the thought of not seeing him for a while after last night. And he did say it'll only be a few days.

His lips quirk. "Or I could stay with Damon."

Cheri smiles. "How about I take you boys out for brunch to say thanks."

"Uh, okay," Maddox says, sounding a little unsure.

I agree to it even though I need to get home to study. Blowing it off again after not doing any last night is going to sting when I fall behind, but Maddox seems out of his element with Cheri. Maddox says she's a hippie and expresses free love and whatever, but it has to be hard finding out your mom's not really your mom.

We walk one block to a diner, and Cheri starts in on us as soon as the waitress takes off with our orders. "So, I hope you don't mind me saying anything, but your dad gave me the impression you two weren't together."

Maddox already told his parents we broke up? That was always the plan, but I didn't realize he'd do it so soon.

"Ah, about that," Maddox says. "I didn't realize Dad had blabbed. When I took Damon home with me, we were just friends. Now we're ..."

My eyes widen. What *are* we? He says he wants to date me, sure, but it's too early for the boyfriend title. One night together doesn't make a relationship.

"More than friends," he finishes.

I can live with that.

"It's a long story," I say. And I'd really like to hear the end part that I'm missing. "What's this trial you're involved in?"

Cheri's hands shake with a small tremor, but she pulls them into her lap under the table to hide them. "It's a clinical trial for new medication to slow down the advancement of MS. Because mine's advanced faster than anticipated, I'm the perfect lab rat."

"Hopefully it works," Maddox says.

"I won't even know which group I'm in. I might be in the control group who are given placebos, but I've got nothing to lose. Literally. I've already spent my life savings on treatment."

"You don't have insurance?" I try to keep the judgment from my tone.

"My insurance covers some but not all."

"How are you paying for the trial?" Maddox asks.

"The cost of the trial is covered by the pharmaceutical company running it."

"Then we should really hope it works," Maddox says.

When our food comes, Cheri turns the subject back to Maddox and his life. He says how he's always had the desire to travel, and her face lights up.

"You must get it from me," she says.

He matches her smile. "You're probably right."

I don't think something like that is genetic, but I don't say anything. I'm not that much of a dick. They've found some common ground to bond over. I'm not going to shit all over that.

By the time we finish the meal, Cheri has practically mapped out a trip for Maddox with all the things he must see and do when he gets the chance. It sounds amazing, and I find myself wanting to plan it together—travel together. But I know it's way too soon for that. I think I've inserted myself into Maddox's life too much already by inviting him to stay with me for a few days. That might be the manwhore's quota of clinginess for a while.

The waitress comes back with our check, and Cheri reaches for it. "My treat, remember?" I almost get a thank you out when she reaches into her bag. "Oh, shoot. My wallet isn't here." She rummages some more but comes up empty. "I must've left it in my suitcase back at your apartment."

Maddox chuckles, as if it's not the first time Cheri's forgotten something. "Don't worry about it. I'll get this one."

"Thanks, honey. I should get going. I need to be at the hospital in fifteen for my first appointment."

Maddox reaches into his pocket and pulls out a key. "Here, I had this made for you while you're staying. Can you find your way back to the apartment? I, uh, need to talk to Damon for a sec."

"I'll be fine. I've been to New York plenty of times. You two stay here and finish up." She stands and glides out the door. Even though she's dressed for early spring in New York, she has that hippie swagger where she seems to float.

"So, that's my birth mom."

"Crazy," I say absently, still staring at the door.

"What's that look for?"

I school my features into passiveness. "Look? I didn't realize I was doing a look."

"She's trippy, huh? I'm surprised she's going for treatment. She always came across as the hippie I'll-do-it-naturally type. Like she could cure MS with acupuncture."

"I'm guessing that was the family drama you mentioned?"

"Yeah. I was so pissed I had to get out of the house. That's why I ended up in Matt's motel room."

"But you're cool with it now? I notice she just said she's been to New York plenty of times, but I'm guessing she never came to see you when she was here."

"It's weird. After my freak out, I no longer saw my hometown as the thing that held me back all those years. It was the place that adopted me and welcomed me as one of their own. Without sounding like a pretentious douche, it changed my whole perspective on that place. I used to see a dead end, small town, and I never understood how the people there could see it as a home. But I do now. I mean, I don't want to move back there or anything, but the thought of going back doesn't induce claustrophobia anymore."

"Getting clarity isn't douchey. Sometimes a punch to the gut is what you need to gain real insight."

"When I'd had time to cool down, I went back to the house to talk to Cheri, and she wants to be more active in my life and get to know me. I don't know how I feel about it yet, but I want to take the chance while I have it."

"I guess she had her own sense of clarity with her illness. How are your parents dealing with this?"

He pauses in thought. "I don't think they're happy with the way it came out. Cheri kind of blindsided us, and she didn't talk to them about it first. But Dad told me not to hold a grudge against the three of them for too long. I told him I wasn't gay to see if he'd do the same."

"You *what?*"

Maddox shrugs. "It was the right time."

"Are you sure you want to stay with me the next few days? You could stay with Cheri and bond or whatever. We can catch up next week when she's gone. I only offered because your couch looks seriously uncomfortable."

"It really is. Besides, choosing between staying with a woman I hardly know who I happen to share DNA with or sharing a bed with a really hot guy while I continue to explore my newfound love of sucking cock, it's really no contest."

A laugh-slash-shocked noise comes from beside us, and we turn to meet the waitress's amused, if not slightly taken off guard, stare.

"For fuck's sake," Maddox hisses under his breath.

"I'll get this," I say. I throw a credit card in the check holder and hand it to the waitress. When she disappears, I laugh. "Seriously, babe. Maybe you should scan your surroundings before talking dirty."

"Wanna go back to my apartment so I can do all the dirty talking I want?"

"As tempting as that is, I *really* need to go home and get some studying done. If I get a full day in, I can give you all of my focus tonight."

"Okay, but how am I going to get through all of today with this?" He grabs my hand and pulls it into his lap under the table.

I groan as my own cock twitches. "Well, now thanks to you, I'm going to be in a similar state."

"You're welcome."

"You tease now, but for the next three days, you're mine."

It's been longer than three days. Almost a week, to be exact. It turns out Cheri had a bad reaction to the clinical drug, so they've had to keep her in the city longer than anticipated.

Having Maddox in my bed at night is great, and normally, I wouldn't complain, but—

"If I'd known you were going to make me watch this crap, I might not have invited you to stay with me," I say.

"Shh."

I know he did not just *shh* me.

No joke, the guy likes cooking shows. I mean, I get he likes to cook, but if I have to sit through any more of this, I want to be stabbed in the eyes with a paring knife. The reason I even know what a paring knife is, is because I'm watching the fucking cooking network. I'm rarely home as it is, and when I am, I have to endure this?

With our feet up on the coffee table, only wearing boxers, and our thighs flush against each other, I know I shouldn't complain. I get to come home to a hot guy, who—if I make it home before he's asleep—is eager to suck my dick. The least I could do is endure watching a little cooking.

"There's numerous ways goat's cheese can be used in a dish

and so many complementing flavors." The guy on the TV rattles off the different things you should use goat's cheese for. I'm living a real-life Forrest Gump moment where Bubba is listing off all the different types of shrimp.

Shoot me. Please.

Nope. Can't watch it anymore.

I lift my arm and wrap it around Maddox's shoulder casually, as if that's my end goal, when really, my target is the remote beside him. I can't let him know what I'm up to yet.

His hand goes to my thigh and squeezes. We've only been officially seeing each other a week, but I already know what that squeeze means. *"We can fool around after this is done."*

My hand on his shoulder skims down his arm and back up again, each time getting closer to the remote on the side of the couch. I breathe in deep and hold it as my hand slides down again. It's within reach now. I lean into him a little bit more so I can—

Maddox slaps my wandering hand. He doesn't take his eyes off the screen as he says, "I know what you're doing, Dik. Don't even."

Pretending I have no idea what he's talking about, I lean in, my lips going to his neck. "Don't even what?"

He shudders under my breath on his skin. "Out of both of us, I'm the only one who can cook, so watching this helps you by giving me ideas on what to make for *your* dinner."

"Fuck dinner. I'd rather eat something else."

Maddox laughs, but it dies when I push him down on the couch and climb on top of him. If I can't change the channel, I'm going to at least have fun while he watches stupid cooking.

I run my nose down his neck and chest, peppering soft, open kisses as I go.

He grunts when I lick his nipple and suck it into my mouth, making it go hard. "Okay, I agree. Fuck dinner."

I grin and make my way up to his mouth. I can't think of a place I'd rather be than right here. Maybe somewhere without cooking shows, but if I can just ...

My hands go above his head, right next to the—

He tears his mouth away from mine. "Bastard!"

We struggle for the remote. I pin him down with my forearm across his chest and stretch above him, trying to reach my target, but he jabs me in my ribs with his finger. I flinch and almost fall off him onto the floor.

Maddox laughs his ass off, but I regain my balance and pin him to the couch. I try to hold back my own laughter as he writhes underneath me, trying to get on top and win the remote.

"You may as well let me change it over," I taunt. "You're not exactly watching it at the moment."

"It's the principle of the thing now. You can't come in here and just take over."

"My TV, my choice."

"I was watching it first."

"What are you, five?" Even though I think we might be having our first disagreement-slash-argument, we're both still laughing, and we're both hard. The thin material of our boxers isn't hiding anything.

"We established my immaturity when we met, remember?" he says.

"Maddy, baby, babe. Can I please watch the baseball game?"

He groans and throws his head back on the couch in defeat. "Even I know not to get in between you and your baseball."

"Oh my God, I could kiss you."

"If I have to endure nine innings, you should do more than just kiss me."

I roll my hips, our cocks rubbing against each other, and I try to hold in my moan. "There should only be about three innings left, and I can multitask. I can watch and get you off at the same time."

He's breathless now, so close to the edge as I continue to grind against him. "Prove it."

"Gladly."

I switch the channel over to baseball, but I never see a second of it. Turns out, I couldn't care less.

Three days staying with me turned into six, and now it's nine. Cheri's still having issues with her meds, which sucks, but living with Maddox is surprisingly awesome.

It works because we barely see each other, and if he hadn't been staying with me, I wouldn't have seen him at all. Of the nine nights he's been at my place, I think we've spent a total of four of them together.

Tonight, I'm dragging my ass home at midnight because I had a late class which meant I needed to stay late at OTS being everyone's bitch boy by doing their filing and scheduling. Come graduation, I'll have my own assistant and won't have to do the mundane shit ever again.

The hope I have that Maddox is awake is dashed when the only light on in my apartment is the lamp next to my couch.

I drop my bag in the living room and make my way to my bedroom where it's obvious Maddox tried to stay awake. His phone is on his chest, still gripped in hand. An arm is under his head, his biceps bulging. My gaze drops to his abs and then lower, where only a sheet covers him. It's sad to say this isn't the first time I've found him this way after coming home.

"Babe?" I whisper.

Nothing. He's out. So tempted to wake him with a blowjob, but I'm quickly learning Maddox likes his sleep. If it was me, I'd take sex over sleep any day. Maddox doesn't want to wake for anything.

Having him in my bed gives me the same endorphin spike I used to get from playing baseball. They used to say my smile on the mound was because I was cocky and overconfident. No one knew it was just me being in my element. My smirk was my trademark, and since I injured my shoulder, I didn't even know I still had it in me. I thought it died along with my career.

Maddox has a way of making me smile without even realizing I'm doing it, and I could definitely see myself coming home to him in the future.

Undressing and climbing into bed, I throw my leg over him, and his cock twitches against my thigh.

Maddox turns in my direction, but he doesn't open his eyes. "I tried to stay awake," he mumbles.

"I know. I'm sorry I'm late."

"Dinner. Fridge. Hungry."

"I'm not hungry. Thank you though. You're amazing."

"Yeah, I am." He still hasn't opened his eyes, and I wonder if he's sleep talking.

"Go back to sleep."

"Mmkay."

"I'll be home early tomorrow. I'll make sure of it."

Ten past seven, and I'm walking in the door. That deserves a prize. And as soon as I enter my apartment, I get it. The aroma of garlic becomes overwhelming.

"Thank God. I was hoping that smell was coming from my kitchen," I say. There's no response. I turn the corner and stop in my tracks. Maddox is *naked* apart from my plain black apron tied around his neck and waist. He moves around the small space as if he owns it. He also has earphones plugged in his ears, so he hasn't heard me come home.

I fold my arms across my chest and lean against the wall, watching his firm ass the whole time. By the time Maddox notices me, my cock is at full attention. Maddox's eyes lock with mine, and I can't stop my smile.

"Do you often cook naked?"

"Huh?" he yells and takes out an earphone.

"Do you always cook naked?"

"I'm wearing an apron. No safety or sanitary violations here."

"Not why I was asking." My eyes roam down his body and back up again. "I'm thinking I should try to get home earlier if that's the case."

Maddox's expression turns heated. "It's uh … I had plans. I knew you were coming home early."

"*Had* plans? Why past tense?"

He sighs. "How about I tell you after stage one of my plans. Because that I can still do."

"Is it dinner?"

Maddox steps closer. "Nope."

"Shower?"

"Guess again." He stops a few inches away.

"Kiss?"

Lips land on my neck. "Getting closer," he murmurs against my skin.

"Blowjob?" I ask, my tone filled with hope.

Without another word, Maddox sinks to his knees. *Fuck, yes.* I don't know how I went over a year without sex. Because I've been busy, it's been three days since I had Maddox's mouth on me, and I feel like a starved man getting his first meal in months.

He gets to work, dropping my pants and underwear to my ankles and taking me in his hot, wet, mouth.

"I'm quitting school," I grunt.

Maddox pulls off me and looks at me confused. "Huh? You have like one month left."

"Because if I quit, it means I can come home earlier and get this every night instead of falling into bed exhausted and passing out." I knew it was stupid to start something this close to the end. All I want to do is spend time with Maddox. Instead, I'm cramming for finals and attending classes I have no interest in but have to finish to get my degree.

"Soon," Maddox says and goes back to working me over with his tongue. He's picked up some tricks since staying with me, and I can't get enough. I will never have enough of Maddox O'Shay. He's becoming addictive. Or, more specifically, his mouth is. My hand runs through his blond hair, grabbing what I can of it.

After that first night together, and every night since, my insecurities diminish more and more, but the thought of fucking him makes them reappear, and neither of us has mentioned the possibility of going further. I want to, so bad, but we're comfortable with this for the time being. Except right now where I can see his bare ass. The thought of taking it has me coming in his mouth.

He swallows and licks me clean. He even helps me pull my boxer-briefs and pants back up while I try to catch my breath. That's when I notice the look of guilt on his face.

He turns to go back to cooking.

"What's up?" I ask.

"So, funny story …"

My heart sinks. "Was that a goodbye BJ? Is Cheri gone from your apartment?"

"Uh, no. Actually, we went to lunch today and she, uh, needs a few more days, but this isn't about that."

Relief floods me, because I don't want him to leave. Does it make me a bad person that I'm thankful his mother is sick? It means he gets to keep staying here, without me having to tell him I want him here. I'm worried admissions like that will scare him off. For a supposed manwhore, he's adjusted to our situation well, but part of me wonders if he's freaking out about being thrust into a semi-serious relationship when we agreed we'd take things slow. We haven't used the B word yet, but we're practically living together. I keep waiting for "I need space" to come out of his mouth.

I can feel that I'm getting ahead of myself, but I've always been a relationship guy. I've had my share of hookups, but I want someone to come home to at night. I want serious. I resisted Maddox for over a month, so it feels like we've started in the middle. Being thrust together hasn't helped in trying to go slow, but the thing is, I don't give a shit about slow anymore.

Fuck, don't say any of this aloud. He'll run away faster than Usain Bolt.

We haven't even had sex yet. Well, sex-sex. We've mastered blowjobs.

Maddox looks away as he says, "You know how we decided not to tell Stacy about us yet because she's intense?"

Right, another thing—we haven't told my sister or family we're seeing each other yet. "I believe the word we used was insane, but yes, go on."

"When Cheri came to take me to lunch today, I wasn't thinking and introduced Stacy as your sister—"

"Shit. She knows?"

"Yup." Maddox looks behind me at the clock on the wall. "And she's coming over for dinner. In like fifteen minutes."

"She's going to yell at both of us."

"Hey, I already endured my share at work. This is all for you. Aren't you glad I gave you a blowjob first?"

"I need a lot more than a blowjob to be able to deal with my sister."

"Maybe you can fuck me later then."

While my jaw drops to the floor, Maddox walks into the bedroom. My feet trip over themselves trying to follow him. When I manage to get to the door, Maddox is already pulling on his jeans and putting on a shirt.

"We don't have time now," he says in an obvious tone. "Your sister's going to be here soon."

"But ... and—"

"Before you ask, yes, I'm sure, no I won't freak out, and I know you'll stop if I don't like it."

I don't have any words for him. The thought of fucking him has my spent cock waking up again. But then the idea weighs heavily in my chest, and I begin to wonder what I'm doing with Maddox. Being someone's first is stressful. Hell, my first time didn't go so well, and it ruined it for me forever.

My college boyfriend and I were both virgins and underprepared. It hurt. *A lot*. Even now, with all the lube in the world, it's difficult for me to come that way.

What if Maddox doesn't like it?

He approaches me and wraps his arms around my waist. "Why are you freaking out right now?"

"How do you know I'm freaking out?"

"You think I can't read you? You could read me the minute we met."

Instead of answering, my mouth comes down on his. He responds with a groan and opens for me. Our tongues mash together, and we tumble onto the bed, me pinning him beneath me.

My mouth leaves his and moves to the stubble on his cheek and neck.

"I need to shave," he says.

"Don't. I like it rough."

"Are we talking about my skin or the way you like to fuck?"

I groan. "There's so many things I want to do to you right now but won't."

Maddox throws his head back as my lips trail down his throat. "We don't have time," he agrees.

"I just need you." Not sex. Not a blowjob. Just him.

We continue to kiss, making out like teenagers, until the timer on the oven blares through the apartment, followed by a knock on my apartment door.

"Told you," Maddox says breathlessly. "Now she's gonna know we were fucking around. Look at your hair."

I stand and catch my reflection in the mirror over my dresser. He's right. My cheeks are flushed, my hair a mess, my lips swollen ... fuck. "You get the door. I'll get the oven."

"Deal." Maddox pulls himself up and does some strategic rearranging so Stacy won't be able to see his hard-on.

I do the best I can to flatten my hair and straighten myself up before getting the garlic bread out of the oven.

"You're in so much trouble." My sister's voice comes from the entryway to the kitchen.

"What are you going to do? Beat me up?" I ask, without turning her way.

"Oh, I don't need to do that. I've done one better."

"Hi, Damon, honey," says a feminine voice I know well.

I spin and see two people I haven't seen in a while. Not because I avoid them, but because I'm always too busy to make the trek to Long Island. "Mom. Dad." *Shit.*

Maddox appears in the small space that's only getting

smaller by the second, and he runs a hand over his hair. "I didn't cook enough for all of us."

"It'll keep for tomorrow. We're going out for dinner," my sister announces. "Mom and Dad can't wait to get to know Maddox better." In other words: they can't wait to grill him.

Stacy flashes her trademark grin. It's part-triumphant, part-smug, and part-vindictive. No one does punishment like my sister.

Ten days, and this is how it ends. Probably. My parents are great, but like Stacy, they can be intense. It's terrifying for new boyfriends to endure. If Maddox survives this, nothing will scare him off.

CHAPTER SEVENTEEN

MADDOX

This is a big step. Although, to be fair, Damon's already met my folks.

I'm worried I'll make an ass of myself. I want his family to like me. Not as Stacy's friend, but as their son's boyfriend.

Huh, boyfriend. First time I've thought of us that way. I wait for the panic to kick in, but it's absent. Look at me being all mature and shit.

"Hi," Stacy singsongs at the restaurant hostess. "I made a reservation this afternoon under King. Nine people."

"Nine?" Damon and I ask in unison.

"The Davidsons are coming," Damon's mom says.

My eyes go to Damon to confirm what I suspect, and his skin pales. Yup. Eric and his family are coming to dinner. Brilliant.

"The rest of your party is already here," the hostess says.

Even more brilliant.

As we're led to our table, I lace my fingers with Damon's. "You okay?" I ask quietly.

"Yup." He's lying. I squeeze his hand, but he shakes it off.

Fucking Eric.

Damon whispers, "I'm sorry for what you're about to witness."

I have no idea what he means until Eric and his brother, Julian, jump out of their seats when they see us. Julian goes straight to Stacy and wraps her in a hug.

Eric approaches Damon. "Hey, brother." They shake hands and go in for a man-hug. My hand fists at my side. I don't understand why Damon keeps up appearances.

Eric moves onto me and holds his hand out for me to shake. If it weren't for Damon's pleading eyes, I'd tell Eric to fuck off. Instead, I behave like a good boy and shake his hand.

"Nice to see you again, Maddox." Eric's tone is about as genuine as a politician making campaign promises.

"You too." *Fucker.*

"Hey," Julian says and shakes my hand too, "you run out of women or what?"

I smile politely when what I really want to do is beat the Davidson brothers to a pulp. Although, I know that's not fair to Julian. The few times we've met, he's seemed like a decent guy. "Stacy got to you, didn't she?"

"She paid me ten bucks to say that. Figured I'd get it out of the way so I can hit the bar." Julian turns to her. "Hand it over, woman."

Stacy rolls her eyes and hands him a twenty. "Buy me a drink too."

"And me," I call after him.

"I guess we're getting our own drinks," Eric says to Damon and slaps his chest.

"Let's go."

I suck in a deep breath as I take the seat next to Stacy. I'm left with her, Damon's parents, and Eric's parents. I turn to my supposed best friend. "I hate you," I mutter so only she can hear.

She leans in and kisses my cheek. "Love you too."

"So this is the new boyfriend," Mrs. Davidson says.

"The new boyfriend Damon didn't tell us about," Damon's mom says. She pierces me with the green eyes Damon inherited. "We had to hear it from Stacy."

"We're really new," I say and swallow hard.

"Eric says he met you a few weeks back," Mrs. Davidson says.

Ooh boy. I don't know what lies to keep up with now, so I say nothing before I can put my foot in my mouth.

Julian appears at our side and places drinks in front of us. "You know what's crazy, I thought you two would end up together." He waggles his finger between Stacy and me.

Damon and Eric take their seats, and I slide my hand on Damon's thigh to try to reassure him. We can do this. We can get through this dinner.

"No Kristy?" Stacy asks Eric, nodding to the empty seat beside him.

"Whoa, whoa, whoa," Julian says. "Don't try to change the subject, missy. You and Maddox. What's the deal? How did he end up with your brother when that night we all went out, my friends bet on when you two would get together?"

"Why does everything have to be about sex? Why is it so hard to fathom Maddox and I are purely platonic?" Stacy asks. "Nothing has ever happened between us, and nothing ever will. Even if he wasn't with Damon." She turns to me. "You know I love you, but the thought of kissing you would be like kissing Damon. Or even Julian."

Damon screws up his face, but Julian says, "Hey, I'm offended. I'm hot."

"See"—Stacy gestures to Damon—"that's how I feel about Maddox."

"I wish I could disagree, but best friends kissing fu—dges up friendships," I say and flick my glance to Damon's parents. They appear prim and proper and probably not as cool with the swearing thing as my parents.

Meanwhile, I can feel Eric's glower without having to see it, and Damon lets out a frustrated sigh. Granted, I'm having a major dig at Eric, but no one else would know that. If I kissed Stacy, it *would* fuck up our friendship, so I'm not lying.

"How did you and Damon meet?" Eric's mother asks.

Stacy answers with a giggle. "Funniest story ever."

"Stace," I warn, but I can't tell her why she can't tell the story.

This is so fucked.

"So, when Maddox—"

"I needed a fake boyfriend to go to an ex's wedding." I glare at her. There are so many reasons I don't want the story to be told.

"An ex-*girlfriend*," Stacy says. "He lied and told her he was gay to break up with her when they were eighteen. Maddox didn't know he was bi until he met Damon." She laughs again.

I love Stacy to death, but she really has to learn to pick up on social cues.

Damon's parents stare at me weird—like they don't approve I've never been with a guy before. Or maybe they're pissed because I lied to Chastity about being gay.

I open my mouth to say something to explain my actions five years ago, but Eric beats me to it.

"Favorite pastime of Damon's—hitting on straight guys."

What did he just say?

"What did you just say?" Stacy asks. Guess it's true, when you hang out with someone a lot, you start to think alike.

Damon chugs his beer.

"It was a joke. Geez," Eric says, but there was no joke in it.

Stacy stands and yells, "It's you, isn't it?"

"Stacy," Damon says. "Stop."

Betrayal shines in her eyes. "Oh my God, it makes so much sense. You used to be so close. You really think Damon tried to *turn* you?" she yells at Eric.

I grab her wrist and pull her back down into her seat. Our eyes meet, and that's when she knows she's right. And that I know all about it.

"Bullshit," Julian says. "Eric's not that ignorant."

I scoff.

"Can we please not do this here?" Damon asks. His eyes dart around the small restaurant.

"Stacy. Outside," I say.

"But—"

"Now." I never use a serious tone with her, and my bark makes her flinch. She relents and storms out ahead of me. "We'll be back." I turn to Damon. "You want to—" I tip my head in the direction of the entrance.

He shakes his head. "This is all about to come out, so I better be here to tell my side of it."

I feel like an ass leaving him to it, but Stacy needs to cool off, because I know her. She was two seconds away from flinging herself across the table.

Stacy's pacing when I get outside. "Why didn't you or Damon say anything?"

"It's not my thing to tell. And Damon didn't say anything because he's trying to protect your families. You do everything together. Imagine how awkward Christmases would be if you all knew how homophobic Eric was."

"*Why* does Eric think like that? I don't understand."

"You should ask Damon. Or go back in there and hear it for yourself. But you can't go making a huge scene in there like you were about to."

She shakes her head. "When I set this up to torture you two, I thought the worst that was going to happen was you'd be grilled, you'd sweat, we'd all laugh at you, and that would be it. I didn't think ... fuck. I really am a horrible person."

"You totally are."

"Hey, I'm feeling terrible about my shenanigans for once. Have some sympathy."

I step forward and hug her. "You're a horrible person in general, but in this case, you didn't know what you were doing, so you can't be blamed."

"Thanks. You make me feel so much better," she says dryly.

"It's what I'm here for."

"Can you just tell me? Please?"

"Seriously, not my thing to tell."

"Eric's the reason Damon didn't want to date you at first, isn't it?"

"Yup. But my charming personality won him over."

Stacy snorts. "Can I ask you a serious question?"

"Only if you want a sarcastic answer."

She shoves me. "Are you and Damon serious?"

"You may want to sit down for this."

Her eyes widen. "Oh God, you're breaking up with him, aren't you? Shit, I thought this might've been going too far, but—"

"Stace. You'll need to sit down, because I want to get serious with him. I haven't felt this way about anyone before. Not even Chastity."

"Aww, you could become my brother-in-law," she screeches.

I step back. "Whoa. Way too soon. I meant serious as in maybe calling each other the boyfriend label."

"The manwhore in you isn't dead after all. So close."

"Ready to go apologize for embarrassing your brother?"

She groans. "I guess."

CHAPTER EIGHTEEN

DAMON

As soon as Maddox and Stacy are out the door, I begin to sweat.

"What's going on, you two?" Mom asks.

"It's nothing," Eric says.

"Bullshit it's nothing," Dad growls.

"Guys, stop," I say. I love my family, but they're all overprotective of me. It's a King trait. Stacy may make inappropriate jokes, but she's always the first one to defend me. Even when I ask her not to. My parents are close behind her. They're awesome for it, but sometimes I need them to back off.

"He kissed me," Eric says.

Kill. Me. Now. "Actually, you kissed me." *And you liked it. Yeah, don't say that.*

"When was this?" Denise, Eric's mother, asks.

I exhale loudly. "A year ago. It's over, guys. We don't need to talk about it."

"Is that why you two haven't been as close like when you were kids?" Mom asks.

"No. We're not close because he doesn't like the fact I'm

gay," I say. "Things haven't been the same between us since I came out in high school."

"You came out in college," Mom says.

"Not to him."

"Because you had a thing for me," Eric says.

This is what shits me off—he has a point. Any other straight guy, I could call bullshit. The only two straight guys I've had a crush on were Eric and Maddox, and it turned out Maddox wasn't so straight after all. Any other guy, I could call them out for being narrow-minded and conceited. But the truth is, I spent most of my teenage years fantasizing about the stupid jerk that is Eric. That doesn't mean I ever acted on it. Or hinted. Or fucking manipulated him. I was overly conscious not to do any of that, because I didn't want anyone to know how I felt.

My cheeks heat. No one says anything, and I get the impression everyone at the table suspected my crush even if I did try to hide it. Maybe I sucked at covering it up, and that in itself could be seen as an act of manipulation on my part.

Stacy and Maddox arrive back at the table, and Stacy hugs me from behind. "I'm soooo sorry," she whispers.

"I know," I reply and pat her hand.

Eric leans forward in his seat. "Look, it happened a long time ago, and we're both over it. We didn't tell you because we knew something like this could come between us all. There's no lines being drawn here. No sides."

My parents turn on their best friends who they've known for over thirty years. "I think you understand if we leave dinner here for the night," Mom says in a polite tone that doesn't sound anything like how she normally talks to her friends.

"Mom, Dad," I say, "don't let this get between our families. With all due respect, I appreciate you guys sticking up for me, but it's between me and Eric. I've pretended he doesn't exist for over a year now. I can keep doing it. Don't ruin an otherwise great thing because of me." I don't think I've gotten through to them. They remain stoic. With a sigh, I turn to Maddox. "Looks like we'll be eating the dinner you cooked after all. Let's get out of here."

"Gladly," he says.

"I'm coming too," Stacy says.

"Stace, can I crash with you tonight?" Julian asks. "I wanna go with you guys."

"Sure."

This is not how I wanted this conversation to go—I didn't want this to happen at all.

Solidarity. Sometimes it's the best thing in the world, but this time, it's making me feel like shit.

"Are you okay?" my sister asks on the walk back to my apartment.

"I'm fine," I snap.

"Yeah, sounds it."

"You two didn't need to come for moral support," I say to her and Julian.

"Eric can spout all he wants about no lines being drawn or sides being taken," Julian says, "but that's exactly what happened back there."

"Don't turn on your brother for me," I say.

"How can you say that?" Stacy yells.

"Because I can deal with homophobia. It happens. It's been happening to me since I came out. It's part of being born this way."

"Now who's quoting Lady Gaga?" Maddox mumbles.

I ignore him. "Maybe Eric is confused or bi-curious, or maybe he's just an ass. But say he is confused. Say he has been for a long time. We all practically outed him back there and then walked out on him. Real supportive."

Julian stops dead in his tracks. "Oh, shit."

"Yeah. Oh, shit is right," I say. "I don't like what Eric did, and I will probably hate him forever for making me doubt myself, but I'd never wish what happened back there on him. Not ever. I don't care if he's the one who technically started it. No one deserves that. I can't be the one to be there for him, but you can. Go support your brother, asshat."

"You don't mind?" Julian asks.

"Thanks for backing me, I appreciate it, but this isn't a game of taking sides. Besides, I have to torture my sister for setting up this ridiculous dinner in the first place to try to scare my boyfriend off." I turn to Maddox. "Did she succeed?"

"Fuck no," Maddox says. He steps forward and brings his mouth to mine in a soft kiss.

"Okay, that's weirder to see than I thought it would be," Stacy says. "Not because you're two guys, but because my best friend is kissing my brother." She shudders.

"Boyfriend, huh?" Maddox asks me.

"Unless the label freaks you out. I know you're not a fan of those."

"I like the boyfriend label." He kisses me again.

"Have a good night, guys," Julian says, and Maddox and I pull apart. "Stace, we going out one weekend soon? Party it up old-school style."

Stacy's face lights up. "With wine coolers, cheap chasers, and horrible dance music? I'm in."

"I want in too," Maddox says.

"I'm out," I say.

"You're no fun," Julian says.

"He never has been," Stacy says.

"Catch ya next family gathering," Julian says.

"If there is a next one," I say as he backtracks to the restaurant.

We continue to walk, the mood a little lighter than it was. "You should've said something sooner," Stacy says.

"Sure. *Mom, Dad, your best friends' son is a bigot, but I suspect it's because he likes guys. Thought you'd like to know.*"

Stacy stops walking again. It's going to take all night to get back to my apartment at this rate. "Damon. No one should be forced into enduring his behavior. I don't care how close our parents are or how confused he is."

Frustration bubbles out of me. "He has issues he needs to deal with. They're his issues. Not mine."

"But when they affect your ability to have a relationship—"

"Does it look like it's affecting us?" I wrap my arm around Maddox.

"It did in the beginning," she states.

"How much did you tell her?" I whisper in his ear.

"Stace. Drop it, okay?" Maddox says. "We're great. Damon had more issues than just Eric—like my inability to commit to anyone. He thought I was just looking for a hookup. And yet, tonight, I openly admitted to being in a *relationship*. I'd say we're more than good. So much so, I'm tempted to walk you home to your own apartment."

She screws up her face. "TMI."

"All I said was *apartment*," he argues.

"But I know what you're implying. Can I at least come back for dinner? I'm starving, and Maddox's cooking is awesome."

I wrap my other arm around my sister. "Come on then."

CHAPTER NINETEEN

MADDOX

The love I have for Stacy dims with every passing minute. We've eaten dinner, we've laughed, we've mocked, and it's been great. Adding Damon into our dynamic, or rather, adding me into theirs, is easy. Damon tends to play mediator between Stacy and me, and now it's fun for us to watch him get riled up.

But it's getting late, and all I want to do is go to bed and show Damon how serious I am about being his boyfriend.

Stacy pours herself another glass of wine, and Damon and I share a glance. Our desperation for her to leave is mirrored in each other's stare.

"God, you two couldn't be more obvious if you tried," Stacy complains. "Last glass, I promise. Then I'll catch a cab and go home. Alone. Again."

"You're single by choice," I say. "Don't try to pull sympathy from us."

"It's not my fault this city is full of morons. They're all either Wall Street wannabes who think their shit don't stink, struggling artists who work in the food industry to afford rent, or divorced guys with more baggage than the turnstiles at JFK."

Her face screws up as those last words fall from her mouth. "Where are the guys who use their hands to work? Big and strong."

"Jared's in construction," I mutter.

That's all it takes. Stacy downs her glass of wine. "Thanks for dinner. Love you both."

"We can walk you home," Damon says.

She waves him off. "It's two blocks. I'll catch a cab."

And easy as that, I love her again. I kiss her cheek and walk her to Damon's door.

"Stop pushing me," she grumbles.

"Sorry."

"No, you're not."

"No, I'm not."

As soon as she's gone, I turn to Damon.

"Dishes?" he asks.

"Later. Or never. I'm okay with either of those options."

He smirks and stands from his small dining table, wiping his mouth with a napkin. Wordlessly, we walk—okay, practically run—for the bedroom.

Damon spins in time for me to tackle him onto the bed, and we land with an *oomph*. "Someone's eager," he says against my lips which are trying to attack him.

"Yeah, I am. Been thinking about this all day at work. Do you know how hard ... er *difficult* it is to hide a hard-on in work pants? Every time Stacy told me to get her something, I told her to fuck off."

"She probably didn't notice a difference in your attitude."

"True."

Damon cradles my face, and his thumb trails my jaw. "Maddy ... if you're not sure about this or have doubts—"

"I don't. I want this."

"I was going to say if you are you can fuck me instead."

I pull back. "But you don't …"

"I don't *never* do it. I just prefer not to. It's hard for me to come that way."

"I won't make you do something you don't get off on. And I've been preparing for this."

"Preparing?"

"I've watched a lot of gay porn this week when you haven't come home until late. At first, I was all *How does that not fucking hurt?* but they seem to enjoy it. I want to try it."

"Seriously, had you not blown me earlier, I could've come in my pants right now." He kisses my neck. "So hot," he murmurs. "But so you know, porn can be misleading. They generally edit out the prepping part."

He pulls me down and then rolls on top of me. In charge and in control—this is the Damon that turns me on.

I try to lift his shirt up and over his head, but he refuses to let my lips go.

"We have to go slow," Damon says. "I want to make it good for you."

"Doesn't mean you can't get naked."

"Yeah, it does. I need restraint, because fuck, all I want to do is bury myself in you."

"So, do it."

Damon starts by undressing me agonizingly slow and kissing every inch of my skin. Open, wet kisses go from my collarbone to my nipples and down my stomach. He purposefully avoids my cock as he takes my pants off, and a tortured noise gets stuck in the back of my throat.

I want to fucking cry when he leaves the bed. "Where are you going?"

"I have an idea." He wanders over to his closet and starts rummaging through the bottom.

"Is it your turn to look for a tie?" I quip.

"Nope, but I did remember something Noah gave me not that long ago. I was being a miserable asshole, so he threw it at me and told me to go fuck myself. *Literally*." He pulls out an unopened box. "I never used it."

"A dildo?" I ask, my voice pitching high.

"It's smaller than me but bigger than my fingers. It'll be better for, uh, stretching you."

A nervous laugh escapes. "I love it when you talk dirty."

"We don't have to. Just figure it'd be less painful for you."

I shrug. "What's that old saying, *in for a penny, in for a pound*? Get it? In for a *pound*. See what I did there?"

Damon shakes his head. "You're a dork."

"But I'm your dork."

Damon's reaction is exactly what I'm hoping for. The heated stare he gives me when we're in bed makes me wonder why I've never done the relationship thing before—other than with Chastity. It was different with her, because everything was about *her*. There was no leverage; no equal balance. This thing between Damon and me makes me understand what Mom meant when she always used to talk about giving up her dreams to be with Dad. I still want to travel, but right now none of that matters. Being with Damon is more important.

Why explore the rest of the world when the person who makes it go 'round is the man standing in front of me?

That'd be totally romantic to say aloud if Damon wasn't holding a silicone dildo ready to shove in my ass right about now.

Damon throws it on the bed and moves to the bedside table for lube and condoms. Then he reaches back and removes his shirt.

"Finally, we get to the good part," I say. When he drops his pants and boxers and steps out of them, I sit up and take his hard cock in my hand. As I go to wrap my mouth around it, he stops me.

"I've already had that pleasure tonight. This is about you." He pushes me down on my back and lands beside me, pulling my hip toward him so we're facing each other on our sides.

Warmth spreads along our naked skin. His mouth covers mine, and our tongues tangle as a callused hand runs down my back. Even years after his baseball career ended, he still has rough hands. I can't hold back the moan when his finger slips into my crease and presses against my hole. Ever since I told him I was into ass play, he goes there every chance he gets. I half-suspect he's been preparing me for this—easing me into the idea. I now crave the pressure there, and when he hits that spot inside me, I swear sex has never been that awesome. But it'll be different this time. More.

When his finger leaves me, I let out an unmanly whimper. I cover it by grunting—deep and guttural.

Damon knows what I'm doing and chuckles. "Just a sec, baby."

The telltale sound of the lube cap opening has my cock leaking precum. Hmm, interesting. I've developed a Pavlovian response to *lube*.

I don't have time to dwell on that because Damon's back, his mouth on mine and his fingers sliding inside me.

"Goddamn it, sonofamotherfucking fucker," I ramble.

Damon smiles against my mouth. "I love when you don't make sense."

Something takes over me, and I officially have no control over my hips which thrust forward. Our cocks bump and rub against each other, and it's so, so good—too good.

"Wait, wait, wait. Too fucking close."

His fingers slip out of me, and it gives me time to catch my breath. He fiddles with the lube again, and then the cool, soft feel of silicone trails down my ass. Forget catching my breath; I've forgotten how to breathe entirely.

"I'll go slow," Damon murmurs.

I tense to brace myself.

"Need to relax or it'll hurt."

I nod.

"Maddy, you're still tense. Kiss me."

Our mouths distract me from the pressure between my ass cheeks as Damon inserts the toy inch by inch. The sting of stretching makes my arousal waver, but I know if I breathe through it it'll be worth it as soon as—

"Oh fuck." It brushes against my prostate, and even with the sting still there, I want more.

Instead of moving it, though, Damon leaves it in me and moves his hand in between us, gripping our cocks together and stroking in slow pulls.

My chest rises and falls in shallow pants, and my face and skin burn up.

"You're so hot when you're turned on," Damon says and tightens his grip.

"You mean when you're trying to fucking kill me." I throw my head back enjoying the fullness in my ass and Damon's hand on my cock. "Fucking hell."

"I know you're close when you start dropping too many F-bombs." His hand releases us and goes back to the toy. He moves it in and out slowly, and I can feel him watching me for a reaction. "Does it hurt?"

I shake my head vigorously. "Fuck no."

He continues to torture me with it—in the best way possible—until I'm breathing so heavy I can't talk. "Can you take more?"

The same time I go to answer, he pushes the dildo back inside me harder. "Yes!" Fuck, yes. I can't tell if it's my mouth or my head that chants "More, more, more."

"Roll over," Damon whispers.

I shudder in anticipation as I turn over onto my hands and knees. Staring at him over my shoulder, I watch as he rubbers up and covers his cock in lube.

"Still with me?" Damon asks.

"Hurry up and fuck me, jackass."

Damon laughs, and in one swift move, he removes the toy from my ass and lines up his cock. He pushes in, and I tense against the invasion. He's a lot bigger. I take a deep breath.

"Babe?"

"I'm okay," I choke out. "How far in are you?"

"Just the tip."

"Fuck. Okay." Another deep breath. I can do this.

Damon doesn't push in any father but starts massaging my ass and lower back, trying to get me to relax. He squirts more lube in my crease, and it works enough for him to slide in a bit more. His groan has my cock twitching. The poor thing is confused. It doesn't know whether to be turned on or go flaccid from the pain in my ass.

"I can stop," Damon says.

"No, don't." I'm anything if not determined. "Keep going slow." I close my eyes tight and rest my head on my forearm.

Just when I think this isn't going to work, Damon reaches that glorious spot deep inside me. The stretching pain diminishes as Damon's hips roll in small, shallow thrusts, making his cock rub over my prostate over and over again.

"More."

"You sure?" Damon asks.

"Yes. I need ..." The words die as Damon tests out a bigger thrust. It feels so fucking good. "Keep going," I pant.

Damon keeps moving in and out of me, slowly picking up his pace.

"Fuuuuck," I grunt.

"So hot. Tight." His voice is strained.

"I ..." I can't form words. Nope. Brain is gone. Words no longer exist. I'll be lucky if I can grunt like a caveman.

"What do you need?" Damon asks. "You need me to touch you?"

Fuck, yes. Friction on my dick is exactly what I need, but I can't do it myself. My fingers are scrunched in the bedsheets, holding on for dear life while Damon's hips piston and thrust deeper. The pain is completely gone and replaced with a growing need for more. More touching, more fucking, more, more, more.

Apparently, I'm a greedy bottom. Interesting.

I have no idea if my "Yes" comes out aloud or not, but Damon reaches around me and starts stroking in time with his thrusts which are now frantic and needy.

Every time he slams into me, pleasure zaps down my spine. Heat pools in my groin, and my balls draw up tight.

"Maddy," Damon warns. He's close.

We're on the edge together, both trying not to let go. I explode first, my orgasm taking me by surprise. I shoot everywhere—the bed, Damon's hand, and my stomach.

"Oh, thank God," Damon says and shudders above me.

When he's done convulsing, he collapses onto my back. Unable to hold both our weights, thanks to my muscles wobbling like Jell-O, I fall in a heap onto the mattress.

Damon rolls off me onto his back, breathing heavy, and I wince when his cock leaves me. Yup, gonna be sore tomorrow, but right now I couldn't care less.

"I don't think I've come harder in my life," I mutter.

"I *know* I haven't. Or maybe it's been too long. I don't remember what sex feels like." Damon's chest glistens with sweat as it rises and falls in fast breaths.

"I ... uh, should clean up, but I can't move."

"Five more minutes," Damon mumbles. He doesn't even get up to ditch the condom. Just ties it off and dumps it next to the bed.

"Okay."

Only ...

"Babe," Damon whispers.

"Gothefuckaway," I slur.

"We fell asleep."

"Then why are you waking me?" I grumble.

"Shower, then work. It's morning."

"You fucked me into a coma."

"Uhh, yeah, good luck getting all that cum off you now it'll be dry and gross."

"Damn it."

The ache in my ass makes me flinch when I climb out of bed.

"Are you okay?" Damon asks.

"Never better," I say, downplaying it. I make my way to the bathroom to get the hot water running while I take a piss. My body aches everywhere, but it's not all unpleasant. When Damon joins me in the shower, he steps up behind me, and his hands massage over my shoulders and down my back. I moan and throw my head back on his shoulder while he continues to massage my tired muscles.

"If I get a massage every time you dick me out, it should become a nightly occurrence."

His lips land on my neck. "I'm okay with that arrangement. Your ass probably won't be, though."

"Right. Umm ... will it always take that long to uh ..."

"Adjust? Nah. Now you know what you're expecting, it'll be easier to relax and let it happen. Are you sore?"

"A little."

"Will a blowjob help?"

"Help my ass?" I ask with a laugh. "Probably not. But there's no way I'm saying no."

Damon spins me so I'm pinned against the wall of the shower, and he sinks to his knees. Just like the first night I hooked up with Damon, I wait to become uncomfortable or for that feeling of wanting to escape. It's like I'm expecting it to hit me each time I try something new with him. But as I stare down at him, with his gorgeous mouth wrapped around my cock and his big green eyes watching me in amusement as I can't control my moans, all I can think is I could definitely get used to this.

I take a sip of my wine and stare at the woman who gave birth to me. I'm happy I've gotten to know her these past couple of weeks, but I still don't see her as anything other than my crazy aunt. And I still have so many questions.

"Do you know anything about my birth father at all?"

Cheri plays with the cloth napkin in her lap. "He said his name was Jimmy."

"Of course. Couldn't have been something random that might not be hard to track down like ..."

"Rumpelstiltskin?"

I laugh. "Right."

"Would you really want to find him if we could track him down? I tried when I found out I was pregnant, but I had nothing to go on."

I shrug. "I dunno. Probably not. Wouldn't mind knowing if there were any genetic problems I'd have to be aware about. What if Jimmy's an alcoholic with diabetes who has a heart condition? Shouldn't I know these things?"

Cheri sighs. "As someone with a permanent illness, I don't think you should worry about that stuff. When it happens, you deal with it. Don't spend your life being scared of something that may or may not happen."

"That's good advice." I take another sip of wine when my phone vibrates in my pocket. "Sorry, I should check that."

"Go ahead."

Damon: Fun fact. Walking into an empty apartment and yelling SURPRISE when no one's home isn't as fun as you'd think it would be. Where are you?

Now there's a visual.

Maddox: Thought you were working late? I'm at dinner with Cheri.
Damon: Damn. I guess it's my turn to wait for you to get home.

"Is that Damon?" Cheri asks.

"I'm grinning like an idiot, aren't I?"

"Yeah. You are." She matches my smile. "He makes you happy, and that's a good thing, hon."

Damon: Okay, I'm officially bored already. How do you do it?

I snort. "Sorry. I'll just text him back to say I'll be home in an hour."

"We can leave now if you like?"

"You haven't even touched your soup yet." I've devoured my dinner, though.

"It takes a while to eat these days. Too fast and it comes back up again. Plus, the medication is screwing with my appetite. I could sit here and nurse this bowl of soup all night."

"Shit, I'm sorry. Can I get you anything? I feel like I'm not doing enough. I can come to doctor's appointments with you. Or I can—"

Cheri shakes her head. "You're doing enough by letting me stay in your apartment and keeping me company. You don't owe me anything, Maddox. Our lunches and dinners have been the highlight of … well, my existence lately."

A lump lodges in my throat. "I'm happy to get to know you and glad you finally told me the truth."

She reaches across the table and grips my hand. "I don't deserve you. Giving you up was the best thing I could've done, but that doesn't mean I don't regret it. I doubt you would've grown up to be such a great person if you were on the road with me all those years. And now I'm here"—tears fall from her eyes—"I feel horrible that you've had to take me in."

"Hey, it's okay. You're going through a hard time, and we're family. It's what we do for each other."

"You should go home to Damon. Go have fun. I'll finish my soup eventually, settle the check, and then head on back to your apartment when I'm done."

I'm torn because while I should stay to make sure she gets home okay I really want to go home to Damon. "I know this time you were going to get the check, but how about I go pay and you use your money on a cab back to my apartment so I won't worry about you getting home?"

"I seriously don't deserve you."

I stand from the table and lean into her, kissing the top of her head. "Don't worry about it. Catch up again soon? Come for lunch again one day you're feeling up to it?"

"Definitely."

After settling the check, I can't get home fast enough. When

I walk through the door, Damon's fresh out of a shower, only wearing a towel.

"You're home." A grin lights up his face.

My eyes rake over him, from his wet chest down to his happy trail.

"How's Cheri?"

"Huh?" I pull my gaze away to meet his amused expression.

"Cheri. She doing better?"

"I think she's okay. She doesn't really talk about it much. I can tell the side effects are kicking her ass, though. She can barely eat anything or do anything ..." I check my watch. One thing about seeing Cheri go through this is it makes me realize I need to take her advice. Don't worry about the future so much and go out and have fun. "You should get dressed. We're going out."

Damon's smile falls. "Where?"

"Out." I've been wanting to drag Damon to the batting cages for a while now. I want to see him in his element—where he claims he's most happy.

He eyes me warily the whole time he gets dressed and all the way to the subway too. "Okay, seriously. Where are we going?"

"It's a surprise." One I hope doesn't freak him out like the last time we were at a baseball field.

"If you can't already tell, I'm not a big fan of surprises."

Of course, he isn't. "Wouldn't have guessed," I say.

When we arrive outside the sporting complex, Damon tenses.

"Come on. You need to show me how you almost became famous."

He rubs the back of his neck as I drag him inside. "I'll be rusty."

"You'll still be better than me." I've always been one of those guys who can play any sport. I pick shit up easily, but I was never a prodigy. Never enough to be great at any of them. "Come on, Lion King."

A hand clamps over my mouth. "Please don't say that too loudly." Damon's eyes dart around the nearly empty place. He doesn't remove his hand until I nod.

"You really don't like that name, do you?" I ask. "What are the chances of anyone spotting you here?"

Damon shrugs. "It happens sometimes—like at Chastity's wedding. When I say I was everywhere for a while, I mean, I was *everywhere*. I was the next big thing before I'd even made it to the majors. I don't like the billions of questions it comes with when someone recognizes me. *What happened to your career? Where did you disappear to?* They treat me like a has-been, but I'm not even that. I'm an almost-was, and I think that's even worse."

"Yeah, I can see how that would suck." When he doesn't reply, I squeeze his hand. "Did I make a mistake bringing you here?"

"Nah, I'd love to hit the cages with you. It's just, anything to do with baseball makes me happy and bitter at the same time. Puts me in a weird mood."

It'd be hard to hate something you love so much. "If you want to leave at any time, we're gone."

With a nod, he leads the way.

At the cages, Damon blows out a loud breath and runs his hand over the row of bats lined up outside the cage.

"Is this a 'If you build it, he will come' type thing?" I ask. "You waiting for a bat to speak to you?"

"Nope. The bats who speak to you are shit, because they won't stop talking to keep their eye on the ball."

"Funny guy."

"You started it." Damon picks up a bat and closes himself in the cage.

If smashing out ball after ball is his definition of rusty, I would've been in awe when Damon was in the peak of his career.

My gaze—surprisingly—isn't stuck on his firm ass the whole time as he takes swing after swing. From his long arms to his powerful muscles, he's amazing with a bat. And now I'm thinking about *his* bat and wondering how much longer it'll be before he gets over it and we can go home.

I never thought baseball could be a turn-on.

He comes out of the cage sweaty but happy. His entire face glows, and his posture is somehow proud and relaxed at the same time.

I hope he'll look at me like that one day, because I'm coming to realize I really fucking care about the guy standing in front of me.

"I thought pitchers were easy outs?" I ask. "You kicked ass in there."

"I was decent at hitting. Not the best on the team, but I held my own. God, I've missed this." His nostalgic tone and flushed glow makes my heart break for him.

Baseball was his life and now he has to live without it. He can go to games and watch from the sidelines, but the way he talks about it, it's as if part of his soul died when he was injured and couldn't play anymore. He speaks of the game as if it's a living, breathing thing.

"When was the last time you played?"

Damon's shoes apparently become fascinating to him. "Since the injury. I went through all that rehab, hoping, but when the doctor said I'd never regain full movement, it hurt too much to even try to recondition myself. Both physically and mentally."

"How is the shoulder holding up?" I ask.

"Not too bad. How about we hit the night field at the back where I can pitch to you. Let's see if you can hit my fastball." His face morphs into that of a child on Christmas morning, and I realize we won't be going home any time soon. I think in the world of priorities for Damon, it goes baseball, sex, food. But if this makes him smile like that? I'll gladly stay here all night if he wants to.

"Pretty sure I won't even be able to hit your slow ball," I say.

"That's not a thing," he says and tries not to laugh.

"All right, but go easy on me."

He doesn't go easy on me.

Bastard.

The first ball flies past me before I can even blink.

"Come on," Damon taunts, "that was only eight-five." He points to the display, lighting up his speed.

"I'm so glad I'm wearing a helmet for this."

"You have nothing to worry about. My precision has always been on point."

"And you're so modest about it."

Damon sighs. "You think I'm bad now. Can you imagine how I was four years ago?" He looks at the baseball in his hand and squeezes it tight. Even from here the deep concentration line on his forehead is prominent.

Slowly, I walk toward him. "What's up?"

"Nothing," he murmurs, still looking at the ball. "Just ... this was my whole life. I've spent so long being angry at myself, at the world, at my coaches—even though I never told them I was in pain. I kept trying to rationalize that they were the professionals, they should've seen the signs. I know it was my fault. My cockiness and the pressure became too much, and I thought I was invincible. And it's true I miss it. Standing here, holding this ball, I really fucking miss it. But, you know what?"

"What?"

"It doesn't feel like home anymore."

I smile. "That's a good thing, right?"

"A really good thing." He sniffs and lifts his head, and I pretend I don't see the glimmer in his eyes. "You ready for more?"

"Bring it. But, uh, not too hard."

He grins.

This time, I'm ready. I'm going to hit—

Bam, the ball flies into the net behind me.

He continues to throw bullets at me, but toward the end, I manage to get a few hits, and I'm proud to even accomplish that. Damon's either too tired, sore, or he's going easy on me.

"I think I better call it," Damon says after a while. "My shoulder's starting to pinch."

"Thank God. I don't know how much longer I could keep embarrassing myself."

"You did better than I expected. That, or I really suck now."

I wrap my arm around him as we make our way out to the front. "As if you weren't going easy on me toward the end there."

His face has guilt written all over it, and for a competitive guy to give that to me ...

I lean in and kiss his cheek. "I might keep you. You're good for my ego."

CHAPTER TWENTY

DAMON

God, I hate coming home late. It never used to faze me, but now, knowing Maddox is at home waiting for me, I hate it. Only a few more weeks and I'll be coming home at a reasonable hour. Of course, by then, he'll be back in his apartment which will suck.

When I walk through the door, he drags me straight into the bathroom and starts undressing me.

"Missed you too," I murmur.

"We're seeing your friends tonight or did you forget?" His hands continue their assault on my clothes, and I can't wait to have them on me.

"I forgot. When do we have to be there at?"

"Ten minutes ago," he says. "But they're going to have to wait, because for the last three days I've tried to wait up for you and passed out instead. I need you in me."

And I'm done for. My mouth crashes down on his. He shaved today, so his smooth face is different from the stubble I'm used to, but I still love it. Love his lips, his tongue. I groan into his mouth. "Wait." I pull back. "We need—"

"Lube and condom already in the shower. You can't call me a boy scout; I'm just horny. I ... uh ... went shopping."

"Shopping?"

"You'll see." Maddox pulls me in under the spray and kisses me hard.

My tongue meets his, and my hands wander over his hard body. His abs contract and harden beneath my fingers. When they go to his ass, there's—

"Is that a butt plug?"

His newfound love of ass play is a novelty to him. It's like a game, figuring out how many different ways he can come.

"Little to no prep time. I'm ready." He reaches for the condom and rolls it on for me. Then he grabs the lube and massages a generous amount on my cock. I'm close to blowing already, so I have to stop him.

"Wrap your legs around me." It comes out like an order, and I half-expect Maddox to tease me further to watch me squirm and complain, but he must be hornier than I expect, because he does as I say without demanding I use my manners first.

Maddox moves so his back is flush against the tile wall. When his legs go around my back, I hold him up with one hand, while the other reaches around and pulls out the plug, letting it drop to the floor. Then in one swift, glorious motion, Maddox's tight heat surrounds my cock.

"You have to come fast. Not only am I close to coming, but you're fucking heavy."

Maddox laughs, and the movement ripples down to my toes.

"So not helping." I breathe deep to pull me back from the edge.

"I got this," he says. Reaching between us, he takes himself in his hand.

My head falls to his shoulder as my hips move in short and

shallow thrusts. I want to close my eyes to try to make this last longer, but I have an awesome view of Maddox's hand wrapped around his cock. He rolls his wrist on the upstroke and rubs the precum from his slit down his shaft and then repeats the same motion over and over again. If I wasn't about to blow my load, I'd be able to watch that for hours. His thumb swipes some more precum, and he lifts his finger to my mouth. I love the taste of him on my lips.

My hips pivot forward and pick up pace.

"This angle," he pants. "I'm gonna—" He's cut off by his orgasm ripping through him. His ass clamps down on me, and I grunt as I chase my own release. I can't take much more, but I don't want this to end. It's the perfect dilemma.

My legs threaten to fall out from underneath us when I shudder and Maddox's ass milks my dick. Maddox grabs onto my shoulders for leverage as I pound into him with what I have left. When I finally still, my arms are heavy, my legs weak, and I notice a pain in my right hamstring. "Fuck, I think I pulled something."

"If it doesn't cause an injury, it isn't fun."

I slip out of him and practically drop him, but he finds his balance fast when his feet hit the tiles. "We need to get cleaned up and go."

We rush as fast as we can and are out the door in five minutes, but Wyatt's place is on the Upper West Side near Columbia, so we're forty-five minutes late when we finally arrive. It's not a big deal considering our catchups are always casual, but with the way I'm now limping, thanks to the shower romp, they're all going to know why.

"Whose place is this again?" Maddox asks.

"Wyatt's. Blond guy, long hair."

"Ah, the surfing analyst."

"Except he doesn't surf. And I don't think he's an analyst. I don't understand his job."

Wyatt's building is so old the buzzer to get in only works to let the people know you're there. They have to physically come out to let you in, so I hit the buzzer and wait.

"Now, am I going to have to remind you that you will be around other humans tonight, and Wyatt lives in a one-bedroom apartment, so most likely, someone will be listening at all times?"

"Are you implying I'm not able to keep my mouth shut about your sex injury from dicking me out—"

I sigh when Wyatt laughs. Of course, he had to open the door in the middle of Maddox's sentence. "Yo, Noah," Wyatt calls out down the hall to his ground-floor apartment. "You owe me twenty bucks."

Maddox's cheeks pinken. "I'm never speaking again."

I frown at Wyatt. "What are you talking about?"

"I bet twenty bucks that Maddox was a bottom. Noah reckons you're too *straight* for that."

"Uh ..." Maddox's mouth opens but nothing else comes out.

I shrug. "If they're betting on you, it means they like you," I say to him.

"Okay ... thanks? I think?"

Wyatt's dining area and kitchen are small, but he has a loft bed in the corner, so he turned his actual bedroom into a large living room—large for New York anyway.

Rebecca and Skylar are on one end of the couch, and Noah and Aron are on the floor, sitting close together. Noah and Aron have a weird relationship, and they refuse to talk about it to anyone. I think they may have slept together, but they deny it.

Maddox and I squish in on the couch next to the girls.

"You're one of us now," Skylar says to Maddox.

"One of you?" he asks.

"Damon told Rebecca, who told me, who told everyone, you two are officially together now. So, that means you're one of us."

"One of us. One of us," Noah chants.

"Do I get to learn a secret handshake? If there's no handshake, I'm not interested."

"Here's a handshake for you," Noah says and flips him off.

Maddox laughs. I'm glad he takes Noah's shit in stride. He can definitely rub people the wrong way. Although, half the time I expect he purposefully does it to push people away.

There's no group of people I'm more comfortable around than these guys—not even my own family. And Maddox fits in easily. We sit there basically slinging insults at each other all night, and it's obvious they approve of and love Maddox. Like I'm beginning to think I do too.

Two more weeks fly by, and poor Cheri is still stuck in New York. Maddox says she's getting nausea from the treatment, and they're trying to counteract the vomiting with other meds, but nothing seems to be working. She has the option to pull out of the clinical trial, but without it, her MS might get worse, and she doesn't want that.

She thinks she might be here another week at least. By then it'll be six weeks total, and I'm selfish enough to say I'm thankful for her being sick. Okay, not thankful—that makes me an asshole. I don't like that she's sick, but it's the reason Maddox is still staying with me.

If there was a way to keep Maddox in my apartment without Cheri being sick, I'd take it.

You could always ask him, dumbass.

Or, I could be a huge chicken shit and hope that once Cheri

leaves, Maddox will want to stay and say it himself without me having to ask.

The time living with Maddox has been better than I could've expected, but it's not like he's there by choice. Anyone would choose a big, comfy bed over sharing one room with an aunt-slash-birth-mother person and sleeping on a tiny couch.

If I tell Maddox I'm ready for the ninth inning when he's still in the second, it's going to get awkward.

Has that stopped me from searching apartments in between SoHo where OTS is and Midtown where his office is? Nope. Has it stopped me from wanting to make future plans and fantasizing about coming home to Maddox every single night? Nope.

I know not to say these things aloud. Maddox would run the other way. It's only been five weeks. A great five weeks, but still. It's way too soon. Especially for someone like Maddox who isn't normally a long-term guy.

I text Maddox when I leave the office, because I know he went out tonight with my sister. When I walk the few blocks home, I arrive outside my building at the same time a cab pulls up.

"I think this belongs to you," a slurred, high-pitched voice yells.

I turn to find Maddox stumbling out of the cab. Behind him, both Stacy and Eric's brother, Julian, are squished up against the window.

"Looks like you guys had fun," I say.

"Awthsome night. Woulda been betterer if you were there."

I try not to laugh as I wrap my arm around Maddox's slumped shoulders and pull him to my side so he stops swaying. "Awthsome and betterer? How drunk are you?"

"About ten and a half drunks."

"That's the right amount of drunks," I say and drag him upstairs to the apartment.

He doesn't make it to the bedroom. He falls onto the couch and breathes a sigh as if he's comfortable, even though he's half hanging off the thing.

"I'll go get you a glass of water and some Tylenol."

Maddox bolts upright into a sitting position. "Do I remind you of Eric?"

I freeze in my steps, halfway to the bathroom. "What?"

He waves me off. "Never mind. Forget I said anything."

I stalk over to him. "No, what did you mean by that?"

"Hanging out with Julian ... he said some things about his brother. Might've said I looked ... wait, I want to get the wording right." He speaks low in a mimicking voice. "'You look a fuck-ton like my brother. Can anyone say *Eric's replacement*?'"

Fucking Julian.

"Is this why you're hammered right now?" I ask.

"Naaah. We were all drunk waaaaay before that. Seriously, wine coolers with cheap chasers is *not* a good idea. The chasers tasted like lighter fluid. I'm surprised Stacy was still standing in the end."

"Julian becomes an ass when he's drunk, so I'm sure he didn't mean any of it. Or, he was so drunk, he actually thought you looked like Eric—"

"I thought it too, you know. When I first met the asshole. My initial reaction was to wonder why you wouldn't hook up with me when I was clearly your type." His speech is no longer slurred—this conversation sobering him right up.

I join him on the couch and push him down, my body blanketing his. "You are not Eric's replacement in any way. You're both blond and have blue eyes, but your similarities end there. You might've been an asshole to your high school girlfriend, but deep down, you're kind"—I lean in and kiss his cheek—"thoughtful"—a kiss on his neck this time—"awesome. And nothing like Eric ..." I take his mouth with mine, and yup, I totally get the lighter fluid taste in my mouth. "What the hell did you guys drink?"

"Who the fuck knows," he mumbles.

"Want to go to bed?"

"Fair warning, I'm way too drunk to get it up."

I burst out laughing. "I meant to sleep."

"Mm, sounds good."

CHAPTER TWENTY-ONE

MADDOX

I sound like an old man as I drag my ass out of the bedroom. The groans that come from my mouth could be confused with a zombie looking for its next feed.

"I'm never going out with Stacy and Julian again," I grumble.

Damon's laugh comes from the kitchen, but it echoes in my ear as if on loudspeaker, and I grunt.

"Coffee?" he asks.

"IV drip."

More laughter. Ugh. As I enter the kitchen, not only is Damon's laugh deafening, his smile is blinding.

"How is it that I'm twenty-three but pulling hangovers of a forty-year-old?"

"Maybe because you practically drank a swimming pool of alcohol? And don't even try with that *I'm never drinking again* crap. We both know you will."

I nod. Slowly. "Probably."

"So, uh, do we need to talk about last night?" Damon's voice is quiet, and for a quick second, I freak out about what I possibly could've done that needs discussing, but then it floods back to me.

"Shit. I went all insecure on you, didn't I? I didn't mean ... I mean, I ..." Fuck, I don't know what to say. I didn't mean to freak out on him, but I was drunk, and Julian said all that shit about me looking like Eric ...

Damon's arms wrap around me. "Now you're sober, I want you to hear this again. You're not Eric. You have to remember that he and I haven't been close since high school. We were good at keeping up appearances for our families, but that was all. They can say we were inseparable up until *the kissing incident* all they want, but it's not true. It hasn't been the same between Eric and me since I came out to him. Yeah, we were still friends but not how it once was."

"So, you won't care if I tell you he called off his wedding?"

Damon steps back. "He what?"

I shrug. "Julian said after that awkward as fuck dinner, his brother called off his wedding, moved back to New Haven, and got a job with one of his Yale buddies. He says Eric's running away."

"It's what Eric does best," Damon says. "Look, there would've been a time where I cared and felt sorry for the guy, but he only ever cared about himself. I don't want him to suffer, but I don't want to be involved in his life anymore. In fact, if you reminded me of Eric, it'd be a turn-off because of what he put me through."

"Are you sure?" I avert my gaze.

"If I didn't like you for you, do you really think we would've survived the last few weeks living together in this shitty apartment?"

This apartment really is shitty. "I cannot wait to have my shower back. And my kitchen."

Damon purses his lips. "Right."

"Don't get me wrong. I'm more than grateful for you letting me stay here, but I'm ready for my own apartment."

"Of course." He steps back and leans against the kitchen bench. "How's Cheri's treatment going?"

"She called yesterday and said they've finally got her levels to even out. She's on the perfect cocktail mix of MS and nausea meds. She'll be out of my apartment by Tuesday. I was going to tell you last night, but clearly I was more focused on other things."

"Like getting drunk with my sister." His tone has turned distant. Cold.

"Priorities," I say dryly, trying to break the sudden freeze he's directing my way.

Damon folds his arms across his chest. "So, you're leaving."

"Uh, yeah, but not until Tuesday. We still have the weekend. Unless …"

His eyebrows shoot up. "Unless what?"

"You tell me. You've gone all weird again. You want me to leave earlier? I know I've stayed longer than originally said, but—"

Damon's jaw hardens. "That's not why … Uh, forget it. We have until Tuesday. We should make the most of it. You know, when you're less hungover."

I'm *too* hungover to try to decipher his shift in demeanor. "What's going on? Just tell me."

"I was …" He breathes deep and gets his next words out in a rush. "I was kinda hoping you'd stay."

I stare blankly at him, wondering if I heard him correctly. "Stay?" I croak, my throat dry and trying to constrict into a tight knot.

"Fuck, I'm freaking you out." He leads me to his couch and sits me down. "It's too soon. I get it."

My mouth has forgotten how to work.

"Maddy, it's okay. Forget I said anything."

"It's not that I don't like being here. It's just really soon to be thinking about that step. And it's ... you know ... really, really serious."

"Maddox," he says slowly. "You don't need to explain. It's only been five weeks. I'm getting ahead of myself. I promise you, I'm cool with it."

His words sound genuine, but that doesn't stop the guilt from hitting me when disappointment clouds his eyes. I don't want him to feel rejected, and this has nothing to do with him. These past weeks staying here have been great. I haven't felt overwhelmed or crowded or trapped. Having said that, the thought of making it permanent makes this apartment seem extremely small. Did the walls just move closer?

"Wow, okay, you're really freaking out," Damon says. "I knew you wouldn't like the idea, but I didn't think it was *that* bad."

"I'm not freaking out."

His lips quirk. "Want me to take a photo of your face right now? You look like you're going to faint."

"It's the hangover," I lie.

"I'm not going to force you to move in with me. We'll do it when you're ready."

If we did this now when I'm not ready, it'll end in disaster. I'll probably freak out and run away like I did with Chastity.

"And I still have you until Tuesday," Damon says, leaning in to kiss my neck. His lips trail down. "If you go brush your teeth, I might show you how much I love having you here."

I scramble off the couch as fast as my tired body will let me and rush to the bathroom, but even after brushing my teeth, I still smell the stench of sweated alcohol. "Just going to jump in the shower real quick."

I've barely stood under the spray for thirty seconds when strong hands wrap around me.

"We can always get started in here." Damon's gruff voice has my cock hardening. "I only have two finals left before graduation," he says in my ear. "You know what that means?"

I shake my head and shudder as tingles shoot down my spine. "Nuh-uh."

"I've got barely any studying to do this weekend." He reaches around and grips my cock, giving it a firm pull. "I hope you're ready for a two-day fuck-a-thon."

"Can't wait."

On Monday, Damon arrives home earlier than usual. "No naked cooking tonight?" he asks with a smirk.

I jump off his couch. "What are you doing home? I mean ... hi. But I mean ... I would've had dinner cooked already if I knew you'd be home early."

"It's our last night. Figured we need to make the most of it."

I grin. "Pretty sure we made the most of it all weekend. I'm surprised Stacy didn't pick up on me walking funny all day."

"She probably did, but acknowledging it would've caused images in her head that she'd prefer not to think about. She can barely handle us kissing."

"True."

"Anyway, we have cause to celebrate. Thanks to you, after I graduate next week, I'm starting out with one more client than the other noobs." Damon steps forward and kisses me.

"Who?"

"Matt has officially signed with OTS. I thought he would've told you."

"Nah, haven't heard from him since he went back to Philly."

"I'm going to be the main agent on Matt's case because he requested me, but with his high profile, they've got a senior associate on it too. They want to play up the almost-famous gay baseball player representing the infamous gay football player angle."

"Congrats. That's awesome."

"Watch out, Matt and I will be the next couple the tabloids 'ship together. And we already have a celebrity couple name thanks to you. We'll be the Matt Damon of football."

"I'll kick Matt's ass if he comes near you. He says I have a free pass after what happened in college."

Damon hums a low moan. "I love it when you're jealous."

My eyes roam over him. "I love it when you're home early." I pull him toward me.

His stomach rumbles. "Dinner first?"

We did barely eat this weekend. "Want me to cook or—"

"Nope. We're going out for dinner. Somewhere nice."

I groan. "Do I have to wear a tie?"

"I can help with that."

Damon's already wearing a suit, so when I get dressed, he approaches with a thin black tie of his. He smiles as he slides it around my neck and starts to tie it.

"I've heard it's easier to tie it on yourself and then slip it off loose," I say.

"I know, but then I wouldn't be able to touch you—like when I did this at Chastity's wedding. I was looking for an excuse to get close to you. Your tie wasn't even crooked ... much."

"But you avoided me after you found out about my dream."

"You were freaking out. I didn't want to make you uncomfortable."

"I almost kissed you then—when you were tying my tie—even though no one was watching. The kiss on the dance floor had nothing to do with putting on a show and everything to do with the fact I *wanted* to kiss you."

Damon finishes and tightens the tie around my throat. "I've never been so glad that you were an asshole to your high school girlfriend."

I lean in and do what I wanted to outside that church almost three months ago. My mouth claims his. He cups the back of my head and presses our bodies together.

He didn't bring up the whole moving in together thing again this weekend, but part of me wonders if the constant sex was his way of trying to convince me living with him would be awesome. And it would be. There's just something holding me back. Maybe it's what has always held me back—that inexplicable restlessness I've had forever. The thing is, though, when I'm with Damon, I don't feel restless. I'm content. I'm happy. It's the happiest I've ever been.

Then *why* am I holding back?

"We should get to dinner," he murmurs.

I nod. "Yep. Dinner."

With a hug and a promise to keep in touch, Cheri goes back to being my flighty aunt who travels with the circus. Okay, not circus, but psychic fair is still close enough. I'm thankful to have gotten to know her better over the last few weeks, but my parents will always be my parents. I make a mental note to visit them more often. I owe it to them to be more present in their lives. Call more. Visit more. The thought of going back to Clover Vale no longer makes me antsy. Whether it's because I no longer have to keep up with a stupid lie or I have closure on why I never fit in, I'm not sure. Maybe a bit of both.

I finally have my apartment back, and the first thing I do is use my shower which has hard water pressure and a wide enough head to actually do its job. The shower in Damon's apartment is the worst ... unless he's in there with me.

Even though I'm used to Damon's apartment being empty a lot, the silence when I get out of the shower makes me uneasy. I don't like it. It makes my studio apartment too spacious, and I didn't think that was possible. For a small space that's full of furniture, it's never been this bare.

It's not until I'm halfway through making my dinner that I realize I'm cooking enough for two people. Habit I've picked up over the last few weeks, I guess. Instead of wasting the leftovers, I decide to take the food to Damon's place. Just because I'm not agreeing to move in with Damon, doesn't mean I can't take my boyfriend dinner after his final today. He'll put in some hours at OTS and will come home late, so he most likely won't eat.

When I'm finished making dinner, I put it in a microwaveable container and head to SoHo, but Damon's not in his apartment when I use the key I still have.

Knowing he could be hours, I eat my share and watch TV but end up going to bed when eleven p.m. hits.

"Maddy?"

I startle awake at Damon's voice.

"Did Cheri have to stay longer?"

With a yawn and a stretch, I sit up in bed and rub my eyes. "Nope. I just ... wanted to be here. What time is it?"

Damon doesn't answer me—his wide smile probably won't let him talk.

"Time?" I ask again.

"Two."

My brow furrows. "Why are you home so late?"

He's never been *this* late.

"I didn't want to come home to an empty apartment."

I reach for him and pull him down on top of me. "I'm still

not ready to live together, but I don't want you to think I don't want to be with you."

"I don't think that."

"I only had a few hours at home on my own, and I didn't like it. I want to stay here even if I'm not living here. I want you to stay at mine too—after you graduate. Getting to Columbia from the East Village is a pain in the ass."

Damon smirks. "I thought you didn't compromise."

"I do when I like the compromise."

"It's a really good compromise." He leans in and kisses me, and it's the type of kiss that lets me know I won't be going back to sleep anytime soon. His tongue dominates mine, controlling and strong.

I groan. "If you're going to fuck me, you better hurry up and take your clothes off."

I've never seen anyone move faster, but when he joins me, he takes his time as his mouth moves over me. His hands are gentle, his kisses tender, and I realize it's more than sex tonight. I'm not here because someone's in my apartment, and Damon isn't letting me stay because I have nowhere else to go. It's just us.

Stacy appears over my shoulder when I'm packing up my desk to leave the office for the weekend. "Here are the listings Damon wanted me to look at." She thrusts a stack of papers in front of my face.

"Listings?"

"Stacy," Greyson, our boss, barks.

"Shit. Gotta go. I've circled the ones I love."

"What ones you love?"

But she's gone, already entering our boss's office, and I'm left staring at apartment listings.

Three grand in Midtown, three and a half thousand in South Central, three thousand two hundred in SoHo, all two-bedrooms, all out of Damon's price range. Available now, available next month, available in a few weeks.

I try to make sense of it, but I can't.

I know Damon's getting a raise with his promotion, but it's not that much, and the only way he'd be able to afford these apartments is if …

He's looking at apartments for us even though I told him I wasn't ready?

What. The. Fuck.

Yes, I've stayed with him every night this week since Cheri left, but I told him—repeatedly—that it didn't mean I wanted to move in.

I gave an inch and he took a mile. This is why compromising never works. This is why relationships are total bullshit.

He's making plans *for* me? After he knew what Chastity put me through?

CHAPTER TWENTY-TWO

DAMON

When I get an urgent message from Maddox telling me I'm needed at home ASAP, I hope it's a sex emergency, but knowing Maddox, he would've at least added an eggplant emoji if that were the case. Which makes me wonder what have I done wrong and what am I walking into when I get home?

Please let Stacy be pulling one of her over-the-top pranks.

Only, when I walk through the door, I know this is not a prank. Maddox is pissed as hell, pacing my apartment.

"What happened?" I ask.

"Why don't you tell me?"

"Umm, I literally have no idea what you're talking about."

"We're not moving in together. It's too soon."

My forehead scrunches in confusion. "I know."

"Don't make plans for me without talking to me first. Chastity used to do that, and it fucking pissed me off."

"I wasn't making plans," I say.

"Seems that way to me."

"You know I've thought about us living together—I've

spoken to you about it—but you said you weren't ready. I backed off."

"Then why is Stacy giving me apartment listings?"

"I don't know why she's giving you listings." I asked her to check out a few apartments for me, but I didn't mention anything about Maddox joining me.

"Now you're lying?"

"Back it up here a sec. Stacy gave you listings and said?"

"*Give these to Damon.*"

"And that means I'm making plans for us how?"

"I can't ... I can't be here. I have to go."

"Don't leave. If you'd let me explain—" If I even knew what was going on.

"I don't think ... I'm not cut out for this like I originally thought," he says. "I'm not good at relationships and people making plans for me that I don't want—"

"That's not what's happening. Maddy. Seriously stop for a second."

He doesn't listen. He's too riled up. "I let Chastity do it for way too long. You're the one who told me I need to stand up for myself, so this is me doing it. I won't let anyone interfere with my life again."

Okay, now that pisses me off. "I call bullshit. You let everyone but me interfere. You went to a wedding and pretended to be gay for your ex. You ran home to PA when your mom demanded, and you gave up your apartment to your aunt when she asked for it. And Stacy ... she's the worst of all of them. She interferes all the time."

"Yeah, but I love her."

Ouch.

His words feel like ice in the pit of my gut.

Yeah, we haven't said the L word yet. Yeah, I've known I loved him for weeks now. At least I had the smarts not to say it, because clearly, we're not heading in the same direction as each other. Fuck, I don't even think we're in the same zip code.

"Good to know," I mumble.

His eyes widen when he realizes what he said. "Damon, I didn't mean—"

"Maybe you should go," I say. "Clearly, you're not ready for whatever conclusion you've jumped to, and I don't want you to say something you'll regret and I don't want to hear. I'd rather talk to you when you're not losing your shit."

"I think I have a right to lose my shit over this."

"Over what? I haven't done anything."

Maddox scoffs. "Yeah, okay, keep telling yourself that." He reaches into his back pocket and throws folded papers down on the coffee table. With a shake of his head, he leaves, and I get the feeling I've fucked up somehow. I'm just not sure how.

I flop down on my couch and pull out my phone. Stacy doesn't answer when I dial her, so I leave an angry message for her to call me back.

Then I reach for the papers Maddox threw down and unfold them. The listings are all wrong.

"What the fuck?" I say to no one.

Grabbing my phone again, I pull up my email and look at the link I sent Stacy. Shit! I sent her the list I was looking at before Maddox told me he didn't want to live with me yet. When he said he wasn't ready, I searched for more affordable places within my budget. I sent her the wrong saved list.

Shit, shit, shit.

I hit dial on Maddox's number this time, and it goes straight to voicemail. "Doesn't anyone answer their fucking phones anymore? Maddy, call me back. I understand why you're freaked out, but it's a misunderstanding. I swear. Stacy had the wrong listings. Babe, please call me back."

When I hit end, my knee bounces. I try Stacy again.

"Two phone calls in ten minutes? Someone better be dead. I'm dealing with a crisis of my own here."

"Has Maddox called you?"

"Nope. Haven't seen him since work."

I explain to her what I did and how Maddox jumped to conclusions.

She whistles. "I thought they were out of your price range, but I thought you must've been getting a super raise when you graduate. Living with Maddox never crossed my mind. You asked him to move in with you already? I'm surprised he didn't run immediately."

"Not helping, Stace. Tell me how to fix this."

"Let him cool off."

"How much have I fucked up here?"

"It was an honest mistake, but getting through to Maddox when he's in avoidance mode is difficult. Trust me."

"Thanks," I mumble and disconnect.

Even though she told me to leave him alone, I don't want to. I stand and get ready to run after him—turn up to his apartment and make him listen. It's literally a misunderstanding. Had I actually done what Maddox thought, I'd understand why he was mad, but I didn't.

My feet pause halfway to the door. What if he doesn't believe me?

Fuck it, it's a risk I'm willing to take. I'm not going to sit back like I did with Eric and wonder what I did wrong, how I could've fixed it, or if everything was my fault. Not when it was a mistake.

The need to salvage what Maddox and I have fuels me forward, but by the time I get to Maddox's apartment, my confidence has dwindled. The knock echoes in the small hallway, and I'm tempted to run away. That wouldn't be creepy at all when Maddox opens the door to no one.

Only, after three minutes of knocking, it's clear he's going to ignore me or he's not home.

Hoping it's the former, I sink to my ass and put my back against his door.

"I don't know if you can hear me," I say, "or if you're even home. But I want you to know I'm not going to let you run away from this. From us. It was a misunderstanding." I sigh. "I may not be able to play ball anymore, but for the first time since my injury, I look forward to the future. After I graduate, I'll be making other sports hopefuls follow their dream, and I'll get to live vicariously through them. If it weren't for you, I never would've seen it that way. I would've kept looking at my future as punishment for not listening to my body and for being weak and not good enough. You gave me my happiness back and made me realize that just because baseball is over for me, doesn't mean my life is. You gave me that, Maddy. And I love you for it. I've probably just scared you off even more by using the L word, but it doesn't make it any less true. I'm in love with you, and that means I'll be willing to wait forever for you to catch up to me. We'll do everything at your pace. I just want to be with you."

My head bangs on the door repeatedly as I close my eyes. He's not going to open the door.

"He's not home," an elderly voice says.

My eyes fly open and meet the neighbor Maddox talks about. She stands in the doorway of her own apartment.

"He's not?" I've been talking to a door? Great. Just great. "Do you know where he is?"

"No. There was a lot of slammin' doors and grumblin', and I came out to see what was going on. He muttered an apology and ran outta here."

"Thanks, Mrs. Jacobs."

"He'll forgive you, honey. Fights happen to the best of couples. I fought with my husband up until the day he died."

"Umm ... okay."

"Let him come to you."

With a nod, I get to my feet. Back out on the street, with no idea where to go, I head home and do the only thing I can do.

Hope.

CHAPTER TWENTY-THREE

MADDOX

The last place I thought I'd find myself was back in Clover Vale, PA. My bank account suffered a major blow, forking over three hundred bucks for the Uber to get me here.

I didn't get in until late, so the parentals haven't had the chance to grill me about why I'm home for the weekend.

Five years ago, I ran from my problems, and now I'm back to where I began, running again. I wonder if in five years I'll have to take a girl to Damon's wedding and pretend to be straight.

Damon's wedding … Nope, I'd never survive seeing him marry some other dude.

My brain likes to confuse me. It made me yell at Damon for going behind my back to look at apartments, but now it's the thing telling me that Damon didn't actually rent a place for us; he was just looking. It told me to run home to PA and switch off my phone, and now I'm lying here wondering what the fuck I'm doing.

I try to get the image of Damon's face out of my head—the face he pulled right after I said I loved Stacy in a way that implied I didn't love him. It's not at all what I meant. Stacy is like family to me, and that's why I let her interfere. Yet, when

Damon did it, I couldn't see past my issues with Chastity that I never dealt with.

Damon's nothing like Chastity, and I broke his heart anyway.

What the fuck is wrong with me?

I'm running away from the best thing that ever happened to me because of a fucking teenage relationship I was too chicken shit to put an end to. Why was I reluctant to break her heart, yet last night, I had no problem telling Damon I didn't want a relationship with him.

Which is bullshit, because I do. I want him more than I've wanted anyone or anything.

So, why is it so hard for me to let go and allow it to happen?

Because you're scared of being trapped again.

I thought Damon would never do that to me, but then those listings ...

So what? Just because he was looking at listings doesn't mean he was forcing me to move in with him. He wasn't holding a gun to my head or giving me an ultimatum. He was literally looking for somewhere we could live together, because he wants a life with me.

That monster.

Fuck, I'm an idiot.

I'm about ready to give up on sleep, when Mom startles me, and I realize I must've fallen asleep after all. There's drool on my pillow, and it takes a minute for me to realize I'm at home and not in New York.

"All right. You've had enough sleep now," Mom says.

"Sleep? It feels like I haven't slept at all."

"Time to milk the cows."

I throw my pillow over my face. "We don't have cows. We don't live on a farm."

"With the way you talk about how country we are, I get confused sometimes."

"Mom," I whine.

"Oooh, he brings out the teenager in him." The bed dips as Mom sits on the end.

"Out with it. What boy or girl has you running back here?"

I lean up on my elbows, and the pillow falls away from my face. "Dad told you?"

"That you're not gay? Yeah. Also told me that my future son-in-law was a no-go."

"You like Damon better than you like me. Admit it."

"Well, *he* used his manners. Spill it. What did you do to piss him off?" she asks.

I groan. "I don't want to talk about it. And how do you know it was him?"

"You have a visitor downstairs. I don't think you're going to get out of talking about it."

Damon's here?

I scramble out of bed, still in the clothes I was in last night. My feet bang loudly against the stairs. Damon stands from my parents' couch, his hands go to his pockets, and his head hangs low.

I hate that I'm the one making him second-guess himself—something I promised I'd never do. I told him I wouldn't be like Eric, and then I go and shut him out.

Fuck.

I rush over to him and practically knock him down as I kiss him hard. He stumbles back, but his hands go to my waist, and his mouth takes everything I give.

I try to express everything I feel for him, everything I want to say, because I'm not sure if I can admit it aloud yet. I love him. This is true, but the thought of saying it out loud makes the walls close in—just like they've always done. Only difference is, this time, when I remind myself that it's *Damon*, all that doubt, the claustrophobia, the itchy feeling of wanting to escape disappears completely.

If I focus on the Damon part and not words like love and forever, I don't freak out. I want it. Everything.

Mom clears her throat, and I force myself to pull back. "I'll uh, let you boys talk it out," she says.

When she's gone, Damon turns to me. "I was expecting more yelling, maybe accusations of being a stalker, and maybe a *I never want to see you again*, but a kiss?"

"How did you know I was here?" I ask.

"Tracking app on your phone," he says simply. When my mouth drops open, he smirks. "What, I can't make jokes?"

I shove him.

"I was going to let you cool off and give you space, but well, I'm me. I called around to like ... everyone. I found out you were here, and I told myself to stay away. If I drove you to escape to PA, something had to have been seriously wrong. But you have to know I didn't do what you think I did."

"I don't care anymore."

"Huh?"

"I'm not like you. I've never thought of something I wanted and just gone for it. I don't travel because I'm content to sit back and complain without actually making an effort. You know what you want and you go for it. I've always admired you for it, so it makes sense you would've been planning for the future and looking for possible apartments—"

"That's just it. I wasn't," he says.

"You weren't?" Why does that fill me with crushing disappointment?

Fucking hell, I *want* to live with him now? I shake that thought off and tell myself to come back to that later.

"I was looking for me," Damon says. "My lease is up next

month, and we both know I hate my apartment. I asked Stacy to check out a few buildings near your work, but when I sent through the list, I accidentally sent her the one I saved *before* you told me you didn't want to live with me. I don't want to pressure you into anything you're not ready for, and I've been chasing you down trying to tell you that. I'm pretty sure I'm in a relationship with your apartment now though. I gave it a killer speech last night, hoping you were on the other side of the door listening."

I burst into laughter. "Speech? Do I get to hear it?"

"Nope. It's between me and your door. But it had lots of apologizing and groveling, and now you may never see that side of me."

"I treated you as if you were Chastity, when you're not. You wouldn't hold me back or make me do something I didn't want to do. Last night, I was too freaked out to see it rationally and went into flight mode because it's my automatic reaction to everything. But I don't want to run away."

Damon wears a grin that lights up my Goddamn world. "You'll come home with me now?"

"How did you get here?" I move to the front windows and see a Beemer outside.

"Borrowed Noah's car. I would've been here sooner, but he decided to lecture me about fucking it up with a guy who could put up with my shit."

"Noah loves me more than you," I sing. "When do you have to have Noah's car back by?"

Damon shrugs. "Dunno. He rarely uses it. Who has a fucking car in New York?"

"When's your graduation?"

"Wednesday."

I smile. "What are the chances of getting two days off from OTS?"

Damon fake coughs. "I think I feel the flu coming on. Where are you going with this?"

"Do we need passports to cross over into Canada? Niagara is what, four, five hours away?"

"Maddy, what are you planning?"

"I'm planning to jump in headfirst with my eyes closed and hope for the best. I'm acting instead of wishing for more, and I want you to do it with me." I swallow hard and force myself to say the words I've been too scared to admit. "Because I love you."

A breath gets caught in Damon's throat. "Your door blabbed, didn't it?"

"Huh?"

"Can we state for the record that I told you I loved you first? It just happens that I told your door instead of you."

"You told my door you love me?"

"I fell in love with you weeks ago but didn't want to scare you off."

"Even when you scare me, I promise I'll come running back," I say. "It might take a while for my irrationality to be drowned out, but I will always overcome it. I know that now. You're worth it."

Damon steps forward, wrapping his arms around me and bringing his forehead to mine. "If we're making promises to each other, I promise to not get ahead of myself, to consult you on everything before acting, and also to follow you wherever you want to go ... unless baseball is on."

"Of course."

"I'm even willing to go to *Canada*. If that doesn't tell you I love you, I don't know what else will."

"It's a hardship, I know."

"Guess we have a road trip ahead of us."

"I'll make snacks!" Mom yells from the kitchen.

"I think she was eavesdropping," Damon says.

I lean in and whisper, "Lucky I didn't mention the road head I plan to give you."

Damon glances around the house as if looking for something.

"What?" I ask.

"Was waiting for someone who overheard you to jump out."

"I really should learn to shut my mouth."

"Or put it to good use."

When our lips meet, I'm in a tortured heaven. I can't believe I almost walked away from this. This guy owns me, and it's killing me that I fucked up.

"Maybe we should save this for Canada," Damon says. "You know, where your parents aren't eavesdropping or watching."

"The next five hours are going to be the longest of my life."

CHAPTER TWENTY-FOUR

DAMON

Apparently when Maddox is sorry, he really fucking means it. We're both exhausted and covered in cum and sweat by the time we're done. We checked into a hotel overlooking the falls two days ago and didn't waste any time. We haven't seen the light of day since. With room service and a spa bath in our hotel bathroom, it's been totally worth calling into work and pretending to be sick.

"I can't move," he says.

"Then don't."

He's on his stomach, his head buried in his pillow, and I'm panting next to him.

"My phone," he grumbles.

"Is that your way of asking me to get it?"

"Yes."

With an exaggerated sigh, I climb out of bed and smack his naked ass. "You're lucky you're good-looking."

"Or what, you wouldn't fuck me?"

"Oh, I'd fuck you, but I wouldn't fetch your phone." I locate it on the floor near his discarded pants and throw it at him.

While I stand here admiring him, he types out a text. Even

though I'm spent, I want to tackle him and wrap myself around him.

I find my jeans and get dressed instead, using my shirt to clean up as much as possible. We should probably take a break. I pull back the curtain to stare at the falls, but my own phone goes off with an alert, letting me know a new apartment listing was just added that matches my search.

"Your sister's texting, wondering why I'm not at work and if we sorted our shit," Maddox says.

"Did you tell her we're in Canada?"

"Yup. She yelled at me for leaving her out. I told her we haven't left the hotel room in two days, and now she's thanking me."

I laugh. "You're only with me to freak out my sister, aren't you?"

"Nah, that's just a bonus." He holds out his hand and beckons me back to bed, but I don't move.

"Shouldn't we go see the falls at some point? Isn't that why we're here?"

"Says the guy on his phone."

I lift my chin in his direction, gesturing to the fact he's doing the exact same thing.

"What are you looking at?" he asks.

"Apartment listings," I say absently.

Maddox frowns and opens his mouth to say something but changes his mind.

"What?" I ask.

"Come back to bed. We'll do the falls tomorrow. We can spend all day in Canada and drive back to New York in the afternoon."

"Isn't the point of traveling to see things and do touristy shit?"

"Nope. It's to make memories. And you know what I'm

going to think about when someone talks about Niagara Falls? I'll remember my awesome boyfriend fucking me until I'm legless."

"Well when you put it like that ..." With a flick of my wrist, I pop the button on my jeans and am naked again within seconds.

"I have a confession to make," Maddox says as soon as I climb into bed next to him.

My arms snake around him and bring him close to me so his head is on my chest. "You're actually married and have three kids."

"You know about Stella and the triplets?"

"Stella? Really?"

He shrugs. "First name I could think of. What I was going to say is I think I knew I loved you weeks ago."

"You didn't say anything."

"Uh, you were fucking me with a dildo when it happened. Didn't think it was the best time to bring it up."

I burst into laughter.

"But really, I don't think I understood that's what it was at the time. I remember thinking you were everything to me, but given the circumstances, that might've been my dick talking. Only now I realize it was the first time I knew you were my future, and that doesn't scare me."

"Fuck, I love you."

Maddox grins. "I know."

"Nice *Star Wars* reference."

"I told you the originals were better. They're quotable."

"But the effects are shit."

"I don't think I can live with you anymore."

"You *don't* live with me," I point out.

Maddox swallows hard. "I want to do it. I want you to move in with me."

"Okay, how did we go from almost breaking up over the idea of moving in together to you asking me to move in?"

"It wasn't the moving in part that freaked me out. I assumed it was, but when I thought about why I came home, it wasn't because you wanted to live with me. It was because I thought you were manipulating the situation to get what you want."

"I—"

He cuts me off before I can interrupt. "I know that's not what you did, but at the time, *that's* what drove me away."

"I'm worried it's too soon and you'll freak out again, but I do need a place to live. If you're unsure, I can get a six-month lease somewhere and we'll reassess then."

"I have a cheap apartment, and even though it's small, it's enough for us. Might need to buy a wardrobe to fit somewhere because my closet barely holds all my shit. But with your promotion, and me paying half my rent, if we saved for a few years, we could buy a place in Brooklyn or somewhere cheaper. Or go on a really expensive round-the-world trip."

"Look at you, planning a future," I joke, but inside I'm doing a frickin' happy dance—an embarrassing one with awkward white guy clicking and finger pointing.

"I don't like fighting with you."

That sobers my internal dancing a little. "I agree, fighting sucks, but there'll only be more fighting if you're truly not ready for this."

"I am ready. I promise. And if I become uncomfortable again, I'll let you know before I blow up."

"You know what one good thing is about you blowing up? The makeup sex." Sex with Maddox in general is awesome. I can't get enough of him.

"Well then, maybe you're a dickhead." He smirks.

"Are you picking a fight right now so I can fuck you again?"

"Is it working? Assface?"

"Honestly? I don't know if I can get it up again. You've fucked me dry."

Maddox sighs. "Fine. I'll order us some refueling food, and then I'll call you names until you can't take it anymore."

"You're the perfect man."

"Thanks, Dik."

"Wait, are you using my initials or calling me another name?"

Maddox winks. "Figure it out yourself."

CHAPTER TWENTY-FIVE

MADDOX

I shouldn't be nervous. After all, I'm not the one who has to walk across a stage today. Nope, I just have to sit with my boyfriend's parents and watch as Damon graduates law school.

"It's so cute you're scared of Mom and Dad," Stacy says beside me. Damon just left us to go sit with the rest of his class, while we wait for his parents to turn up before we take our own seats.

"I'm not scared," I lie. I lie my ass off. I want them to love me.

"You don't need to be. It helps I've been talking you up for years. Hey, maybe I'm psychic and knew you were going to end up with my brother."

"Maybe you should join my crazy birth mother on the road with her psychic fair."

"Stacy," a feminine voice says from behind us.

"Hi, Mom."

Here we go.

After Stacy's parents hug her, they make their way over to me. And *smile*.

"Maddox," Mrs. King says and hugs me. "It's good to see you again."

"You too," I murmur.

Mr. King shakes my hand and squeezes my shoulder with his other hand. "If you boys need help moving Damon into your apartment next month, let me know. I can drive into the city."

"Uh ... I ... oh, okay. Thank you, sir."

Damon's father grins. "Call us Henry and Cindy."

I manage a nod.

"Sir," Stacy mocks beside me.

"Shut up." I nudge her.

Cindy purses her lips. "Maddox, I hope you don't mind, but ... we ... umm ... We invited the Davidsons."

"Why would I mind?"

"Well, Eric's not coming, but Denise and Jeff are. They weren't sure you'd be okay with it after—"

"I have nothing against them at all. But, uh, it's probably good Eric's not coming. Damon doesn't need that today."

"I still don't know why he didn't tell us," Henry says.

"You know how overprotective Damon can be. He didn't want Eric to be treated like the bad guy for making a mistake."

"Doesn't make what Eric did right," Stacy says.

"Never said it did, but I can't help feeling sorry for him."

"Let's not get into it here," Cindy says. "We're here to celebrate."

Stacy and I follow her family into the crowd to find some seats.

"You don't really mean that, do you?" she whispers.

"That I feel sorry for Eric? Yeah, I do. I accepted my feelings for Damon easily, but I struggled with it at first—putting a label on it and defining it. Doesn't give Eric a right to act like a dick, and if he comes near Damon again, I might have to get violent, but I understand where he was coming from."

Stacy scoffs. "You? Violent? Okay."

"You're forgetting my form of violence—I get you to do it for me. My little attack dog, you." I wrap my arm around her and give her a noogie.

"Careful or I'll turn my violence onto you."

"Never. You love me."

"I do. I'm happy to have you in my life."

My eyes narrow. "But?"

"No but. You're my best friend." Tears pool in her eyes.

"Are you dying?"

She shoves me. "I can't be serious every once in a while?"

"No."

"Whatever, I hate you again."

"There's my Stacy."

We watch the commencement speech and wait three hundred hours for Damon to take the stage. My leg goes dead at one point as pins and needles shoot down to my feet. Stacy laughs at my pain. Yeah, she really loves me. But not as much as the guy claiming his degree right now. The pride I have for Damon rivals that of his parents.

"Wait for it," Stacy says.

Dread replaces the proud feeling warming my stomach. "What did you do?"

She grins.

"Stacy ..."

As Damon crosses the stage to accept his diploma, the world slows down. It's like a scene from a movie where the hero knows what's going to happen but can't stop it in time.

A confetti cannon goes off early.

Stacy jumps up and down and claps. She's not seeing what I am. The cannon is too close to the stage. Yeah, it's shooting paper, but put that much pressure behind it and it can turn into the weight of a baseball. And that weight launches itself at my boyfriend's head.

Stacy pales when her brother drops to the stage. Gasps come from the audience, but I'm already halfway through the crowd to get to him.

Damon's out cold.

"Babe," I say frantically. Weird, I never call him babe—that's his thing—but in my panicked state, it slips out.

My hand cradles his cheek. With a groan, he leans into my hand but doesn't open his eyes.

"Someone call an ambulance," I say.

"Ambulance?" Stacy croaks next to me. She followed me up here.

"What did you do?" I yell at her.

"It was a ... it was a prank. I paid a guy to set off the confetti early so it happened when Damon was called. It wasn't meant to—"

"Goddamn it, Stacy."

"I'm okay," Damon says, suddenly awake. He tries to sit up. "But the ground is upside down." He lies back and closes his eyes.

"Shit, he probably has a concussion," I say.

When the paramedics arrive, which takes way too fucking long for my liking, I don't hesitate climbing in the back of the ambulance with him. He's in and out of consciousness the whole way, complaining of the bright light every time he opens his eyes.

As soon as we get to the hospital, they take him for a CT scan, and I'm told to wait in the ER.

Illogical and selfish as it is, all I can think about is the fact Damon and I are going to miss the hockey game tonight. I was going to surprise him and finally get him that meet and greet with my brother-in-law—*the hockey god*, or whatever.

I take out my phone and message my sister what happened, letting her know we wouldn't make the game, but the King clan enters the ER waiting room before she can respond.

For the first time since I've known Stacy, she looks sheepish. "I'm sorry. It wasn't meant to do that. It was a 'Yay, Damon!' type thing. No one else got confetti with their names. I wanted to do it for him."

"Maybe no one got confetti because no one should've been on stage when the cannons went off," I say.

"How was I to know that?" she whines. "The guy I paid off should have."

I can't be mad at her. This is who Stacy is.

"This does make me think I should ease up on the pranks."

"Ya think?" I ask.

"I mean, paying off people costs a lot these days."

I shake my head. "You're a horrible human being."

"Yep." She smiles but it falls quickly. "Is he going to be okay? I do have half a heart and know it's inappropriate to joke about this if I accidentally killed my brother."

"Paramedics said he's showing signs of a concussion but should be fine," I say.

"But they're not doctors," Stacy says. "EMTs know shit all."

"Makes me feel a lot better. Thanks, Stace," I say.

"Shit. Sorry. I'm sure he's going to be fine."

We wait in that waiting room for over an hour. In that time, I pace, drink acid-flavored coffee, and glare at Stacy.

"King family?" A doctor asks, coming into the waiting area. We all stand. "Damon's got a mild concussion—a lot less serious than we originally thought."

I release a loud breath of relief.

"We need to keep him overnight for observation, but he can have visitors. Who's first?"

I look at his parents but they're looking at me. "I guess that's, uh, me. I'm his partner."

"Aww," Stacy croons. "That's the first time I've heard you refer to him as your *partner*."

"Shut it," I say through gritted teeth.

I'm led back to a room where Damon's fully conscious. His graduation gown is folded on the seat next to him, and he's in his regular clothes.

"What, no sexy hospital gown for me to perv on you?"

"I'm going to kill my sister," he says.

"Get in line." I approach and kiss his cheek. "So, concussion, huh? Is that one of those conditions where I'm not allowed to give you bad news?"

"Don't think so. Why? What's the bad news?"

"I was going to surprise you tonight. Tommy gave me tickets to the New York versus Boston game."

"I'm fine." He tries to get out of bed but as soon as he sits up, he wobbles. "I'm good. Seriously. I wanna go to the game."

I push him back down. "You're not fine. You have a concussion. We can't go where there's bright lights and lots of noise. You can meet Tommy another time."

"Or right now."

My brother-in-law stands at the entrance to Damon's room, along with one of his teammates and my sister.

"Jacie told us what happened," Tommy says.

"Holy shit," Damon says. "You're ..." His gaze flits between Tommy and his teammate. "And you're Ollie Strömberg. Do concussions cause hallucinations? Don't you two have a game right now?"

"We're not due at the rink for another hour," Tommy says.

"I've had a concussion before," Ollie says. "When I was on the farm team. Almost cost me my career. When Tommy said what happened, I said I'd tag along. Tough break, man."

Tommy puts his arm around Ollie. "And this guy is also interested in setting up a meeting when you're back on your feet."

"My current agency is screwing me on a contract extension, and there's been rumors of a trade," Ollie says.

"Uh ... umm ..." Damon stammers.

I lean in and whisper, "Dude, you're a sports agent. Be cool. One would think you've never met a famous athlete before."

Damon shakes his head and then winces. "Sorry. Kinda wish this wasn't happening while I had tiny jackhammers going off in my head, but yeah, definitely. Meeting."

While they talk over the details of when they can meet, Jacie comes to me and wraps her arms around me. "Hey, little brother."

"Don't you mean *cuz*?"

"Whatever. You'll always be my weird little brother."

I laugh. "Thanks, Jacie. I see you managed to dump the kids for the night."

"Mom and Dad are happy to see the grandkids, and Tommy and I got a hotel room. You want to come out for drinks after the game and catch up?"

I glance at Damon in bed and hesitate. "I should probably—"

"Yes, he'll go out," Damon says. "Visiting hours will be over by then, and you never see your sister. All I'm going to be doing is getting woken up every two hours to make sure I don't die."

"My boyfriend's a little dramatic," I say to the others, and they snicker.

"Seriously, Maddy. Go out. I'll be fine."

I turn to Jacie. "Text me where to meet you after the game."

The conversation turns to hockey, so my sister turns to me. "You know, I always thought the gay thing was a lie to break up with your crazy high school girlfriend."

I laugh. Hard. "Here I thought I'd fooled the entire town when I'm starting to think no one believed me. I don't know if Mom and Dad told you, but I'm not gay. I'm bi. It's a long confusing story."

"As long as Damon makes you happy, we'll all love him."

"He does."

"We better get to the rink," Tommy says after a while. "Feel better, and we'll see you at the next family get-together."

"Like there's many of them," I say.

"Maybe you all could come to Boston for Thanksgiving," Jacie says.

"Okay, I'll see you in six months," I say dryly.

"We'll organize something in the off season," Tommy says.

"Sounds good," Damon says, and I love that he immediately knows it includes him too. When they leave, Damon slumps back in his hospital bed. "I need to get my sister back for this."

"Oh no. He's gone to the dark side. Fight it! Don't stoop to our level. Save yourself!" My dramatic crying has a nurse coming to check on Damon.

I chuckle and wave her off. She tells me to keep the noise down.

"I bet she's fun at parties," I say.

Damon ignores me. "I could be hanging out with Tommy-fucking-Novak and Ollie-fucking-Strömberg tonight instead of being stuck here. Vengeance needs to be served cold, and I have the perfect plan." He turns to me and grabs hold of my hand. "I had a surprise for you tonight too. Where's my phone?"

"I have it. They gave it to me in the ambulance." I pull it out and hand it to him. It takes him a while to find what he's looking for because he can't focus on the screen without wincing. He gives up and hands it to me. "It's in my email. First one in the starred file."

"A cruise? To Bermuda?"

"You know how Matt signed with OTS?"

"Yeah?"

"We hired a PR firm to help his case. Part of his marketing strategy is to clean up his image. We figured the best way to do that is to get himself a boyfriend."

"I'm so confused. What's this got to do with the cruise?"

"It's a setup and a PR stunt. Matt will be there with his new boyfriend. They'll be photographed together, and it'll be leaked to the press. We're going to spin it so he's a good ol' wholesome gay man in love, instead of what that gossip rag made him out to be which was … well, a dirty manwhore and the abomination all those crazy church people claim we are."

"Okay, so who's going to be his boyfriend?"

Damon grins. "Noah."

A laugh escapes. "Noah? Poor Matt."

"As un-PC as this is, they hit all the targets. Gay, interracial, and Noah's from a prominent family, so they can't accuse him of being a gold-digger after Matt's money. They're kind of a PR's wet dream."

"How did you get Noah to agree to this?"

"I reminded him how bored he is being the rich trust-fund guy. Plus, he finds Matt hot. I get to go along with them on this cruise to oversee everything, and I bought an extra ticket for you, because I know how much you wanted to travel and see the world. It's only Bermuda, but hey, it's not Canada."

"That should be a tourism slogan. It'd work for anywhere. 'Come to West Shittyville, Ohio. There's nothin' to do, but at least it ain't Canada.'"

Damon winces. "Fuck, don't make me laugh."

I lean in and press my lips to his. "Thank you."

"I've had it organized for weeks, because I wanted to do this for you. If I had the choice between following you wherever you wanted to go or pitching a no hitter in a Major League Baseball game, I'd choose you. Every time."

"Shit, that was practically a marriage proposal coming from you." I kiss him again until I realize ... "Wait. How exactly are we using the cruise to get back at Stacy?"

"When I asked her to organize the week off from work for you so I could surprise you, she said how much she wanted to come. I might be sending her an early birthday present in the form of her own room on board."

My eyes narrow. "I still don't get it."

Damon cocks his eyebrow. "What's your high school friend Jared up to lately? Think he'll be interested in a free cruise?"

A smile breaks out. "You're more evil than both me and Stacy combined."

"Yeah, I am. Don't mess with the Dik."

I almost choke on my laughter. "You're the best fake boyfriend a guy could've ever asked for, and after tonight, you'll be the biggest sports agent in town. I'll do some recon for you with all of Tommy's teammates and see if anyone else needs a new agent."

"If you keep finding me clients, I may have to hire you as my assistant."

I shake my head. "Bad idea. We'd never get any work done."

"True. I love you, Maddy."

No matter how many times he says it, I can't hear it enough. It doesn't freak me out, and the idea of being with him forever doesn't make me antsy. I crave him, more than I've ever craved anyone or anything in my life. I always used to think relationships meant compromising what you want for something somebody else wants, but I never realized that when you meet that one person who becomes your priority it's not compromising because you'd willingly do anything to make them happy. Just like I know Damon would do the same for me.

I kiss him again. "You remember when we first met and I told you I felt like I don't belong?"

Damon nods.

"I found it—where I'm supposed to be. It's with you."

CHAPTER TWENTY-SIX

DAMON

I heave the final box on top of the others and let out a breath. "Done. Finally."

Maddox stands in the middle of his—no, *our*—apartment with an adorable scowl on his face.

"What's up?" I ask.

"What's *up*? Oh, I don't know. How about the fact I have no apartment left? How much crap do you own?" He holds his hands out and turns in a circle. Granted, there are boxes piled up everywhere, and there's barely a clear path to the bathroom ... or kitchen, but it'll be fine once I find homes for everything.

"Whatever we don't have room for, I'll put in a storage unit."

Maddox falls back on his bed amongst a heap of boxes. There's just enough room for him to squeeze his lithe body in between them. "We're gonna need a bigger boat."

"*Jaws* reference? Really?"

He throws his arm over his eyes.

"Babe, are you freaking out?" My heart pounds, and the same doubts I've had since we got together creep in. I'm worried I'm pushing him into something too serious before he's ready. I thought we were over this, but maybe it's all too real for him now that it's actually happening.

"Yes."

The weight on my chest plummets to my stomach. "About me moving in?"

In a rush, he sits up and stares at me wide-eyed. "What? *No.* I'm freaking out about not having enough room and practically living on top of each other. Maybe ... maybe we should look for somewhere with more space."

I rub my sore chest in relief. "This is fine for now. If we can endure this for a year—two tops—and put aside what we normally pay for rent, we'll have a down payment for a place in Jersey or Brooklyn."

Maddox gasps. "You dare suggest I move to *Jersey*? You really are a monster."

"I know. I'm the worst," I say dryly. "Jersey is not *that* bad." But hey, I should be thankful he's only worried about the Jersey part and not the sharing a mortgage part.

"How can you call yourself a New Yorker?"

I ignore him and lift my shirt to wipe the sweat off my face from lugging boxes all day. When the shirt falls back in place and I lock eyes with Maddox, his tongue darts out and wets his top lip.

"Like what you see?" I mock.

"Mmhmm. You should come over here and share this ginormous bed with lots of space ... oh, wait ..." He gestures to the crap surrounding him.

I try not to laugh. "Sarcasm isn't good for you, you know."

"Lies. Sarcasm is great. You can say anything and pretend you're joking. People think I'm hilarious when in reality I'm just an asshole."

"Yeah, but you're my asshole ... That sounded extremely wrong."

Maddox snorts. "Maybe that should be in our wedding vows."

His words throw me, and when I take a step backward, my foot gets stuck on the lip of a box and I go crashing to the floor—what's left of the floor anyway. My hip digs into the corner of a box, and a sharp stabbing pain fills my head. I still occasionally get residual effects from the concussion. Doctors say it should go away soon—along with the daily headaches, thank God.

"Shit." Maddox is by my side in an instant, hovering over me and cradling my face with his hands. "Are you okay? Is it the concussion? Are you dizzy?"

"I'm fine," I grumble and sit up. "I tripped over a stupid box because you said wedding vows as if it's a possibility. You shouldn't do that to a guy."

He leans back on his knees in front of me. "Why wouldn't it be a possibility?"

"Because you're *Maddox*."

"Like that's a reason?"

"Let's look at the facts." I run through the reasons, keeping score with my fingers. "You ran away from your hometown so you didn't have to marry Chastity. You wouldn't sit still during her wedding ceremony and admitted to feeling more comfortable in a graveyard than in a church. You could barely get the boyfriend label out of your mouth at first, so I'd hate to see what you'd be like with the word husband. And you practically broke up with me when I suggested we live together."

"But that was before."

I shrug. "I just figured being with you meant no wedding in the future, and I'm okay with that. I want a life with you. That doesn't mean it has to include marriage."

"I want to marry you, though."

I replay his words in my head over again, because they don't make sense. *I'm* not ready for that, so surely he can't be. We've only been together a couple of months. That's way too fast, and—

"Fuck, I don't mean now," he says with a laugh. "Or soon. Geez, role reversal. You look like you're going to pass out. I mean for the first time in my life, I see a future with someone and want the possibility of spending the rest of our lives together."

His words shouldn't surprise me—Maddox is always changing the expected—but the fact he's even thought about the long run makes me love him even more.

"I don't think getting married is *necessary*," he continues. "But that doesn't mean I don't want to do it. Especially when I know you'd like to get married someday. The operative word being *someday*. Isn't marriage the whole point of a relationship? It's like the end goal or whatever."

"I never … I …" I don't know how to get the words out. "I never expected you to change who you are for me. The end goal can be anything we want it to be. House, marriage … kids, if you want them. Or not. We can choose our own future, and it doesn't have to fit in a box or have a label or match society's expectations."

"I thought you liked labels?"

"Maybe you taught me labels don't matter. What does matter is you. And me. Nothing else."

Maddox's eyes fill with awe as if I just gave him the world. I'll gladly make it my life's purpose to keep that look on his face. "Nothing else," he murmurs.

"Except maybe how we can find room to fuck when all these stupid-ass boxes are in the way."

Maddox tackles me to the ground. We haven't had sex since the concussion, so he's a little overeager. My head hits something hard, and I wince at the pain, but I don't care. I want Maddox's lips.

Before his mouth meets mine, he pulls back. "Wait. You're not supposed to have sex with a concussion. No strenuous activity."

"I just moved a shit ton of boxes."

"And you have a headache. I can tell by the concentration lines in your forehead." He trails the lines, and his fingers feel amazing on my skin.

"The headache's because we haven't had sex in years."

He laughs. "Try a week."

"Feels like years. It's a *mild* concussion. I'm good to go. I promise."

The smile Maddox gives me is innocent while his burning gaze is anything but. He presses his mouth to mine, but there's only tenderness. And it's over way too fast. "I'm going to be a good boy and wait until you're better before I attack you."

I let out an involuntary whine. I want him *now*.

He clamps his hand over my mouth. "We have forever, Damon."

Even though I still want to jump him, his words settle in my chest. I smile up at the guy who's become everything to me and relent, because how can I complain when he's promising me something I never thought he'd give me?

"Forever?" I ask.

"Yes, Dik. Forever."

THANK YOU

Thank you for reading *Fake Out*

Trick Play (Matt and Noah's story) is coming soon!

CONNECT WITH EDEN

If you want news and updates of upcoming releases, follow me!
http://edenfinley.com

BOOKS BY EDEN FINLEY

ONE NIGHT
One Night with Hemsworth (M/F)
One Night with Calvin (M/F)
One Night with Fate (M/F)
One Night with Rhodes (M/M)
One Night with Him (M/F)

FAKE BOYFRIEND
Fake Out (M/M)
Trick Play (M/M - coming soon)

STEELE BROTHERS
Unwritten Law (M/M - coming soon)

ROYAL OBLIGATION
Unprincely (M/M/F)

ACKNOWLEDGMENTS

I want to thank all of my betas: Kimberly, Edie, Shelly, Michelle, Karma, and Janice.

Deb Nemeth for the wonderful editing and helping me bring Damon and Maddox more depth.

Thanks to Kelly from Xterraweb editing—you are always the best.

To Lori Parks for one last read through.

Leslie Copeland, for everything! From talking me off the ledge, to the quotes, to being an awesome new friend!

And definitely Kellie from Book Cover by Design. You are a rockstar for getting me out of my jam.

Lastly, a big thanks to Linda from Foreword PR & Marketing for helping get this book out.

Printed in Great Britain
by Amazon